As The Stars Fall

A Book for Dog Lovers

Steve N Lee

Blue Zoo
England

For my four-legged best friends.
And yours.

Can You Keep a Secret?

There's something magical about losing yourself in a story, isn't there? When you tell people about *As The Stars Fall*, please don't give away its secrets so others can discover the magic for themselves.

Thanks,

Steve

Chapter 1

Dog shivered on the edge of the curb, his brown coat sodden, raindrops drip-drip-dripping off his nose. The cruel cold gnawing on his bones, he stood transfixed, clinging to a splinter of hope like a hanged man clings to his final breath. He ached to escape this torment and continue his search, but instead, he waited. Hoping.

Rain bounced off the asphalt with tiny splatters, then gushed through the gutters running down either side of the road. Cars growled along the street as gruffly as the people growled along the sidewalk, and drenched black buildings reared all around like monstrous beasts glaring down on their prey.

In the midst of it all stood Dog. Wide-eyed, he gazed at what he knew could never be his — never — yet he couldn't help but dream, so he stared. Stared at a round-faced man sheltering under a blue awning twenty feet away. A round-faced man shoveling doughnuts into his mouth.

The man's tongue slithered out, licking the white powder and red goo from his lips. Dog licked his lips too, even though there was nothing to wipe away.

Oh, that smell! Sugary, fruity, fresh, warm. A string of drool dangled from Dog's mouth and dribbled into a shallow puddle by his front paws. He dreamed of what it might be like to have just one bite of such a wondrous delicacy.

Hunger twisted his gut like some crazed creature trying to claw its way out. He hunched over, a whimper escaping.

Dog didn't like to beg, to admit he'd failed; he was a big dog now and big dogs didn't fail. Since losing his mother, he'd sniffed out something to eat every day — everything from a half-eaten burger dumped in an alley to a handful of potato chips crushed into the sidewalk. However, over the last five days, he'd found nothing, even though he'd trailed the streets until his paws hurt.

Sitting back on his haunches, Dog gazed at the man, tilting his head to one side and making his big brown eyes even bigger.

The man dipped his hand into a paper bag, pulled out another doughnut, then savaged it, white goo oozing out and dribbling down his chin. Dog could almost taste it. So sweet, so creamy, so... Dog melted inside as the man wolfed down chunk after chunk.

The man lifted the last morsel to his lips as his wandering gaze fell upon Dog.

Their eyes met.

The man froze, mouth agape, then dropped his hand from his lips.

Dog wagged his tail, flicking water up from the sidewalk.

"Hungry, huh?" The man held out the scrap.

Wow, that was easy. If only every day were filled with such delicious miracles.

Wagging his tail harder, Dog trotted toward him.

The man scowled, yanking back his foot to kick. "Get the..."

"*Cookie trick! Danger! Danger!*" screamed a voice in Dog's head. Rump down to make himself a smaller target, he scuttled beyond reach. Kicks hurt. Hurt so much.

Tail between his legs, Dog skulked along, scanning everything and everyone, wary of what might be lurking in the gloom that drenched him as thoroughly as the rain.

He always had to be alert.

Someone called out behind him. He flinched and glanced back as one boy shouted to another. Even though the boys were a long way off, Dog scurried on. Boys were cruel. Being tempted by a cookie that time had cost him dearly. He'd limped for a week after falling for that trick.

8

He quickened his pace.

Danger was everywhere. Slashing claws, gnashing teeth, punishing fists and feet... any of them could come at any moment.

Though far worse dangers were out there.

He shuddered and peered around again, praying he wouldn't see the Gray Man about to pounce.

Only ordinary people hustled along the street — people who barely noticed him. Dog sighed with relief and tramped on, as he always did. The world was hard, but at least understanding his place in it was easy: he was a nobody from nowhere, as insignificant as a shadow in twilight's last glimmer.

He reached the building where the five fake-people stood motionless in a big window all day, every day. It wasn't their lack of movement that gave them away as fake, but their lack of a proper scent whenever the door opened and warm air wafted out. Other than changing their clothes once in a while, they did nothing, yet passersby often found them so fascinating they stopped to gawk.

Today, a young woman gazed at them from beneath a red umbrella, as if the fakers had a deep secret to share with those willing to join their pack.

Dog tottered over and slumped against the building, gasping for breath, legs shaking from weakness as lack of food sapped his energy. Hanging his head, he closed his eyes for a moment's rest. There had to be something to eat somewhere, some scrap a stranger had tossed away or dropped. Anything. Just a crumb to stop the grinding pain in his belly and give him the strength to do what he had to do.

Lifting his head, he scoured the scents drifting on the air, homing in on the source of each for his eyes and ears to expand on what his nose was telling him: a man who'd dined on fish for lunch, a crushed can containing a few drops of sugary liquid, a woman wheeling a bawling child sitting in its own poop...

Nothing edible.

He eyed the mute, motionless fakers in the window, then the mute, motionless woman staring at them. No one was doing *anything*, so what was going on? Could she see something he couldn't?

He didn't get people — they fixated on the strangest things. Every day, they bustled around, clinging to boxes and bags obviously filled with precious things. Then the next day, back they came for even more boxes and bags filled with even more precious things.

Yet despite their endless hunt for precious things always being so fruitful, they never seemed happy. At least, not the people he came across. It was a mystery, and while Dog loved a good mystery, all his pondering on this one had failed to reveal a conclusive answer: people were either plain out-and-out crazy or simple creatures easily distracted by the most fleeting of whims. Sadly, neither boded well for establishing any sort of relationship with any of them.

The red-umbrella-woman did a double take, noticing he was watching her. She eyed him up and down.

Dog gently wagged his tail. Some people seemed to like that, and while it didn't work often, when it did, they threw him a scrap of sandwich or a bit of cookie, or, on rare occasions, gave him a little pat. He always hoped for food, yet bizarrely, sometimes a pat felt even better. It was like, for a few seconds, he was no longer invisible and that made him glow inside. Maybe people weren't the only ones who were crazy.

The tiniest sneer flickered across the woman's face as if it was insulting to share the same space with him. She turned her back and flounced away.

Dog sighed. Sometimes being invisible was preferable to being seen.

Desperate to find something to eat, he pushed away from the wall, but lightheadedness suddenly swept over him and he staggered sideways. He caught himself before he fell, then slumped back against the building. Soon. He'd search again soon.

Dog closed his eyes to gather his strength.

"Dog," called a woman's voice.

His chest heaving, Dog gulped air while he rested his weary legs.

The voice came louder. "Hey, dog!"

Dog opened his eyes at the sound of a raised voice and turned his head to investigate. A woman stalked directly toward him, draped in a jacket made of the blackened skin of some flattened animal.

He gasped, his eyes popping wider.

The woman strode closer and closer, her long brown hair soaked and plastered to her head.

The jacket, the hair, the purposeful approach... oh boy, was she scary. Dog trembled.

If he pushed off the wall to run, he'd collapse, so he did the only thing he could — he screwed his eyes shut, cowered to be as small a target as possible, and braced for the shower of kicks that would inevitably come.

He waited. Shaking.

The voice softened. "You okay, little fella?"

Praying he could be invisible again, Dog held his breath. If he didn't move, didn't even breathe, maybe the scary woman would leave him alone.

After a few seconds, with the rumble of traffic the only sound, he dared to peek through one eye, hoping the danger had passed.

The woman was crouched only a few feet away, staring right at him.

He whimpered.

"Stay there." She raised an open palm toward him. "I'll try to find a store for some kibble, okay?"

If she took just one more step, that hand would be within striking distance to clobber him. He couldn't run, but he had to do something. Maybe he could drive her away to give him the time he needed to recover.

He growled.

"So there's still some fight in you yet, huh, boy? Good." She straightened up. "Stay there. I'll be back."

She strolled away. Unlike the other people who scurried through the rain like it was hot and would scald them, or shuffled hunching over in a futile bid to stay dry, she glided with an animal-like grace, the weather seeming to mean nothing to her. A moment later, she vanished around a corner.

Dog gulped a huge breath. Oh boy, that was close. Talk about a lucky escape. However, in case she came back, he had no choice but to leave as soon as possible, whether he was ready or not.

Easing off the wall, he let his legs take his full weight to check if he could stand without falling. He swayed, then held steady, so he trudged on. He glanced around to make sure the woman wasn't coming back, then shuffled over to the curb, peering across the road and farther down the street.

There it was.

His heart beat that little faster, a flicker of hope dancing inside it. Maybe today would be the day and he'd find a message waiting for him. A message saying they were okay, they were back, they were searching for him just as he was for them.

Maybe...

Yes, today felt like a good day. He was sure today was going to be the day. The best day ever.

Hope soothing his aches, his tail swept up from between his legs and a renewed bounce filled each step. Yes, today was the day. After all, it was only logical that all the bad days eventually balanced out with good days. And only a fool argued with logic.

Gaze fixed on his goal, he trundled out into the road.

A deafening honk blared.

Dog jumped and whipped his head around as a blue bus thundered straight at him. He darted across to the other sidewalk as the vehicle tore past just inches from him.

Safe, Dog gulped a deep breath and watched the bus disappear.

What must it be like to travel inside such a machine? Surely it was only for the bravest of people, those who lived for adventure. But that was another mystery for another day. Only one thing mattered now, as it did every day at this time: had he been left a message?

He'd been disappointed so often he almost didn't want to check, but he *had* to. Hope laced with despair churned inside him as he dodged around the people dashing around in an attempt to stay dry.

Yes, today was the day. He could feel it.

And then, straight ahead, there it was.

He quickened his pace, eager to learn the secrets it kept.

Chapter 2

It stood near the entrance to the park, where it always stood. Silent, commanding, conspicuous. It never moved, never made a sound, never did anything except stand in the same place all day, every day, making it ideal for what they'd needed.

The red fire hydrant gleamed in the rain.

Dog sniffed the air as he drew closer and scoured the scents. He ignored some, filtered out others to investigate further, then moved on to what remained. Scent after scent after scent.

Ten feet away, his shoulders slumped and he slowed to a shuffle.

There was no new message — no, not today. Just like there hadn't been yesterday, or the day before, or any of the days since that nightmare day when it had happened. His nose was never wrong.

His legs heavy with disappointment, Dog plodded over to the hydrant, sniffing, but already knowing what he'd find.

They were still here — all four of them — but weaker now. So weak, it would soon be impossible for him to tell they'd been there at all. Time was washing them away from the hydrant just as it was washing them away from his memories.

But that wasn't the only reason they were fading. Another scent marked the hydrant. A powerful scent. A dark scent. Dog shuddered. Some monster was overmarking his pack's scent to wipe them from existence, proclaiming his presence, his dominance. Claiming their territory as his and his alone.

The scent was a few hours old, as it usually was by the time Dog arrived. A fresher scent always saw him turn tail and scuttle away. He'd have loved to arrive first thing in the morning to wait as long as possible for his pack to return, yet he quaked at the thought of meeting the monster face-to-face. There was something about that scent, something ominous, dangerous. Something terrifying.

With the area safe from immediate threat, Dog crept right up to the hydrant and sniffed the left-hand side. There she was, his mother. She'd taught him the importance of marking by peeing on things: to let others know he was around, to attract new friends, to claim something as his... so many incredibly useful messages all in one. It was strange people didn't pee on stuff when it was such a simple yet powerful technique. Or maybe they did, but he hadn't yet caught one of them doing it.

Yes, that was another mystery he needed to investigate one day: why didn't people pee on stuff to announce their arrival or stake their claim? One night a wobbly man had peed against the wall in Dog's alley, but he wasn't typical because he'd fallen over as he'd staggered away, so had to be discounted as he was obviously ill. Other than that, Dog hadn't found a single clue that people peed anywhere.

People were so weird. They were alien creatures compared to every other kind of animal he'd encountered. They simply didn't fit into the world. They were... awkward. Yes, that was it — awkward. In how they moved and, if the way they interacted with everything around them was any indication, in how they thought.

Dog studied them every day during his search, and the evidence was overwhelming. Instead of eating all their food or hiding it for later, they left it lying on the ground for anyone to take — thankfully! When they tried to run, it was either all flailing arms with red-faced huffing and puffing or dainty steps with barely a change in speed. As for their sense of smell — oh, the way they squawked if they stepped in a tiny bit of poop because they hadn't smelled it. How could *anyone* not smell poop?

No, with such appalling survival skills, they didn't fit into the world. Not at all. Although, that did go some way to explaining why they worked their butts off to change a perfectly good world into something more people-friendly. With all the effort that demanded, it was no wonder they were so grouchy all the time. He'd have to try to be more tolerant of them in the future — they obviously had difficult lives.

Circling the hydrant, he sniffed all around it, reveling in the scent-induced memories as he picked up the smell of each of his three brothers. Though, the littlest was so faint, he might not even be there tomorrow.

Dog hung his head and whined. He was losing them all over again. The first time had been traumatic enough: seeing them all disappearing into the distance hurt his chest worse than any kick he'd ever suffered. He'd cowered in their box, waiting and waiting for them to come back. Whimpering, trembling, alone. He'd waited days, waited until his stomach gnawed at him so much he couldn't last any longer without eating something.

He'd lost track of how many weeks ago that had been, but these days, when he wasn't searching for food, he still waited in their box, yet not one of them had made it home so far.

And now, with their scents fading more and more every minute, they were being ripped away from him again.

Pain clawed in his chest. He longed to snuggle up to his mother — to have her scent fill his nostrils, her warmth hug his body, her breathing soothe his troubles.

He whimpered. He didn't mean to; it just leaked out.

Glancing around, he hoped a passerby might see him, sense his distress, and reach out and touch him. Just for a second so he knew the world wasn't such a desperate and lonely place, where every being had no choice but to face day after day after day of endless struggle completely and utterly alone.

No one stopped.

No one reached out.

No one even looked at him.

He was invisible.

Hanging his head, tail drooping, he moved around to the other side of the hydrant, raised his leg, and squirted a few drops of pee on an area that wouldn't cover any of his family's scent. If they came, they'd know he was still around and to search for him.

Sniffling away the rain from his nose, Dog closed his eyes and drew in the longest breath he could to seal the scent of his pack in his mind and heart forever. Each unique smell of each family member danced on his senses, conjuring a time of snuggling in a box alive with paws and tails and whimpers and yips and warmth and love.

The instant he opened his eyes, they vanished.

With a whimper, he turned away.

Slouching along the street, he checked the ground next to a building for scraps of food, then crossed over to check the gutter.

Nothing.

Drifting on the wind, the faintest hint of something edible grabbed his attention. Dog tipped his nose up into the air. As though the scent had looped a cord around his neck to lead him, it drew him toward a bench under a tree where people often relaxed while eating, but today the black wooden seat was slicked with water and sat empty.

As he got closer, the smell grew stronger. Fries. Fries sprinkled with salt. Soggy, but still fresh.

Excellent! Not only had he found food, but he'd be able to slink under the bench and out of the rain to dine in style. There was a time when he could run under benches like this one without any effort, but for the last couple of weeks, he'd had to remember to duck to get under or he banged his head. Boy, he had to be such a big dog now.

His disheartened shuffle turned into a hopeful stride, and his mouth watered as he imagined burying his snout in a delicious mound of cold potato. It was his lucky day after all! His nose was never wrong, and it said there were enough fries to fill him, so he'd be able to go home to his box early and shelter from the awful weather.

However, there was another scent too. Not the monster from his pack's hydrant, but something else.

Dog slowed as he neared the bench. He inhaled the scent again, struggling to identify the mysterious smell.

16

Something moved in the shadows beneath the bench. Something big and black.

Dog crept closer, hunched over to peer underneath it. Fries scattered the ground, and something was eating them.

Dog froze.

A big black bird lifted a fry in its beak, tossed its head back, and devoured the soggy strip of potato.

Dog stared at its enormous daggerlike beak as it stabbed at another fry.

Okay, that was a big bird. A very, very big bird. But he was bigger.

He marched forward.

Standing side-on to him, the bird stopped eating and glared from one beady black eye.

Dog prowled forward, a rumbling growl coming from deep in his throat.

Cawww! The bird beat its wings at him.

He gasped and jerked back. Heart racing, he stared at the bird, as confused as he was shocked. This thing did know it was smaller than he was, right?

The bird taunted him by scoffing another fry, and his stomach clenched. He needed food.

Dog bared his teeth, then barked.

The bird devoured another fry as if he didn't even exist.

Dog barked a second time.

And again, the bird ate another one of *his* fries.

Dog snorted. That was the last one the bird was having. He was going to eat fries now, then he was going home to wait in his box.

He inched toward the bird. With his head lowered, he glared at it as a growl rumbled in his throat again.

Any moment, the bird would realize what a mistake it had made, flutter like a fool, and disappear into the gloomy sky.

He stalked closer.

The bird continued eating *his* fries.

Closer...

Closer...

So close he could snap at the feathered beast if he stretched. Maybe he wouldn't be eating fries today; maybe he'd be having bird.

Closer...

The bird flung its wings open and launched itself at Dog. It pecked his nose, then fluttered back under the bench.

Dog yelped and scrambled back. Slipping in the wet, he crashed to the ground, his bottom jaw hitting the concrete, jarring his teeth.

Clambering up, he glowered at the bird. The bird eating *his* fries, nice and dry under the bench.

Its head held high, chest puffed out, the bird glowered back. *Cawww!*

Dog bolted, forsaking the precious food in favor of keeping his nose intact.

Once at a safe distance, he slowed to an amble but glanced back to be sure the bird hadn't followed him out of spite.

It hadn't.

Wise move, too. Not following him was the smartest move that bird had ever made because he was ready for it now. A surprise attack might have worked once, but it wouldn't work a second time.

He glanced back again, just to be sure.

Still not coming.

Why hadn't he bitten the horrible thing? Bitten it and eaten the fries. He could have been on his way home after having had a decent meal for a change.

It was just a bird. A *bird!* He was a big, streetwise dog — or he was supposed to be. What was he doing running away from a bird? What would his mother think? Talk about a wuss.

Maybe he needed to go back and teach the bird what a mean dog he was.

But it really was big. A giant of a bird. What if it hurt his nose so he couldn't smell to find food or his mother? What then?

Yeah, the smart move would be to leave his revenge for another day.

Wuss.

No, he wasn't. He was being smart.

He trudged on along the sidewalk.

A young woman, wearing a ribbed blue coat with the hood up, stood looking in a window at more of those fake-people who never moved. She held a chain in her left hand, the other end being tied around a tawny dog's neck. The woman had mutilated the poor creature — it should have been covered, with luscious curly fur, but most of it had been shaven bare, leaving only balled tufts on its feet, head, and chest. As for its tail... where the devil was it? There was little more than a stump left.

The poor thing looked like a circus freak.

Crazy. People were crazy. It was like an illness — people-crazy. Dog hoped it wasn't contagious.

He stared at the poor beast. Its head bowed, it shivered in the rain.

And Dog thought *his* life was bad.

Maybe it dreamed of having a friend too and of escaping such abuse. Maybe they could start a new pack together and find a place where there was food, freedom, and definitely — definitely — not a bird in sight.

He trotted over and said hello as any polite dog should — he sniffed his new friend's butt.

The woman yanked on the chain, jerking her circus dog closer to her. "Get away, you filthy animal!"

Dog leapt back. Moving over to the curb, he scooted around the pair, giving them a wide berth and eyeing the other dog as he passed. The poor animal looked so pathetic. It obviously knew it was doomed to a life of being nothing but a precious thing: an object someone owned, not a companion someone loved.

Dog's gaze fell to the ground. Even though the circus dog was so abused, at least it wasn't alone. Dog was never going to be loved like the animals he'd seen people dote over in the park, so what was he going to do if his pack never came back? Be alone forever? Never feel a hand that wasn't hitting, hear a voice that wasn't screaming, see a face that wasn't scowling? Was that a life?

He glanced back at the circus freak. Could it be that some sacrifices were worth making, some abuses worth taking, simply to have the company of another living creature?

A smell slapped Dog in the face, snapping him from his thoughts.

He paused midstride. What was that? Could it be...?

He sniffed. Sniffed again.

Turning his head to the left, he sniffed harder, craning his neck to stick his head out farther in that direction.

It was. He was sure it was. He always trusted his nose, and it was telling him the second-best thing in the world it could ever tell him: hot dog!

Chapter 3

Dribs and drabs of people meandered from a green fast-food truck with a giant glowing hot dog hanging over the serving hatch farther down the street. Dog had found food in this area a number of times before, so was today going to be another lucky day?

The scent of succulent cooking pork wafted over: sausages, burgers, hot dogs. Saliva pooled in Dog's mouth. He passed the truck every day, and the smell always drove him nuts. Not just because it was so heavenly, but because he dreamed of how the warm, fresh meat would taste compared to the occasional cold, decaying scraps he found nearby.

Unfortunately, no matter how many times he dreamed of a fresh hot dog, that was all it was — a dream.

Once, Dog had found the truck's back door open, so he'd ventured inside. Big mistake. A man in a white apron had screamed and kicked him so hard his ribs hurt for a week, so he'd never tried again and had given up all hope of ever tasting a fresh hot dog. Like anyone was ever going to take someone like him to such a place for a hot meal.

Though his paws ached from tramping the streets since dawn, he quickened his pace, the thought of food — real food, not dream food — powering his weary legs.

A young man and woman strode toward him hunched under an umbrella together. Walking arm in arm, each stared down at a small flat black board in their free hand on which they tapped with their thumb. Too distracted by whatever was on their boards, they didn't see him but marched on as if he wasn't there.

Dog jerked sideways to avoid being trampled, then hugged a building's wall to avoid people as much as possible.

He scampered along, the giant hot dog glowing brighter and brighter as the scent grew stronger and stronger.

He couldn't get too close to the truck because, following the kicking incident, the aproned man always shooed him away, yet he didn't have to get close because this smell wasn't a hot, fresh smell. No, it was different. Old and cold, it meant only one thing — the food had been dumped because it was unwanted. Unwanted by anyone except him.

It really was his lucky day. At last, all the bad times were going to balance out with good times.

Dog drooled.

Forgetting about the food truck and what he could see, he focused on what he could smell and allowed his nose to guide him past the vehicle.

Ahead on the left, the mouth of a dark alley loomed. He stepped away from the wall toward the middle of the sidewalk, putting some space between him and it as he approached. Except for his own, he didn't like alleys. Too many bad things had happened in them.

As he got closer, he slowed to a shuffle. Sniffing the air, he shuddered. Maybe his nose was wrong this time. Maybe he wasn't just hungry but sick, so his nose was misleading him. Or maybe the bird attack had hurt him so his nose was off its game. Whatever it was, this time, his nose was wrong. It had to be.

Creeping along the curb to stay as far away as possible from the alley, he tensed and dared to peer into the shadow-strewn depths. He didn't want to go in there. He was *not* going in there.

However, now so close to the entrance, his nose confirmed his deepest fear — the food he so desperately needed was hiding down in the darkness.

But that wasn't his biggest problem.

Chapter 4

Dog skulked over to the corner of the building next to the alley's gaping mouth, his heart thumping in his chest, threatening to burst out. He inched nearer to the edge of the wall but couldn't see around. Inched nearer. Nearer still. Tantalizingly close, he craned his neck and leaned so far forward he couldn't stretch farther without toppling over. Finally, he peeked into the gloom-drenched cavern.

He trembled.

He didn't need to see into the shadows to know what lurked there because his nose had already told him. There was his hot dog, yes, but now that beguiling smell had entwined with another scent. One far darker, one he'd come across before, one he dreaded.

The fur on his back stood on end and his legs shook, threatening to give and crash him to the ground. His heartbeat skyrocketing, he gulped.

Oh, yes, he knew what waited down there. A monster. Not a bird, but a *real* monster. The monster that was trying to wipe his pack from existence by overmarking them.

Dog hung his head. He couldn't go down there knowing what waited for him.

His stomach clawed at him, demanding food. Again, he peeped into the murkiness.

No, it was too dangerous. Only a fool would risk it.

But a wuss would say that, wouldn't they?

He was not a wuss. It had been a very big, very aggressive bird that could have seriously hurt his nose, and then what? No nose meant no food, so he'd starve. Simple.

Yeah, a wuss would say that, too.

He was not a wuss!

Then why had he run away from a bird of all things? A *bird*!

Hunger mauled his insides, and his stomach rumbled so loudly people in the next street probably heard it. Dog cringed, imagining the monster hearing and springing at him from the shadows.

He glowered into the darkness. Nothing moved.

Shaking with the nervous energy shooting through his body, he gulped and stepped into the alley, then took another teetering step. He was a big dog now, far bigger than he'd ever been. Big enough to take what he wanted, and he wanted that food, so that was exactly what he was going to do — take it, no matter what was lurking with it.

Dog sucked in the largest breath he could manage. His chest swelled, and he pushed up on all four paws to make himself as tall and broad as possible.

He could do this. He was a big dog now. Big.

He stalked down the alley, scanning the environment. A black metal staircase zigzagged up the side of a wall plastered with dark green algae on the right, while on the left, a blue van was parked between a doorway and two battered dumpsters.

Dog edged farther, each tentative step confirming he was a big dog who could do what was necessary to get what he wanted. Yet, with each step, the buildings stretched up around him, closing in to trap him inside a menacing cage.

His mouth watered, the scent of his hot dog so much stronger. *His* hot dog.

But someone else thought it was *his* hot dog too.

Behind the van stood four trash cans, with a fifth knocked on its side to spew garbage onto the concrete. A monstrous hound as dark as night pawed through the pile.

Dog gulped again, hunching over to make himself small,

unthreatening, invisible, even though he desperately wanted to be big and dangerous.

Hunger forcing him on, he lifted a paw to take another step, but his legs shook so much they buckled. He just managed to catch himself before he crumpled to the cold concrete. He drew another huge breath and strode on, taking the smallest steps he could, even though each one felt gigantic as they hauled him closer to the gargantuan beast.

This monster was trying to wipe his pack from existence by overmarking their scent. A wuss would run away and let that slide, but a big dog would make it pay for that crime.

Dog tottered forward.

As if destroying Dog's pack wasn't enough, now this thing was trying to steal his hot dog. It would pay for that crime too.

Another tiny step.

He'd seen for himself that life was unfair, seen some dogs riding around in cars, cozy and fat, while others haunted the streets, ribs on display for all to count. It made no sense. There had to be balance — win one day, lose the next. It was only logical. Everything had to even out over time, and today there was going to balance. Today was going to be *his* day because he was eating that hot dog. Period.

Dog slunk closer.

The monstrous hound's upper lip arched, and a rasping snarl shook the alley. The thing didn't even look up, obviously seeing him as so little of a threat it couldn't be bothered.

A voice inside Dog's head screamed, "*Run! Run! Run!*"

Although Dog desperately wanted to do just that, he didn't because there was something he wanted even more, something he *needed* even more: food, and to prove he was a big dog others should fear.

His paw trembling, he reached forward to take another teetering step.

This time, Hound looked up. Dark eyes burned with fury and bared teeth glistened as Hound snarled a second time, standing up to its full height. The tip of Dog's nose was barely on the same level as Hound's chest.

With a gulp, Dog stared up at the savage daggerlike teeth hanging over him.

Dog had fought with his brothers when he was tiny, and he'd held his own, and now he was much bigger than he was then. Or was he? Looking at Hound, he felt like a week-old puppy again. Hound was big. So very, very big.

Dog heaved himself up to be as tall as he could be. Though he was still young, he was wise enough to know it wasn't always the biggest dog that got what it wanted, but the dog with the biggest bite.

And he wanted *his* hot dog.

No way could Hound want it more than he did, which meant only one thing: that hot dog was his. *His!*

If Dog's ordeal with the bird had taught him anything, it was to confirm size didn't always win a battle — sometimes it merely came down to who struck first.

Dog lunged.

Chapter 5

Dog hobbled along the sidewalk, holding his left forepaw off the ground. He winced as his right landed on the ground, the impact sending shockwaves through his body, jarring his injuries.

The streetlights cast an eerie yellow light over the dark buildings that walled him in. He never liked to be on the streets this late, but it was taking him longer than normal to struggle back after his encounter with Hound.

He strained to pry his right eye open to better watch for dangers, yet he could manage only a squint through the stinging pain.

Shivering, he gasped for air as he composed himself before pushing himself to take another step. After a few seconds, he lurched forward again, and again he winced at the sharp pain that drove through his body like a stake.

With every step he took, the night sky seemed to sink lower, closing in around him, as if trying to smother him. Its blackness seeped into his body, draining every last drop of his strength and hope as it fought to squash him into the sidewalk, to leave nothing but a stain the rain would wash away.

His legs gave way and he slumped against a brick wall. Though his chest heaved, there wasn't enough air in the entire world to give him the strength to carry on to his alley.

This was it. The end.

He slid partway down the wall, the dark, damp ground seeming so welcoming.

His mother flashed into his mind.

Dog gritted his teeth. A good dog never abandoned its pack. What if she came back and he wasn't there waiting for her?

He pushed to stand once more, yelping as pain stabbed his shoulder.

Panting with the effort, he lumbered another step, battling his way along the sidewalk as clouds skittered across the moon. Finally, he turned a corner, and there, only feet away, was a moldy old box lying on its side.

Home.

Swaying, Dog had to focus to stop himself from toppling over with the relief.

The sight of the filthy box energized his beaten body. He staggered toward it as fast as he could and collapsed inside. He was home. Home!

He hadn't eaten today. Again. Neither had he found a message from his mother or any of his brothers. Again. As if that wasn't bad enough, now he could barely walk.

Every day was nothing but struggle — struggle for food, struggle for warmth, struggle for companionship. And every day was disappointment. *Every day.* There was no such thing as balance. No win one day, lose the next. It was all lose, lose, lose. Was that really all there was to life? There had to be more than an endless struggle. Surely.

Dog gazed up at the blackness still straining to smother him, now so close he could all but bite it.

There had to be something. Anything. But what?

He stared up at the pinpricks of white set in the darkest of heavens. What were they? So many tiny lights in a wilderness of black, it was almost as if they were lights left on to guide lost loved ones home.

Dog didn't have a light to guide anyone to him. He whimpered.

Starving, cold, and so alone, he did the only thing a dog could do — he howled. He prayed his mother or his brothers might hear, because if they did, he could guide them home and they'd be a family again. A proper pack.

While the night grew blacker and colder, he howled. And howled. And howled.

And waited. And waited. And waited...

Chapter 6

Dog slowly raised his head off the floor of his moldy old box, flinching with pain. The sun was up, but gloom still devoured the alley. Lying on his side, he licked the gash over his ribs, wincing as his tongue scraped over the raw flesh. However, the wound had to be cleaned, so he shut his eyes and tensed his muscles, then licked and licked, pretending there was no pain.

A noise he hadn't heard before made him freeze, his tongue still out as it dragged over his wound.

He held his breath, listening as hard as he could.

The noise drew nearer.

Pointing his snout at the opening in the front of his box, he sniffed, then cringed. Unknown scents hung in the air.

He sniffed harder.

People. Strangers.

Oh, no, that was the last thing he needed. No way could he fight after how Hound had injured him. The safest option was to run and hide.

He pushed to get up, but his left front leg buckled and he fell, his face crunching into the floor of his box. As he struggled to get up a second time, the strange noise came again, closer this time. Much, much closer.

Oh, no, no, no, no, no. Not now. Please not now. Not when he couldn't run, couldn't fight, couldn't even stand.

Maybe if he stayed still and silent, maybe, just maybe, they wouldn't see him and would leave him in peace. He'd been invisible most of his life, so a few seconds more shouldn't be difficult.

The noise grew louder, and the scents grew stronger.

Dog hardly dared to sniff for fear the slightest sound would give him away, yet strangely, though the noise was alien to him, it didn't sound like danger. So, what the devil was it?

It was like something he'd heard on the street, yet different. Like talking, but with rhymes and other sounds playing in the background to create a rhythm. Hearing it now, though, it was a lone voice with no other noises — a young voice.

But the sound didn't matter; what mattered was it meant people. And people meant only one thing: trouble.

Two slender legs appeared outside his home. Dog froze, heart racing, mind a whirl of nightmares.

"Daddy," the voice called out, "what shall I do with this moldy old box?"

"Is there anything in it?" asked an older voice.

A young girl looked into Dog's home, long black locks of silky hair flowing in the light breeze, a stark contrast to her porcelain complexion.

Dog gasped. So did the girl.

Still on his side, Dog kicked frantically but his paws skidded on the smooth floor. Bit by bit, he lurched and bucked his way to the very back of his box, as far away from the danger as he could get — children were always so cruel — but as he squeezed against the wall, he twisted his bad leg and yelped.

"There's a dog!" called out the little girl.

"What?"

"A dog, Daddy. There's a little dog. And I think he's hurt."

A hand reached in. Into *his* box.

The voice in his head screamed again, *"Danger! Danger! Danger!"*

Battling the pain, Dog scrambled to push up to run, to hide, to get far, far away. He heaved with all his might, straining and straining, yet his bad leg buckled time and again.

And then the strangest thing happened.

The hand didn't slap him, didn't punch him, didn't claw him. Instead, it rested on him ever so gently. Maybe the gentlest thing that had ever existed in the entire history of the world.

An intense feeling of well-being washed over him, and for a moment, it was as if someone else cared about him, as if he'd connected with another living being and was no longer alone. It was the first time he'd felt like that since losing his family. The feeling was so primal, so overwhelming, he couldn't help but let out a little whimper.

"It's okay," said the young voice. "No one's going to hurt you."

The girl did a weird thing with her face. It was so weird, Dog couldn't help but stare. He'd seen people do it before — to each other, never to him — and he'd always wondered why they did it and what it meant, and now, here was a stranger doing it to him. What was wrong with her that she wanted to make her face do something so weird?

With her lips parted, the girl showed him her teeth. But it wasn't a snarl like he'd seen so many times before. No, this was different. He didn't know what to make of it except that, in a strange way, it kind of warmed him inside. *Weird.*

Footsteps clomped closer, and the older voice said, "A dog? In the box?"

The girl looked away from Dog. "He's hurt. We have to do something."

As if Dog's day couldn't get any worse, another face peered into his home.

What was wrong with these people? He didn't go into their homes, so why on earth did they think it was okay to barge into his?

The second face was that of a man with a thin line of fur across his upper lip. He smelled of man-flowers: the male version of the fake smell people used to try to mask their natural scent. He had the same pale skin tone, which made the dark rings under his eyes all the more pronounced, but was heavier-set than the wisp-like girl.

The man frowned. "Awww. He's barely more than a puppy."

"So we have to help him."

The man grimaced, his gaze on Dog's side. "Ouch. It looks like he's been mauled by another dog."

"Please, Daddy, help him."

"I don't know. If there was some sort of free animal hospital nearby, then of course we could take him, but that..." Daddy sucked through his teeth. "Vet bills can be sky-high for the smallest of things, so something like this..." He loudly blew out a breath. "Oh, boy."

"But he's obviously got no one else, Daddy, only us. We have to help."

Daddy sighed.

"I have my allowance," said the girl. "And the money Grandma gave me for my birthday."

Scrunching up his face, Daddy shook his head. "I don't—"

"I'll do all the work to take care of him," she said. "Honest, Daddy. You won't even know he's there."

"It's not so simple, honey. A dog's a big responsibility. They're more work than you think."

"Daddy, I'm not a little girl anymore; I'm nine now. I can do stuff, if you let me."

"I know you can, sweetheart" — he rested a hand on her shoulder — "but we don't know anything about him or where he's come from. How do we know someone isn't looking for him?"

"If they are, they're not trying very hard."

"Poor little thing. He's just skin and bones." Daddy reached into Dog's home. "Have you been in the wars, boy?"

Another hand reaching into his home was too much! Dog growled, then snapped at him.

Daddy jerked back.

"Don't be scared, Daddy. He won't bite." The little girl reached in again.

Daddy snatched her hand away. "Don't, Mia. He's dangerous."

"No, he isn't." Mia reached in with her other hand and rested it on Dog's side. She showed her teeth to Daddy. "See?"

Dog didn't snarl, didn't growl, didn't pull farther back into his box. He stared up into Mia's face, into her blue eyes that sparkled like the water in the park on a glorious spring morning. He'd never seen eyes that color before. The only eyes he'd ever seen so close had all been brown: the eyes of his mother and brothers.

He studied her. With such gentle hands and sky-blue eyes, there was something strange about this girl. Strange... but warm, soothing, welcoming.

Mia stroked his back, and he let her. It reminded him of how his mother licked him to wash his fur.

"Kai's a good dog. See, Daddy? A good dog." She leaned closer and did the weird thing of showing her teeth again. "Aren't you, huh, Kai? Aren't you, boy?"

"Kai? You've already given him a name?"

"No. He looks like a Kai, so that's always been his name." She continued stroking him and didn't turn to Daddy. "That's why you said Mommy called me Mia, isn't it? Because that wasn't what you'd decided before I came, was it?"

Daddy looked at the girl with a sadness in his eyes. He stroked her long, flowing hair just the way she was stroking Dog.

"That's right, sweetheart. Mommy took one look and knew instantly: Mia. She said it couldn't be anything else."

"So, she'd understand and want us to help Kai, too." She looked at Daddy, her big round eyes pleading more than her words. "Please, Daddy, he's so small and so poor."

Daddy grimaced and shook his head. "Mia—"

"Please!"

Water welled in the bottoms of the little girl's eyes.

"It's not so simple, sweetheart." Daddy gazed away. "Dogs demand a huge commitment, not just expense. With everything that's happened, I think it would be a mistake to rush into something like this."

"But..." She hung her head.

Mia continued stroking Dog, continued soothing his pain, and continued that connection, so he did what a good dog was supposed to do — he leaned around and licked her hand to show his appreciation.

Mia showed even more of her teeth than she had before and made an odd little grunting noise.

Then Daddy did something strange. As he looked at the girl, and how she was showing so many gleaming white teeth, water welled in his eyes too. It was as if he'd never seen such a look on her face and was moved by it. Yet a darkness tinged his expression. A deep, deep darkness. As if he knew the moment would be only fleeting and then that darkness would once more consume them both. As if he knew he had to do something special if he wanted the girl's expression to last for more than just a few seconds.

Chapter 7

Mia's bedroom was the pinkest thing Dog had ever seen. He doubted there could be anything pinker, even if he traveled to the farthest corners of the world. The curtains, pink; the comforter, pink; the wallpaper, pink. But he wasn't pink, so what on earth was he doing here?

Pictures of dogs, cats, and some of the weirdest creatures he'd ever seen plastered most of the pink walls. Many just couldn't be real, especially the fat gray thing that looked like it had caught its face in a door and tried to run away, stretching its nose so badly the tip trailed on the ground. Dog liked his nose the way it was, so if that was what could happen, he'd have to be careful with the doors in the house. How would he ever run if he was in constant danger of tripping over his nose?

The bed was also littered with strange creatures: fake things that only looked like animals because they were furry, yet they didn't resemble any creature Dog had ever actually seen. Many had ridiculous expressions and even more ridiculous coloring — he'd wandered the streets every day but had never seen a bright green dog.

Mia crouched on the floor near the wall opposite the foot of her bed. She eased up the edge of the brown blanket Daddy had laid Dog on and draped it over him, covering the white patch the man in the green uniform had stuck on him while he'd been lying on a cold metal table. That man had also jabbed something sharp into the back of his neck. It hurt for a second, then, as if by magic, the pain in his side and bad leg vanished. That was also when he'd started to feel drowsy. He'd drifted off to sleep for a while, but now, he forced himself to stay awake so he could check what was going on, discover where these people had taken him, and figure out how he was ever going to find his box again.

"This should keep you warm, Kai," said Mia, tucking the blanket around him. "But I'll be just over there" — she pointed to a bed — "so don't worry. I'll be checking on you and be right here if you need me."

Mia showed her teeth again — she seemed to do it every time he looked at her. So strange. Maybe she had some illness that meant she couldn't control her face. Or a mental affliction. Poor thing. It had to be one of the two because it wasn't normal. Just like all the care they were showering upon him. Utterly abnormal. He'd encountered enough people on the streets to know what to expect of them. Something was going on here, but what? Luckily, Dog was good at solving mysteries.

The rustling of large sheets of paper drew Dog's attention to yet another mystery — as if he didn't have enough mysteries to solve already. On his hands and knees, Daddy was working his way backward toward the door, moving in an arc from side to side and laying sheets of newspaper on the polished wood floor. It was obviously for Dog's benefit because Daddy had tripled the layers around the blanket they'd given him.

Dog tilted his head to one side and looked at all the paper. They did know he couldn't understand the strange markings people loved to plaster over things, right?

Or maybe he'd solved another mystery — they thought he could understand because they were crazy.

Yes, that was it. That explained the weird face thing, the weird bringing him here thing, and the weird green-uniform man with his weird sharp thing.

They had people-crazy. Big-time. He'd been abducted by nutjobs.

How the devil was he going to get out of this fine mess?

Mia slid two white ceramic bowls toward his snout. "Here's some water and some food. Please try to eat something. The vet said you'll get better much faster if you have some proper food inside you."

The left bowl was filled with brown, sloppy gunk. It smelled delicious — even better than damp, cold hot dog, which until today he'd thought was an absolute impossibility.

But he didn't eat it.

His mouth watered when he looked at it, yet there was no telling what these crazies might have put in it. It was better to play safe. For all he knew, everything they were doing could be a trick, and the food could be poisoned. Admittedly, this was an odd way to torture him, but he'd fallen for tricks before: the time those boys had tempted him over with a cookie only to kick him and then hurl stones at him when he ran to escape. Oh yeah, he wasn't falling for anything like that again.

That said, it was warm here — cozy — and Mia and Daddy seemed genuine. Crazy, but genuine. Maybe they simply didn't know they were abnormal. Like they believed it was perfectly acceptable to be nice to a stranger for no reason. Nevertheless, he knew crazy when he saw it.

Something else wasn't right, too. Something was masked by the smell of the brown gunk and clouded by his drowsiness, which thankfully was wearing off.

Dog poked his snout up into the air and sniffed, investigating the scents circulating the room.

Something flowery, but not flowers. What could it be?

He sniffed again.

It smelled... wrong, because whatever he could smell was inside when it should have been outside.

Sweeping his nose in an arc, he found the culprit: a plant on the windowsill with, unsurprisingly, clusters of small pink flowers on the ends of stalks that protruded over roundish green leaves. It smelled... how did it smell? He sniffed again.

Not like the man-flowers smothering Daddy, nor like the flowers he smelled in the park. No, these flowers smelled... wild. Like they would refuse to grow in neat orderly rows with all the other flowers but just pop up wherever the devil they pleased. Boy, this place was a complete nuthouse.

Dog yawned, the excitement of the day catching up with him. His eyelids drooped, and it became harder and harder to watch what was going on in Crazy Town. Unable to prevent it any longer, he fell fast asleep.

* * *

Dog opened his eyes to a room swathed in darkness. Daddy had disappeared and Dog's nose said the mound under the pink comforter on the bed was Mia. All was still and quiet – unbelievably quiet. So quiet, something had to be wrong.

The world was always noisy: people walking and talking, cars rumbling, city hubbub.

He strained to hear something, lifting his head and turning it this way and that, panning his ears to catch even the tiniest of noises.

No, nothing. What had they done to all the townsfolk and their machines?

He held his breath, straining harder to hear something, anything.

A rustling drifted in from outside as the wind fought its way through tree branches, and a creature made *wooo-wooo* noises.

What magic had made the ordinary world disappear? And where the devil was he?

The mystery would have to wait because Dog had something more pressing to deal with.

He pushed up to stand, trembling with the effort. His left leg shook as he put weight on it, but it held. Just. He hobbled off his blanket, swayed, but spread his paws and stayed upright.

Dog took a teetering step onto the first sheet of newspaper in the patchwork Daddy had created over most of the floor. Wincing as pain once more stabbed at his left foreleg, he hobbled forward. And again. And again. Slowly, he limped all the way over to the doorway, the only area of the floor not covered by paper.

His claws tapped on the wood as he turned around. He surveyed Daddy's hard work. The papers formed a meticulously constructed design, each piece overlapping its neighbors to cover almost the entire floor.

Yes, Daddy had done an excellent job and should be proud. No way could Dog spoil such a masterpiece, so he cocked his leg and peed on the door.

Once relieved, Dog turned to admire his handiwork. The last droplets of pee dribbled down the door to join the pool on the floor, which had reached its maximum size with not one drop having dampened the papers. Dog sighed contentedly. That was a good job well done, that was. Come morning, Daddy would be so pleased Dog had been careful not to spoil his wonderful artwork.

Dog hobbled back to his makeshift bed. Panting with the exertion, he slumped onto his blanket.

The next morning, the pain in Dog's side wasn't as stabbing, and his bad leg seemed stronger. Lying on his blanket, he stretched and yawned, his mouth gaping wide and tongue curling up. Mia stirred, so he looked over to see what craziness was going to engulf him today.

"Uh-oh." Getting out of bed in her pink pajamas, Mia looked from the puddle beside the door to the papers, then to Dog. Her shoulders slumped.

"All this paper and you pee here?" She pointed at the puddle.

He wagged his tail. Considering his injuries, it was impressive, wasn't it?

Mia put her hands on her hips and sighed.

Resting his chin on his front paws, he studied her. Why wasn't she thrilled he'd avoided Daddy's mosaic? Maybe she wasn't a morning person.

Mia glanced at his empty food bowl. She showed her teeth and clapped her hands. "You ate your supper! Good dog, Kai. Just don't tell Daddy about this little accident, okay?"

Having woken again after his peeing expedition, he'd found it impossible to resist the bowl of delicious gunk, so he'd wolfed it down. Obviously, it wasn't poisoned because he felt fine — better than fine. For the first time in longer than he could remember, his stomach was so full he couldn't possibly be in anything but a good mood. The only problem was he still had no idea why he'd been brought here and why these people were being so nice.

There was only one option: he had to pretend to be nice too, then maybe they'd make a mistake, and he'd discover what was really going on.

Mia immediately did something that proved it was going to be an impossible task to unveil the mystery of why they'd abducted him — she picked up a piece of Daddy's masterpiece and dumped it right in the pee he'd been so careful to keep away from it.

Crazy.

These people were crazy! How would he ever understand them?

After destroying more of the art by laying it on the floor for pee to soak it through, Mia knelt in front of him. "Do you think you're well enough for a little walk today?"

She ruffled the thick fur on the back of his neck and shoulders. It wasn't the delicate touch from the alley, but it still felt good. If she and Daddy kept doing things like that, it was going to be easy for him to pretend to be nice.

"Well, boy? Just a tiny walk to see how that leg's doing, huh?"

Dog wagged his tail. Even though his stomach was full, there was no telling when he'd next find something to eat, so it was time to get on with his daily routine: searching for food and leaving messages for his pack.

Having stretched, he was confident his leg was strong enough for him to walk, so after a couple of deep breaths, he pushed up onto all fours. His bad leg wobbled yet held firm.

"Oh, well done, Kai. And you didn't try to lick off your dressing, either. What a good boy. To think the vet said you might need one of those nasty plastic cones. I knew you were smarter than that."

Mia pulled on jeans and an orange T-shirt, picked up his food and water bowls, then opened her door.

"Come on, boy." She patted her thigh.

Curious about his luxurious prison, Dog ambled over and followed her out.

He hadn't seen much of outside or the inside of the house when they'd arrived, mainly because he'd felt so groggy after the sharp jab in his shoulders. Outside Mia's bedroom, he stopped and stared, his mouth agape.

It wasn't just Mia's room that was brightly colored, but all the walls and doors. Standing on a balcony, he gazed down on the bright blues, reds, greens, and yellows that filled the house, making it a happy place without anyone having to do anything.

Dog looked down onto a living area with brightly colored furniture that complemented the walls. Daddy was below, somewhere to the left. Dog couldn't see him, but he didn't have to — he could already recognize the scent of man-flowers mingled with Daddy's own. There was something else, too. A softer, gentler smell, more like Mia than Daddy, except it was weak, being overpowered by fresher smells. But it was definitely there. Lingering, like his pack's scent on the hydrant.

What could that be? Was there someone he hadn't yet met? He hoped not. Coping with the craziness of Mia and Daddy was quite enough for now.

He followed Mia along the balcony to a wooden staircase.

Placing the bowls on a lower step, she patted the first one. "See if you can do it with your bad leg, Kai. Don't worry if you can't, because Daddy can carry you down." She patted the step again. "Slowly, Kai. Slowly. And if you slip, don't worry, because I'll be here to catch you." She cupped her hands in front of him.

He'd seen constructions like this in the past, yet he'd never actually had to climb up or down one.

Dog lowered his good front leg toward the first step. Supporting his weight, his bad left leg trembled. He concentrated, willing his leg to be strong, but he swayed forward. Mia thrust her hands forward to grab him, yet he caught himself before he fell.

She hovered her hands a few inches from his chest. "Careful."

His paw touched the first step.

"That's it."

Yes, he could do it. Carefully, he lifted himself down onto the step. Mia clapped. "Good job, Kai. I knew you could do it."

He looked at her. She kept making a particular noise — Kai —

42

so it had to be important. If only he knew what it meant. Or was it more meaningless craziness? Maybe it was a nervous tic Mia couldn't control, like the one causing her constant need to show her teeth. What a poor, troubled little thing she was.

Taking their time, they made their way down the stairs.

Safely at the bottom and thus able to focus on investigating the place, Dog peeked this way and that, hoping he wouldn't see a fat-long-nose creature shuffling around like in the picture on Mia's wall. There wasn't one, which was a relief because the last thing he wanted was proof it was possible to have such a bad accident that his nose could be stretched longer than his legs.

"I see the patient's doing better," Daddy said, holding a flat pan in which something sizzled on a hot-making-machine.

Whatever was in the pan smelled unbelievable, producing more tantalizing aromas than Dog could count — meaty, succulent, greasy, smoky... Dog had thought the brown gunk was the most incredible thing he was ever going to smell, and yet, only hours later, here was something positively heavenly filling the air.

Mia sauntered over to Daddy, reached up on tiptoes as he ducked, and kissed him on the cheek. "Oh, he's such a good little dog. I think we're going to try to have a walk later, aren't we, Kai?" She flashed her teeth at him.

"A walk?" Daddy turned from his pan and looked at her, his eyebrows raised. "Outside?"

"No, around the bathroom, Daddy." She rolled her eyes. "Of course outside. Why? Don't you think he's strong enough?"

"I wasn't thinking about him, but... good." He nodded. "Yeah, you go for it."

"Well, the vet said he has to exercise his leg, and I want him to see where he lives now."

"Yeah, it's a great idea," said Daddy, turning back to the pan and pushing the contents around with a flat silvery tool. "You get out there and have fun together."

Mia crouched and ruffled Dog's fur on his throat. "But breakfast first, boy, huh? Breakfast?"

To pretend to be nice, Dog wagged his tail the way people sometimes seemed to like. However, he kept his focus on Daddy's pan, his mouth watering. If wagging his tail meant he could find out what the bit of heaven in the pan was, he'd wag it all day and all night.

Mia refilled his bowls with water and gunk, then put them on the floor at the far side of the table. "Kai."

He didn't take his gaze off the pan.

"Kai, breakfast."

Still fixated on the pan.

"Did he eat his supper?" asked Daddy.

"Yes."

"He might not be hungry, then. Living on the street, he probably got used to eating small amounts."

"But he's got to eat to grow stronger."

"Maybe he needs to pee first," said Daddy.

Mia screwed up her face. "I don't think so."

"No?"

"Nuh-uh."

Daddy frowned as he opened a cupboard. "You sound very sure."

"Very, very sure."

Daddy stood holding a white plate in each hand and looked at her. "You mean he's left a little gift for me upstairs?"

Face still screwed up, Mia nodded. "He kind of hit the paper. And after you show me how, I promise I'll clean up when he has more little accidents."

"Don't panic, it's not a disaster." He went back to preparing food. "I'd have been surprised if he'd held it in all night."

"So you're not upset and he can stay?"

"As long as he gets a job to contribute to the family finances."

"Daddy!" Mia gasped and playfully slapped his arm.

"Hey, why do I have to pay for everything?"

"I don't work, and you let me stay here."

"Yeah, about that. There's a nice little job cleaning up dog poop at the local pound. You've got an interview this afternoon."

"Daddy!"

"What?" With an innocent expression, he glanced at her while serving the food onto the white plates — possibly the drabbest items in the entire room.

"I am *not* cleaning up dog poop every day," Mia said.

"Oh, boy no. Not every day. You get the first Sunday of the month off."

Mia folded her arms and glared at him from under a wrinkled brow.

"Okay, so I'll talk to the boss and maybe get you two Sundays per month." Daddy placed the plates on a table surrounded by four stools with brightly colored cushions. "Dig in. You have to keep your strength up because I hear the pound's got some particularly big dogs in at the moment. Real monsters."

Mia plonked down on a pink seat, the color coming as no surprise, especially as there was a pink cup in that spot at the table, while Daddy took a blue one to her right.

Picking up her silverware, she said, "There's a word for people like you, and it *isn't* comedian."

Daddy winked at her as they started their meal.

Dog still wasn't sure about Daddy. The man had done nothing wrong — in fact, he'd done everything right — yet he was so big compared to Dog and Mia. Until Dog figured out what was going on, it was best to keep a certain distance.

He went to sit on the floor beside Mia. Pointing his snout upward, he sniffed. Both Daddy and Mia had bits of heaven on their plates, and despite having a belly full of brown gunk, he ached to jump on the table and devour all the heaven he could grab before someone shoved him off. But he couldn't. Not because of his bad leg, but because he was pretending to be nice, and a nice dog would sit patiently.

However, the more he sniffed, the worse his craving to jump up became. Threads of saliva hung down either side of his mouth. The smell was driving him crazy. He didn't know what heaven was, only that he ached to have it. But he had to ignore that ache. Somehow. But how?

He thought of shivering alone in his box...

Heaven.

He imagined wrestling with his brothers...

Heaven.

He pictured the monstrous hound in the alley, all snarls and gnashing teeth...

Heaven.

It was no good. Nothing worked. If he didn't have heaven soon, he was going to jump onto the table and ruin everything. He wouldn't be able to stop himself.

Dog screwed his eyes closed, tensed all his muscles, and bit down hard on his tongue, fighting, fighting, fighting the longing.

It was impossible. No matter how much he fought, all he did was smell heaven stronger and stronger.

His only option was to run away and never look back.

He opened his eyes to look for the nearest window but gasped. Mia had reached down and was holding a piece of heaven right in front of his nose. That was why the smell had gotten so strong.

He froze. Was this real?

He sniffed. Yes, it was. But what was it? He sniffed closer.

Heaven was a piece of thin reddy-brown crinkly meat. And, seemingly, it was meant for him.

Was this the trick he'd been wary of? Like the one with the boys and the cookie. Was something bad going to happen if he dared to take it?

Drooling, he peered at Mia.

Mia showed her teeth. "Go on, boy. It's bacon. Try it, you might like it."

Dog leaned forward and slowly opened his jaws. He glanced at Mia from the corner of his eye to make sure nothing had changed, then took the bacon from her.

He closed his eyes as flavor exploded in his mouth. Oh, it really was as good as it smelled. Pure heaven. He gulped it down.

"Mia..."

Mia looked at Daddy, who arched an eyebrow.

"It was only one piece. And he's so poor, he needs it to get better," she said.

"Not at the table, please."

"So, can I be excused, please? I'm not that hungry."

"But you've hardly touched anything."

"I know, but..."

Daddy huffed and frowned. "Okay, off you go."

Mia jumped off her stool, grabbed her plate, and whisked it away to the counter next to the hot-making-machine. While stealing glances over her shoulder at Daddy, she picked two strips of heaven from her plate.

"Mia?"

"Hmmm?" With wide, innocent eyes, she turned to face him and showed her teeth.

Daddy continued cutting into his breakfast and didn't even look up. "Don't put bacon straight in your pocket or it will stain."

Mia giggled. She grabbed a square of white paper from a roll and wrapped it around the heaven.

She showed her teeth again. "How did you know?"

"That's what makes me Daddy."

She skipped over and kissed him on the cheek. "Thank you for Kai."

He shrugged as if this kind of thing happened every day, which Dog was sure it didn't. Maybe Daddy was the type of person who hid his feelings and what he was thinking. Dog would have to remember that if he was going to solve the mystery of why he'd been brought here.

Heading for the bright yellow back door, Mia said, "Come on, Kai."

Dog looked at her but didn't move.

"Kai."

He kept staring at her. Who or what was Kai?

At the door, Mia shook the paper package at him. "Bacon, bacon, bacon!"

He bounded over to the little girl. Constantly shouting "*Kai*" might have been an involuntary mental spasm, but shaking bits of heaven? He knew an invitation when he saw one.

Daddy said, "Are you taking the leash?"

She patted her bag. "I've got it, but I don't think we'll need it in the woods."

"Okay." He went back to his breakfast, then called out as Mia opened the door, "Don't forget your phone!"

"Like I'd forget my phone."

Dog stepped outside and froze. He couldn't believe what he saw. Maybe people-crazy was contagious after all.

Chapter 8

With his mouth gaping, Dog stared at the sight before him. It wasn't a fat-long-nose creature, not even a herd of them, though that would have been easier to swallow.

Standing on an elevated veranda, he poked his head between two of the upright wooden bars supporting the handrail. Craning his neck left, then right, up, then down, he looked in every direction possible.

Where was he?

And more to the point, where were *they*? They were always around — everywhere he went — so what had happened to them?

He twisted, looking around, but no matter which way he turned, he couldn't see any of the huge buildings that always reared over him.

Green.

Everywhere was green.

And blue. So much blue.

Grass, trees, bushes... and sky that stretched on forever.

A bird sang in a tree near the side of the house, where its branches extended out. Foliage obscured the bird, yet he could hear and smell it — one of those black ones with a yellow beak. And unless his nose was wrong — he sniffed to be sure — there was a nest with two baby birds higher up.

The outside of the house was painted white, a stark contrast to the inside and to all the lush greens, earthy browns, and expansive blue surrounding it.

Dog turned back and swept his gaze over a whole new world — a world overflowing with new colors, new life, and new textures. He staggered back as a multitude of new scents bombarded his nose. The city had been his entire world, so he'd believed that was all there was. Imagining there was anything beyond it hadn't just been illogical but downright crazy.

Maybe there was something to be said for crazy after all.

The big question was, though, what he should head toward to sniff first?

"Come on, Kai." Mia scampered along the veranda to a wide wooden staircase that curved down to an ocean of grass beyond which lay trees that blurred into distant hills.

Sniffing and sniffing and sniffing, Dog toddled over to Mia.

She crouched down to him. "Now be careful again. These are steep, so I'll be here to catch you."

Taking their time, they made their way down the steps. There was so much to explore below, Dog couldn't wait to get down there and let his nose get to work. He moved faster the closer he got to the last step and all the wonderful new things he had to investigate.

However, on that last step, with his new world just inches away, he froze. His nose was never wrong, and it was telling him something wasn't quite right.

Leaning forward, paws still safe on the wooden tread, Dog sniffed the grass. That was the source of the problem — it wasn't grass. He'd smelled grass in the park, and this grass didn't smell anything like that. It didn't look like real grass either.

Craning down, he sniffed it closer. There was definitely something wrong with it. Seriously wrong.

He squinted at it. All of the blades were different heights instead of a nice, even length. It was all patchy and clumpy and lumpy too, not smooth, level, and uniform. However, most damningly, there was no chemical smell. At all. He sniffed it again to be sure. No, nothing. This stuff smelled... odd — fresh, earthy, lush. Completely unnatural.

He reached forward with his good front leg and pawed a patch of the uneven, unnatural grass.

Springy.

Soft.

Spongy.

It had to be fake-grass. Though it looked, smelled, and felt good. Did that mean all the trees were fake too?

He took the tiniest of steps, finally placing both of his front paws on the ground, then bent to sniff another patch.

It smelled just as fresh and chemical-free as the other. As did the next area. And the next. Yet each smelled fractionally different — just enough to suggest they weren't all made by the same grass-making-machine, but different ones. It had to demand a huge effort to create so much fake-grass. Why didn't they use the real, chemically fragrant, uniform stuff that grew all by itself in the park?

Having made it about four feet from the stairway in the last seven minutes, Dog moved on to the next clump of grass, searching the other scents that demanded investigation: people, animals, insects, birds, plants... Each clump was a scent museum bursting with exciting exhibits. And he had such a huge area to explore; it could take him all day to smell everything. Fantastic!

"Kai! Come on, boy. There's plenty more stuff to smell where we're going."

He looked up at Mia. She was pointing to where a brown trail snaked into the trees.

Oh, wow, that looked interesting. Everything was bigger over there, so there'd be even better smells. Why hadn't she taken him there already instead of having him waste so much time at the bottom of the steps?

He hobbled over to Mia, his leg moving and feeling much easier, especially with all the fun he was having.

She pointed back at the house. "This is where we live — that means you now, too. If you get lost, just look for the yellow door." She gestured to another house to the side of theirs that had been out of view from his position on the veranda. "The Pagets live there." It was the same size and shape as Mia's, but blue with a black door.

Pointing again, she said, "And next to them is Mrs.—" She stopped and looked at him looking up at her, not the houses.

"You don't need to know all this boring stuff, do you?"

Dog didn't make a sound.

"You just want to play, don't you?"

He tilted his head to one side. For such a small person, she sure made a lot of noise. It was a pity he couldn't understand her because he was sure it would be fascinating.

Mia showed him her teeth, even more than usual. Whatever she was thinking, it had to be special. What she did next only made him believe that all the more.

Mia leaned down to him and whispered in his ear, "Do you want to see my special place?"

Chapter 9

Mia ducked under another branch that arced over the trail, while Dog ambled behind her along a path made up of short stretches of bare earth separated by patches of moss, grass, and small plants, suggesting people used to walk there regularly but didn't anymore. The trail seemed to wind through the trees forever.

"Come on, Kai," Mia called for the umpteenth time as she strode ahead beside a long thicket of spiky bushes.

Having stopped to sniff a yellow flower, Dog lifted his head and squinted at her. That "Kai" noise again? Why did she think he knew what it meant? Crazy!

As if everything wasn't puzzling enough, he had yet another mystery to puzzle over — what the devil did Kai mean?

A wafting scent pulled him from his thoughts. To his right, a gnarled tree climbed into the sky before showering draping branches of delicate green leaves all the way to the ground. He wandered over and sniffed the trunk.

Someone had peed there. It kind of smelled like a dog but also kind of didn't. How could something be both a dog and not a dog? Fake-grass, fake-trees, and now, fake-dogs. The craziness never ended.

"Come on, Kai."

Dog glanced around. Mia stood beside the thorny bushes. He hated those things. All stabbing and sharp and jagged. The time the cruel-boys had tricked him with the cookie, his only escape had been to dive into a thicket of those bushes. It had saved him because the cruel-boys couldn't reach him, but it had sliced him to bits. When he'd gotten back to his box, he'd spent hours licking clean the tiny wounds that plastered his back, sides, and legs so they'd heal properly like his mother had taught him. No, he wasn't going anywhere near that bush.

Turning back, he sniffed the strange pee again. Yes, definitely not a dog, but like a dog. Very puzzling. What kind of a creature was a dog-not-a-dog? He'd ponder that while they continued their walk and maybe have another smell later, if they came back this way.

He stepped away from the gnarled tree to continue along the path.

Mia had vanished.

He spun back the way they'd come. She wasn't there either.

His heart pounded and gnawing emptiness clawed at him from his gut. He was alone again. Except this time, he couldn't be more lost; miles from his beloved moldy old box, he had no clue in which direction it was.

Had he solved one of his mysteries? Was this what these crazy people had intended all along — to drag him from where he knew and was safe, to dump him in the wilderness, miles and miles from anywhere?

What was he going to do now?

He sniffed, praying for a hint of monstrous dark buildings, gloomy alleyways, and grumbling cars, anything that could guide him back to his box.

Trees.

Grass.

Nothing but endless trees and grass.

He whined. Alone again. His mother had warned him people couldn't be trusted and to stay away from them. Why hadn't he fought when Mia and Daddy had dragged him from his box? Why?

Stupid dog. Stupid dog. Stupid dog!

He slunk away from the gnarled tree. As his nose cleared of the last remnants of the dog-not-a-dog pee, he drew in a deep, deep breath, desperate to filter out a scent he recognized — a scent that might save him.

One scent overwhelmed all others: Mia.

She was still nearby. But where?

She hadn't come back past him, so she must've gone farther along the path. How could she have moved so fast that he couldn't now see her?

"Kai?"

He pricked his ears.

"Kai?"

He could hear her *and* smell her, yet the direction of both the sound and scent didn't make any sense — they said she was in the middle of the thicket.

Impossible. He'd been in one of those things and been ripped to pieces, and he was much smaller than she was, so no way could she be in there.

Did that mean his nose was actually wrong for once? When he was lying on that metal table, the man in the green uniform had done all sorts of strange things to him. Maybe he'd damaged his nose.

Dog trembled. A dog couldn't live without its nose. Scent was everything.

Then, as if by magic, a rustling came from the thorny bush and Mia appeared. Or not all of her — her head stuck out from the bottom of the thicket. She looked at him.

"This way, Kai. But be careful, these prickles are sharp."

She disappeared back into the thorny bush.

Dog padded over. He didn't want to go anywhere near that bush, but if Mia could go into it, a big brave dog like him could do it too.

As he got closer, a small archway going underneath the bush became visible.

Dog hunkered down as low as he could and peered in. On her hands and knees, Mia was already almost through to the other side about twenty feet away.

With his belly scraping on the ground, Kai shuffled in. He arced his head from side to side, checking to make sure none of the spikes were close enough to spear him, then he shuffled in a little farther.

From the archway at the other end, Mia beckoned. "That's it. Come on, boy."

Gaining confidence as he evaded the thorns, Dog crawled faster, then faster still. This wasn't hard after all.

With the spiky branches thinning and an expanse of grass only a couple of steps ahead tempting him, Dog bound forward and leapt out of the other side and stood tall and proud.

"Yay!" Mia clapped.

He shook himself to make sure none of the thorns had latched on to his coat to stab him when he next lay down. Satisfied he was safe, he gazed around. What was all the fuss about? It was just another clump of trees. Another clump that looked exactly the same as the clump they'd left behind.

"This way now." Showing her teeth again, Mia darted between some of the trees.

Dog followed her, trotting along to keep her in sight, but also keeping enough of a distance to be safe and avoid any surprises. He thought about Mia showing her teeth so often. It seemed to happen when she was in a good mood. Could that be one mystery solved?

No teeth: bad mood. All teeth: good mood.

So, all he had to do was watch for happy-teeth, and he'd know if a person was likely to be nice to him or not. Amazing. And to think he'd believed people were complicated creatures he'd never understand in a million years.

Beyond the small clump of trees, a narrow path snaked around the end of a gully, a drop on one side, a steep wall on the other. Once at the other side, the trail vanished, and as they dove deeper into the wood, the trees shrouded them in gloom. A queasy lightness rose from his stomach as the shadows closed in around him, darker and darker. If they got lost here, they might never find their way out.

Dog squirted a little pee on one of the trees as a direction marker. To his knowledge, Mia hadn't done that. Foolish girl. Maybe if she saw him doing it, she'd see what a smart idea it was and start doing it too. He hoped so, because he didn't have an endless supply of pee, and there was a tremendous number of trees!

However, Mia didn't seem in the least concerned as she scampered on, so Dog trailed along behind her.

Up ahead, the trees parted and bright daylight shone through the gap. Mia dashed straight for it.

"We're here, Kai. We're here!"

Dog couldn't see her face, yet he was sure it was happy-teeth from ear to ear.

He burst out of the shadows and into the light.

Mia held her arms out wide and twirled around. "This is it, Kai. The most beautiful place in the world."

Mouth agape, Dog stared at the most beautiful place he'd ever seen. Blue mountains soared up on either side of him, while in front of him lay a lake with crystal-clear water the color of Mia's eyes. Breathtaking.

Mia dashed over and knelt beside him. She draped her arms around him and hugged him tightly.

"This was my and my Mommy's special place."

It sounded like Mia was going to say more, as if a story had been started and was begging to be told, so Dog waited. And waited.

Instead of saying anything else, she squeezed him even tighter.

Finally, with a waver in her voice, she said, "Now it's *our* special place. I'm sure that's what she'd want."

The place was stunning, and he was having a wonderful adventure, but Mia's behavior didn't seem normal. Though most of the time she appeared genuinely concerned about him or happy to enjoy his company, every so often a wave of sadness came over her. A darkness that drowned out all that was good. It was the same with Daddy. As if they were both somehow lost and didn't know how to find their way home, even though they were already there, so they floundered in the blackness of loneliness. It was a place he knew only too well — a home that was no longer a home.

Had he solved the mystery of happy-teeth only to discover an even bigger one? What was the root of this darkness and what was he not seeing?

Chapter 10

Dog and Mia spent the morning lying side by side on the grass in the clearing beside the lake. With the sun beaming down, a gentle breeze brushed the water, sprinkling the ripples with diamonds.

Mia pointed upward and did happy-teeth. Big, big happy-teeth. "Bald eagle."

A gigantic brown bird with a white head wheeled high over the treetops.

Mia did happy-teeth. Big, big happy-teeth.

Oh boy, and he'd thought the fries-stealer was a large bird. This one looked so enormous it could eat *him*.

"I love eagles." Mia pushed up on her elbows to watch it.

The bird swooped low over the rippling water and, with barely a *splosh*, snatched up a glinting silver fish in its huge yellow talons. With a few beats of its mighty brown wings, away it soared.

Mia watched until the bird disappeared, then pulled her backpack over to her side to rummage in it.

Dog was happy to lie on the grass. He was warm, dry, and not in the least hungry. It was probably the best day of his life since losing his pack. He couldn't think of a single way it could get any better.

Then he smelled something. Something that convinced him he was one hundred percent wrong.

Mia took out the little package of heaven from her backpack and held out a crispy strip for him. "Are you hungry, Kai?"

For the first time he could remember, Dog wasn't hungry, but heaven was heaven.

With his mouth watering, he reached forward and, taking care to avoid her fingers, took the reddy-brown strip between his jaws. A whirlwind of sensations and flavors swirled in his mouth — salty, meaty, crispy, fatty... he couldn't help but wolf it down.

"Eat it slowly, Kai. The longer it lasts, the longer you get to enjoy it."

She offered him a second piece. He wolfed that down too.

Throwing her head back, Mia did happy-teeth while making a loud *hack-hack-hack* noise.

Dog gasped and scrambled away from her. Cowering, tail down, he eyed her from a few feet away, safely beyond her reach. What the devil was she doing? Was she ill? About to attack him? What was that ungodly sound?

"What's wrong?" she asked.

His head lowered, he stared at her, muscles tensed, ready to run. He ached to check for escape routes, but he daren't take his eyes off her because he didn't know what she might do next. Everything had been so nice, why had she spoiled it?

She made that hacking noise again and did happy-teeth.

Wait, wait, wait... if she was doing happy-teeth, that meant she was in a good mood and wasn't going to do anything bad to him. So, what did that noise mean?

"Come here, silly."

She held out the last piece of heaven.

The girl had only known him a day, and she'd already discovered his greatest weakness. He inched forward, the aroma tantalizing his senses.

"It's yours, Kai. Come and get it." She waved it, and even more of the aroma drifted over to taunt him.

He crept closer, drooling. Craning his neck toward her, he opened his jaws, then delicately closed them around the tiny strip of heaven. Delicious.

For a third time, Mia made the hacking sound while doing happy-teeth.

"What's wrong, boy? Don't you like people laughing?"

If she was doing happy-teeth, the hacking noise couldn't be a bad sound. It was probably another one of her unfortunate mental issues. After all, no one could deny how crazy she and Daddy were.

She pushed up onto her knees and hugged him again. "We're going to be best friends, Kai. Best friends forever."

That strange glow welled up inside him again. It made him feel... wanted.

Dog couldn't count the number of times he'd longed for the warmth of companionship — someone to share adventures with in the day, to snuggle up to in the night, and to count on whatever the time or place. Had he finally found that special someone?

No.

Boy, he was letting things get way, way out of control. He had to stop daydreaming and find out why they'd brought him to their home. People weren't nice without there being a reason. He had to discover what diabolical plan lay at the heart of it all.

In the meantime, however, while he was pretending to be nice, why shouldn't he enjoy the company? And the strips of heaven.

He lay on the grass again beside Mia. She stroked him from the top of his head to the tip of his tail. Over and over and over. While she was doing it, she did the strange thing that first brought her to his attention in the alley — the talk-not-talk-with-rhythm thing.

"You once lived in a moldy box,
With no one to take you out for walks.
But now I'll be your true best friend,
And love you till time meets its end.
Then as the stars fall from the sky,
I'll sing to you this lullaby.
Sweet Kai, little Kai, me and you,
Little Kai, sweet Kai, one not two.
Sweet Kai, little Kai, me and you,
Little Kai, sweet Kai, one not two."

60

The soothing voice, the gentle stroking, and the day's exertion were more than Dog could handle and his eyelids drooped.

Sometime later, Dog awoke to find Mia snuggled around him, fast asleep with her arm draped over his side.

Desperate for clues to solve the many mysteries confronting him, he studied her.

Unlike Daddy, she had no lines in her face. Not one. It was completely smooth like a rubber ball. But it wasn't just smooth, it was innocent — there was no blackness hiding there, only goodness. It was easy for people to mask their real intentions when they were awake, he'd seen that, yet could they also do it while they slept? He didn't think so.

Mia's eyes flickered open. When she saw him watching her, she stroked the thick fur around his neck and did happy-teeth. Happy-teeth just for him.

"We should probably be heading back." She rolled onto her back and stretched, raking the sky with her fingers. "It's getting late, and we don't want you rushing with that leg, do we?"

Dog stretched his forelegs out in front of him while pushing up with his hind legs so his butt stuck up.

"Oh, before we go, there's something we have to do." She took a thin rectangular black board from her pocket. She tapped on it with her thumb, and a picture of a kitten magically appeared on the front.

Mia draped her arm around Dog's shoulders and held up the magic-board in front of them.

"Smile, Kai."

Dog waited for something to happen, yet nothing did. Strangely, though, Mia continued doing happy-teeth as if something remarkable had happened. Crazy as ever!

She tapped the magic-board again and shoved it toward Dog. "Look, Kai, you're famous. You're on Facebook."

The kitten had disappeared and been replaced by a picture of Mia and a very handsome young dog. It was a cool little magic trick, and if Mia was happy, then he was happy because it meant there was a good chance she'd find more strips of heaven. He wagged his tail.

Mia stuffed her magic-board into her pack and they left.

Despite the fact Mia had refused to pee on anything as a direction marker, they made it back to the original path near the gnarled dog-not-a-dog tree without getting lost once.

Dog sidled over to sniff the scent of that creature again.

"Kai," called Mia from farther along the path toward home. "Kai. Come on, boy. Kai."

Every time he stopped for more than a few seconds, Mia made that "Kai" noise. Weird. If only he could work out what she meant by it. He checked to make sure she was still within sight, then sniffed the trunk again.

"Kai."

Wait, wait, wait... she made the noise most often when he was sniffing a tree, so maybe that was what she called the trees. Yes, that had to be the answer. Mystery solved.

Happy he'd ticked off one of the mysteries on his "To Solve" list, he toddled toward Mia, but a boulder drew his attention. He stopped and sniffed it. Yep, the dog-not-a-dog had been there too.

"Kai."

What? "Kai" again?

Seriously? But this wasn't a tree.

He slumped. Maybe "Kai" didn't mean tree after all. Great. The mystery deepened.

They moseyed their way back home. Dog had given most things a good sniff on their way to the clearing, so he only gave them a cursory sniff heading back.

Before they even got to the steps leading up to the house, another new smell wafted through the air to tease Dog's nostrils. It smelled meaty but had a variety of other aromas blended in. Sadly, though Dog sniffed and sniffed, he couldn't detect even the faintest whiff of heaven.

Mia shoved open the back door and, in a ringing, high-pitched tone, said, "We're back."

Daddy was juggling pans again. Maybe that was all he did all day. After all, crazy is as crazy does.

62

"I can see that." Daddy jabbed a wooden spoon toward her. "What's the point of taking your phone if you don't use it?"

He didn't sound unhappy, yet he didn't sound pleased either. No problem, Dog would just use his new insight into people to work out what was going on. He watched for happy-teeth.

"I sent a text." Mia ambled over to him. When she leaned up to kiss him on the cheek, Daddy stooped so she could reach.

"Yes, but a text isn't a phone call, is it?" Daddy arched an eyebrow. "We agreed on phone calls, Mia. If you are going to be out all day, you call every three hours to let me know where you are and who you're with."

"But you knew who I was with: I was with Kai. And you knew where we were going."

Daddy sighed and plunked a big pan down with a bang on the hot-making-machine.

No happy-teeth anywhere. Dog sighed. That didn't bode well for heaven being on the menu.

"If you were worried," said Mia, "why didn't you call me?"

"That's not the deal, young lady, and you know it. The deal is if you have more freedom, you have more responsibility too."

"But I..." She gazed down and fidgeted with one foot, twisting the ball back and forth on the polished wooden floor.

"No buts. That's the deal."

"I'm sorry. I just got carried away with Kai." Her tone suggested that if she had a tail, it would have been firmly wedged up between her back legs.

Daddy sighed again, then drew his hands down his face. He crouched and cupped his hands to Mia's shoulders. "I'm sorry too. I don't mean to be overprotective. I don't want to be one of those daddies. But since..."

Daddy's eyes became watery, and he seemed to struggle to say anything else.

Mia lunged forward and flung her arms around him. "I'm sorry. I promise to call next time. Promise."

"Okay." Daddy turned back to his collection of pans. "Go wash your hands. Dinner's almost ready."

Mia scampered away, her good mood renewed. While she was gone, Daddy filled Dog's bowls, then served the hot food onto plates, which he transferred to the table.

Upon returning, Mia took her pink stool at the table and Daddy the blue, after placing Dog's bowls on the floor, then they all dug in.

"You should have seen how good Kai was, Daddy." Mia looked around the side of the table to where Dog was wolfing down his food like it would evaporate in seconds if he didn't. "You were so good, weren't you, Kai? So good."

"Did you use the leash?" asked Daddy.

"Didn't need it. But, ohhh, he's so slow — he wants to sniff everything. E-ver-ry-thing! The first tree, the second tree, and the next, and the next, and the next. He must have smelled every tree, every leaf, every bit of grass — everything in the whole woods."

"Well, it's all new to him, isn't it? But as long as you had fun, that's all that matters."

"It was fantastic!" Mia beamed and clapped her hands together. "We're going out again tomorrow, aren't we, boy?"

She looked down at Dog as he licked his bowl so clean it sparkled. He then sat down and peered up at her.

Daddy did happy-teeth and cupped a hand to her face. "It's so nice to see you getting out and enjoying yourself again. Mommy would want that, you know."

Toying with her food, Mia stared at her plate. She didn't answer.

It seemed to be taking them forever to eat their food, whereas Dog had gotten through his brown gunk in a flash. Why were they so slow at eating? Weren't they worried someone might steal it if they didn't scoff it down as quickly as possible?

He glanced around, searching for a place he could call his own, a place in which he'd be safe. He wanted to wander around the house because there were so many new things to sniff, but after all the exercise, his bad leg ached. Not to mention he still didn't know what to make of this crazy pair.

The living area next to the kitchen was dominated by a big blue sofa and two blue chairs. The chairs side by side against the wall, a small alcove was formed between their arms — an alcove just big enough for a dog.

Dog ambled over and shuffled inside, then squeezed and twisted until he was facing back out into the room. He lay down. Yes, this was a great spot. The wall protected him from behind, the chairs protected him from the sides and above, and he could see everything going on in the house. This would be his special spot from now on.

Though he was tired and lying down, he didn't close his eyes but watched what was happening at the table.

"There's something waiting for you upstairs," said Daddy, not looking up from his food. He acted as if he wasn't interested in talking, but something about his tone suggested it was quite the opposite.

Mia gasped and looked up, eyes once again sparkling with life. "A present?"

He sliced through a piece of meat. "Well, not for you exactly."

"For Kai?" Mia did happy-teeth. "You got a present for Kai?"

"Well" — Daddy shrugged — "you'll have to wait and see, won't you?"

Mia pushed her plate toward the center of the table and twisted around on her stool.

"Ah, ah, ah." Daddy raised his index finger. When Mia turned back, he pointed to her plate.

"Daddy!"

"You know the rules."

"So why tell me, if I can't go and look?"

"Because I'm a monster." He winked at her as he shoved a forkful of food into his mouth.

"Ohhh." Mia dragged her plate back and, with her shoulders slumped, cut into a piece of meat, making a horrible scraping sound against the plate with her knife.

"The dishes will need doing too," said Daddy.

"Daddy!" Mia thumped her fists down on the table, the ends of her knife and fork banging against the wood.

Daddy did happy-teeth and shook his head. "Hey, don't blame me. Blame the rule maker."

"You're the rule maker!"

"Like I said" — he shrugged — "I'm a monster."

Daddy made a sound similar to the one with which Mia had startled Dog in the wood — the hacking noise.

Mia glared at Daddy. "It's not funny."

"Oh, it is." More hacking noise. "It really is."

They continued chatting over their meal, after which Mia seemed to spend forever playing with a huge pile of pots and pans in a bowl of water frothing with bubbles. Dog couldn't understand why she was wasting so much time and energy doing that, instead of simply licking the last of the food off and having a good lie-down. He didn't like to think ill of anyone, but maybe she just wasn't that bright.

When everything was tidy again, Mia raced across the room for the stairs. "Come on, Kai. Quick."

Dog looked at her from between the chairs.

Frantically beckoning with her hand, she said again, "Kai. Kai. Come on. Kai."

Dog frowned. There was no tree or boulder in sight, so what the devil was this infuriating "Kai" thing?

Everywhere he went, it was "Kai" this and "Kai" that.

Wait...

Had he just solved yet another mystery? Was *he* Kai?

There was only one way to find out: if he followed her and she made that same noise again, then he wasn't; however, if he followed her and she did happy-teeth, then he must be.

He trotted over, scrutinizing her expression.

Mia did happy-teeth. "Good boy."

So, he was Kai. When it came to solving mysteries, it turned out he was something of a genius.

Mia raced up the steps, her feet pounding into the wood so hard Kai could feel them vibrate as he followed her. Something very special was up there for Mia to be in such a hurry. His mouth watered. Maybe that was where heaven was.

66

Chapter 11

A large fluffy bowl-like object lay in the middle of Mia's bed. It was impossible to miss, because it was one of the few things in the room decorated with a blue-and-red tartan pattern rather than pink.

As soon as Mia saw it, she gasped, raising her hand to her mouth. "Oh, Kai, look — it's a bed for you."

She stroked her hand along the tartan rim.

Doing happy-teeth, Mia snatched up some of the other things laid out as if on display. "Kai, look, look, look."

She held up two silver bowls in one hand and in the other an inch-wide band of blue material with a round metal disk dangling from it.

Kai yawned, unable to fathom why Mia had been so excited. As far as he could tell, there wasn't a scrap of heaven in sight.

Mia carried the fluffy tartan bowl over and placed it on the floor where his brown blanket had been, turning the side with a cutaway section in the wall to face her bed. She beckoned him.

Dog sniffed. He couldn't detect a scrap of heaven anywhere but toddled over anyway, hoping there was a secret scent-proof compartment in which Mia and Daddy hid their most treasured possessions.

Mia patted the center of the fluffy-bowl. He looked at her, then at it, then back at her. What was all the excitement about? What did this fluffy-bowl do that was so wonderful? Because so far, he was not impressed.

She patted it again. "Try it, Kai. It's lovely and soft."

She obviously wanted him to do something with the thing, but what?

He did what every dog did with new objects: he sniffed it.

He could smell Mia, Daddy, and a few other people — none of whom he recognized — but no dog or anything else to raise his concerns.

Yet again, Mia patted the center of the fluffy-bowl.

He tentatively lifted a paw over its rim.

"That's it. Good boy."

He rested his paw in the middle and it sank into something spongy. He put more weight on it and looked at Mia.

"Go on. It's okay."

He put his other front paw in, then climbed in completely. Yes, spongy. A brilliant idea struck him.

He walked around in a circle, then around again, then around one last time. Finally, he lay down. Oh yes, he was right — the fluffy-bowl was very comfortable and just the right size. He couldn't help but wonder why they didn't make these as beds for dogs. It seemed so obvious. But then, he did appear to be unnaturally gifted at problem-solving.

"This is yours too, Kai." She held up the blue band and flicked the metal disk, which had markings scratched on it. "Look, this is me: Mia Dubanowski" — she pointed to the scratches — "and this is my phone number, so if you ever get lost, someone will call me and I'll come for you."

After unfastening a silver buckle on the blue band, she hung it around his neck and refastened it.

"Oh, yes, very handsome." She cupped his cheeks and kissed him on the forehead.

So, definitely no heaven, then. He'd have to remember not to build his hopes up for the next time Mia got excited about something.

Though it had been one of the easiest days of Kai's life, the excitement, stresses, and exercise proved too much, especially now he was in his comfy fluffy-bowl and drowsiness swept over him. He snuggled down and closed his eyes.

Wherever his mother was now, he wondered if she was as warm and cozy as he was. Had she ever tasted heaven? Maybe he'd hide a piece under his fluffy-bowl for when they found each other again. She'd like living at Mia's. And his brothers would. There was plenty of room, so maybe Daddy and Mia would help him find them all, if only he could find a way to explain to them that his family was missing and in desperate need of help.

As he drifted off to sleep, the softness of his fluffy-bowl conjured memories of snuggling next to his mother. Where was she? Why hadn't she come back to him?

Chapter 12

Dog's tiny eyes flickered open. He stretched, but the moldy old box was so cramped his paws poked his oldest brother in the side. His stomach rumbled, as it did almost all the time, as he looked up at the ceiling of the box, where the triangle of mold spread from the corner. No water dripped through, so at least it wasn't raining in the alley, which would make searching for breakfast as pleasant as it could be.

As his mother breathed in her sleep, her body rose and fell, gently rocking his head. It was so cozy lying against her belly, feeling her warmth and the calm to-ing and fro-ing of her breath, that he didn't want to move, but... his stomach rumbled again.

He scrambled up, reached out his paws in front of him, and stretched for a second time, then waddled around to his mother's head. He nuzzled her. No reaction. He poked her again. Nothing.

Now what?

He looked up and down the alley. Though he hadn't heard anything happening in the night, maybe someone had passed by and dropped some food. Either he could wait for everyone else to wake up, or he could search for himself. Well, he was a big dog now. Maybe it was time he hunted for food on his own.

Dog dawdled up the alley. He sniffed to his left, to his right, then back to his left. There was nothing he hadn't smelled before, so he continued on his way.

At the tall wooden pole that had wires spreading out from its top, he stopped. Cocking his leg, he jetted a little pee around the base to announce he was around, just as his mother had taught him, then he toddled farther.

Sniffing the ground, he made a complete circuit of the green dumpster halfway along the alley. There had often been a tasty tidbit there, but not today. Oh well.

Wagging his tail, he trotted onward.

A new scent clawed at him from the left. That was more like it. Pointing his nose in that direction, he sniffed harder as his mouth watered. Yes, that would do very nicely.

He looked back down the alley. Should he go back, wake everyone, and tell them he'd found breakfast?

No. His mother and brothers were sleeping so happily, he didn't want to wake everyone only to disappoint them. It was best to check first and make sure he was right — though his nose had never yet been wrong.

Hugging the red-brick wall on his left, Dog trundled up the alley. He stopped when he reached the black wooden gate. One of the five vertical planks making up the gate had rotted at the bottom, so Dog stuck his head through the hole it had created and sniffed to be certain he was in the right place. The scent was stronger at this side, so, happy, he squeezed through.

On the other side, he trotted across a flagstone yard between stacks of white outdoor furniture and piles of crates filled with empty bottles. There, in the middle, someone had scattered ripped-up pieces of bread. A blackbird squawked when it saw him and fluttered away, a scrap of bread clutched in its yellow beak.

Dog wandered over and sniffed the bread to see how fresh it was. Snatching a piece, he tasted it and excitement welled up inside him: this was a good find because the bread was still moist, not hard and dry like the stuff they usually found. Everyone would be thrilled they could have a decent breakfast without having to leave home.

Frantic yelping and barking sliced through the air from down the alley.

Dog jumped. What the devil was happening?

His heart pounding, he shot back to the gate and squeezed through. When he looked toward his box, he gasped. His mother. His brothers. What the...?

Scurrying as quickly as possible, he flew back to help his family.

One of his brothers yelped from inside a cage in the back of a black van. A man in gray carried his other two brothers, one in each hand, to another cage.

Snarling, Mother fought to get at a second man in gray, but the Gray Man had a stick with a loop on the end that had caught her around her neck and was holding her at bay.

Mother lunged left. Lunged right. Bucked up and down. She was a big, powerful dog and jerked the man this way and that, but no matter how she struggled, she couldn't break free.

The Gray Man dragged her toward the van.

Dog tore down the alley, tiny paws pounding into the concrete, rage driving him on, giving him speed he never knew he had. When he was within reach, he leapt and sank his teeth into the back of the Gray Man's leg. He gripped as tightly as he could and shook his head. Ripping, ripping, ripping.

The Gray Man screeched.

He kicked backward, slamming his heel into Dog's side.

Dog cartwheeled across the ground and crashed into the brick wall.

The Gray Man shouted at his colleague and shoved the stick that imprisoned Mother at him. His colleague grabbed the stick and continued hauling Mother away while the Gray Man turned and glowered at Dog.

Dog growled, the fur on his back standing on end. He was going to chew the legs of these bad, bad people and free his pack.

But the Gray Man grabbed another stick with a loop from his van and stormed at Dog.

Dog looked at Mother as she lurched back and forth, snapping, snarling, and slashing, but all to no avail. An empty pit clawed from his stomach and swallowed all his hope. If she couldn't break away from that stick, what chance did a little dog like him have?

What was happening? Why was it happening? Why would people punish his family like this?

He looked at his brothers yowling through the bars of cages, tiny paws futilely clawing to break free.

Mother was trapped. His brothers were trapped. And now, the Gray Man was storming over to trap him.

What should he do?

What *could* he do?

Dog ached to save his family. Ached so much it sliced into him like a knife. But...

There was only one thing he could do. He knew without any doubt it was his only choice, but that didn't stop it from feeling like someone was stomping on his heart.

He looked at his pack one last time, then turned and shot back up the alley, fleeing from everything he knew and everyone he loved.

He bolted as fast as his legs could carry him, yet behind him, the heavy footsteps of the Gray Man hammered into the ground, getting closer and closer...

Kai woke up, leaping to his feet with his hackles raised and teeth bared. Searching for the Gray Man, he spun, ready to charge and rip him to pieces.

But the Gray Man wasn't there.

Kai's heart hammered, and he panted as though he'd been running for hours. Peering into the dark, empty shadows, he twisted this way and that. His pack...

They weren't there either — no one was. Only Mia asleep in her bed.

His shoulders slumped and he hung his head. He'd never seen his pack ever again. And now, even if they escaped from wherever they'd been taken, they had no idea where he was to find him.

He was alone. Completely alone.

Moonlight sliced through a gap in the curtains. He looked up into the heavens at the glowing creamy-white orb. Could his mother and brothers see that wherever they were too?

A desperate urge grabbed him, born of separation and feelings as old as history itself — an urge he could no sooner ignore than he could pull the orb out of the sky. He raised his face upward, took a deep breath, and howled. Howled with all his might.

Mia gasped, lurching to sit upright. She dashed over to him and flung her arms around him.

"It's okay, Kai. I'm here. It's okay." Hugging him, she stroked his head. "It's okay. Don't be afraid. I'm here. I'll always be here."

Her warmth and the calm to-ing and fro-ing of her breathing slowed his pounding heart and eased his panicked panting. He didn't know why, but he felt... safe.

The bedroom door opened a crack and Daddy poked his face in. "Everything okay?"

"I think he had a bad dream," Mia replied, cradling Kai.

"Need me?"

"Nah-huh."

Daddy left.

Kai's panic subsided under Mia's soothing caress. Another urge overwhelmed him, and again, he couldn't resist — he snuggled into her shoulder, nestling in the safety as he closed his eyes and reveled in her caring.

Mia was a strange creature with even stranger ways. She wasn't like any person he'd ever met. Not just because she'd taken him in; it was much more than that. He remembered the joy that had oozed from her on their walk through the woods and the look of awe as she'd watched the gigantic bird soar overhead. Instead of trying to bend the world to her will, no matter the struggle it took, she seemed to appreciate its wildness and revel in its wonder. It was almost as if — he didn't like to imagine it because it was such an outlandish idea — as if she was more animal than person.

The craziness in this place had to be rubbing off on him for him to consider, even for a second, that a person could be innately good. Maybe his dream had shaken him more than he thought.

Mia kept her left arm draped around his body, cuddling him, while she stroked her right hand over the top of his head and down his neck to his shoulders, soothing his fears and driving away his doubts.

Maybe that animal idea wasn't so crazy.

By embracing the wildness in things, the animal, she revealed the animal in herself. It wasn't so crazy when he looked at it like that. In fact, Daddy was a kind of animal too. Not as much as Mia, but there were definite traces. Maybe that was why they were being so nice to him — they were closer to him than to the people in the city. Did that make them outcasts? That would explain why they lived amid the trees and hills and not in those monstrous dark buildings like normal people.

Not that that mattered. What mattered was how he felt in this moment. He'd been an outcast in the city, and now, he'd found other outcasts who'd taken him in. For the time being at least, he was safe, fed, and warm. As life went, that wasn't a bad lot.

Mia pulled away, her eyes sparkling in the moonlight. "It was a bad dream, wasn't it?" She nodded. "Hmm, I get those." She stroked his head and down his neck. "Horrible, aren't they?" She kissed him on the forehead. "Don't move."

She eased up off the floor and padded over to her bed.

Kai whimpered. He didn't mean to, it just leaked out as the sense of security and care padded away with the little girl.

"Don't worry, silly." She shot him a smile. "I'm coming back."

After whipping the comforter off her bed, she spread it on the floor next to his fluffy-bowl, then lay down beside him.

"See, you aren't alone. I'm right here."

She patted the floor of his fluffy-bowl. "Lie down now. There's a good boy."

He looked at the child who was doing so much to make him feel welcome, to show him compassion, to prove she cared. Could it all be real?

Too weary for yet another mystery, he turned completely around in his fluffy-bowl, then snuggled down into it, his back to the cutaway section at the front.

Mia shuffled closer and curled around him, bringing her knees up and draping an arm over his side. He felt her breath on his head. Felt her warmth. Felt the rising and falling of her chest. For an instant, he almost believed he was home in his moldy box with his mother cuddling him.

Kai closed his eyes, basking in the companionship that had eluded him for longer than he could remember.

Mia stroked his side, and just as it had in the alley when he'd first met her, that strange sound drifted on the air. As delicate as the moonlight filtering through the clouds, the sound of talking-not-talking caressed him.

"You once lived in a moldy box,
With no one to take you out for walks.
But now I'll be your true best friend,
And love you till time meets its end.
Then as the stars fall from the sky,
I'll sing to you this lullaby.
Sweet Kai, little Kai, me and you,
Little Kai, sweet Kai, one not two.
Sweet Kai, little Kai, me and you,
Little Kai, sweet Kai, one not two."

Kai pictured his mother and his brothers. He doubted he'd play with them ever again, unless it was in his dreams, so the sooner he went to sleep, the sooner he'd be with them once more. And when he woke?

Mia.

He'd be with Mia.

Chapter 13

Breakfast!" Daddy's voice boomed from downstairs over the sound of Mia quietly talking-not-talking to herself while watering the pink-flowered plant on her windowsill.

She turned to Kai sitting at her bedroom door. "You ready for your favorite, Kai: bacon?" She widened her eyes and licked her lips. "Mmm."

Kai had been sitting in the doorway for the last ten minutes, ever since he'd first sniffed the meat when it was still cold. Now the aroma filling the house declared it was hot, brown, and crispy. He was surprised Daddy had to shout and Mia hadn't smelled it herself.

Kai trotted after the little girl as she bounced out of her room and down the steps, making a strange humming noise to herself like talking-not-talking without the words.

Daddy was dishing food onto plates as they meandered over. "What's the plan for today?" he asked.

He smelled of a different kind of man-flowers again, but flowers all the same.

"Kai's leg seemed okay yesterday, so I think we'll go on a longer walk."

Mia rested on the counter while Daddy turned to the hot-making-machine. Kai watched as her hand slowly snaked toward the plates, but with Daddy facing the other way, it looked like he hadn't seen it.

That was heaven. *His* heaven!

"Mia!" said Daddy, his voice lower than usual as he shot her a sideways glance.

"Hmmm?" Mia's lineless face was the picture of innocence, all big blue eyes and happy-teeth.

"That's your breakfast. Kai's got his own." He scooped something out of a wide pan onto the plates.

"Awww. But he loves bacon. And you said yourself, he's just skin and bones, so he doesn't just love it, he *needs* it."

Without a word, Daddy lifted a bowl that was covering a third plate on the counter.

Mia gasped. "That's for Kai?"

"He's part of the family now, isn't he?"

"It's a small portion."

"It could be smaller still." Daddy reached for a piece of heaven.

"Nooo!" Mia snatched the plate away.

Daddy winked at her.

Mia flicked his back. "You!"

"That's me."

On tiptoes, she reached up to kiss him on the cheek as he bent down.

"I love you, Daddy."

"Yes, well, remember that when I'm old and decrepit and need my adult diaper changed."

Mia frowned. "What's an *adult* diaper?"

"The safest place to hide your wallet during a robbery."

Mia frowned. "What?"

"Never mind. Sit down. It's ready."

Mia put the plate on the floor for Kai: two strips of heaven, a little pile of lumpy, light yellow stuff, and a piece of singed bread smothered in fruity red goo. It all lasted about six seconds.

Daddy put two plates of food on the table and the two of them sat to eat.

"This is just a treat," said Daddy, gesturing to Kai. "In the future, he gets his own food, okay?" He pointed to the far end of the counter and a stack of cans next to a large bag with a picture of a dog on it.

"A weekend treat?" Mia ate a forkful of the lumpy yellow stuff.

"Maybe a once-a-month treat."

"That's not much of a treat."

"You want to go for annual?"

"What's annual?"

"Like Christmas. Once a year."

Mia's mouth dropped open and her eyes popped wider. "That's animal abuse."

Daddy made a hacking sound.

While Daddy and Mia talked, Kai wondered about the room. He could still smell that other scent — like Mia, yet different. It was strongest in the kitchen area, around the blue sofa, and from behind a door upstairs through which he hadn't yet been.

When was he going to get to meet this mysterious person? From how the scent was fading, "like-Mia" hadn't been there for a while, so when were they going to visit again?

After her breakfast, Mia gave Kai a small portion of brown gunk and some brown pebbles that tasted meaty. She then put a bottle of water and some sandwiches in a little pink backpack, promised Daddy she would call this time, kissed him on the cheek, and then, standing with the back door open, called Kai. He trotted over and they left.

At the bottom of the steps where the grass started, Kai cocked his leg and peed on the support column for the banister.

"No, Kai. No!" Mia grabbed his blue-neck-band and dragged him away. "You'll upset Daddy doing it there."

Luckily, he'd managed to squirt enough for a decent message, but he still frowned up at the little girl.

What was wrong? He had to announce his arrival to all the other dogs in the neighborhood and claim the area as their territory. He was doing it as much for her and Daddy as for himself.

She hauled Kai over to a tree thirty feet from the house. "Do that here, please."

Kai sat down and gazed at her.

She patted low down on the trunk. "Here."

He looked from her to the tree, then back to her.

"Pee here." She patted again.

Kai just stared.

Mia threw her arms up and blew out a big breath. Rubbing her chin, she peered around, as if checking no one was watching, then stood closer to the tree and cocked her leg for a few seconds. "Pee here. See!"

She lowered her leg and patted the trunk again.

Kai wandered closer.

"That's it. Now, pee there."

Instead of cocking his leg, Kai sniffed the lower part of the trunk. There was no pee on it. He looked back at her. How was she ever going to protect their territory if she couldn't scent mark? She was going to be a tough one to teach, this one.

"Oh, boy." She shook her head and turned away. "Come on, then."

Mia walked into the tree line with Kai ambling behind. As they made their way through the woods toward Mia's special place, she picked up a small branch and flicked it at leaves as she went along. Kai studied the rhythm of the to-and-fro motion as the stick whipped out and pulled back. Once he could predict where it was going to be, he leapt and snatched it out of the air.

He ran in a circle around her with the stick in his mouth, his tail wagging.

She caught one end of the stick and pulled. Kai hunkered down and thrust his paws out in front of him so he could heave backward with better traction.

Mia tugged. "I'm going to get it. I'm going to get it."

Kai growled in reply. Not enough to frighten, but enough to let her know he meant business.

Mia wrenched the stick one way and then the other, trying to break his hold, but he clenched his jaws tighter. She heaved back and twisted at the same time.

The stick snapped in two.

She fell on her butt, her feet flying up in the air as she rolled onto her back. Looking very silly sprawled in the muck, she made the hacking sound, so Kai ran around her with his prize in his mouth.

But Mia wasn't beaten. She jumped up, held her half of the stick over her head, and chanted, "I've got it. I've got it. I've got it."

Kai dropped his piece and leapt at hers — it was no fun if he had the wrong end of the stick.

Each time he leapt, she whisked the stick high beyond his reach, all the while hacking and hacking.

Slowly, they meandered through the wood, the stick like a new friend who had come to play with them, but by the time they reached the special place, the game had transformed: the stick was no longer a stick, but at one moment a sword, and another, a wand.

"Run, Kai, run. The wicked witch is coming. She'll turn us into toads."

Mia ran around in a wide arc, flailing her wand and making *pshoo pshoo* noises as if something was shooting from it. Kai raced after her, barking his support.

"Onto the dragon, Kai. We have to escape."

Mia dashed to the edge of the clearing and onto a tree that had fallen at an angle and lost all its leaves. Kai leapt up to join her. She scampered along the trunk and then flung herself down onto it, throwing her arms and legs around it to grip it. Kai crouched behind her.

"Hold on tight, Kai. We're flying very high."

Kai barked.

"Breathe fire, dragon. Fire." Mia swung her stick-wand in wide arcs in front of her and made a *kshhh* sound.

"Yay! We got her, Kai." Mia waved her arms in the air. "We got her."

Kai barked. He wasn't sure what was happening, but it was very exciting, whatever it was.

Mia swung her leg over the trunk and spun around to him. She kissed him on the head. "You're my hero, Kai. I couldn't have escaped without you."

He barked again.

She did happy-teeth and ruffled the fur on his neck. "I think such a brave hero deserves a break. What do you think?"

For a third time, Kai barked. Mia seemed to enjoy him doing it, so it was an appropriate response.

Rolling backward, Mia hacked. "Oh boy, you're so clever. Okay, come on, then."

She scrambled up and led them into the center of the clearing, where she rummaged in her backpack and pulled out her magic-board, then tapped on it with her thumb, dropping her pack on the grass.

As if by magic, Daddy's voice appeared. Kai glanced about but couldn't see him anywhere. It was a very impressive trick.

After talking with Daddy, Mia sat on the grass and cuddled Kai, holding the magic-board up in front of them both again.

"Smile, Kai."

And yet again, nothing happened. He liked her trick, making Daddy talk when he wasn't there, but her "smile" trick was a complete flop.

She played with her magic-board for a few moments, then did happy-teeth.

"Everyone on Facebook thinks you're really cool, Kai." She patted him on the back. "Even Johnny Sanger, and he never thinks anyone is cool except him." She stared down at the glowing front of her magic-board. "'Cool dog. Good to see you on FB again. Been too long.'" She did happy-teeth again, as if the words meant more than they did.

"Oh, look." She shoved the magic-board in front of him again. "You've got forty-six likes."

Kai yawned, then nuzzled the backpack. Was it time for a snack yet?

"You can smell them, can't you, huh, clever boy?" Pulling the pack over, she again rummaged inside and broke out a parcel of sandwiches wrapped in foil. They ate.

Kai wolfed down two meat sandwiches, plus a little container of meaty pebbles. The pebbles were okay, but the sandwiches disappeared far too quickly. He looked at Mia, still nibbling on her first sandwich. How could she eat so slowly?

She took another microscopic bite.

How? If he tried to eat so slowly, his jaws would seize through lack of use. If he didn't starve first.

He drooled, gazing at her sandwich.

She twisted away from him. "Hey, you've had yours. Stop looking at mine!"

He stared at the foil parcel on the ground containing more sandwiches.

"Nah-uh." Mia whisked it away and shoved it into her backpack. "We need some for later because dinner's going to be late — I've something else to show you and it's going to take a while."

His mouth watered as he gazed at the pink bag. What was the point of saving them? If they lost the bag, they lost the food. However, if they ate the food and lost the bag, they only lost the bag. It was basic logic.

Of course, he could make the bag easier to find should they lose it by peeing on it, but he got the impression that wasn't an option Mia would approve of.

Yes, he really had his work cut out for him if Mia was going to master even the most rudimentary of survival skills. As it was, she wouldn't last a day on the street by herself. What was Daddy thinking, sending her out so unprepared?

Mia bit half her remaining sandwich away and offered the other piece to him. "Did you really think I wasn't going to share?"

Kai's piece disappeared in an instant.

Still chewing, Mia lay down and snuggled up next to him, digging her fingers into the thick fur around his neck to cling to him. Kai flopped down against her. His leg ached, so he was thankful for the rest.

Nevertheless, with nothing else to fill his thoughts, he couldn't help but return to the puzzle of why he'd been brought here and why he was being treated so well. So well, so far — the memory of the cruel-boys and the cruel cookie trick still haunted him. It probably always would. The strange thing was that the way Mia clung to him made him think she was haunted by something too. But by what?

Chapter 14

After another session of running around and stick waving while Mia shouted about ogres and castles and stealing treasure, she led Kai away from the special place. She made Daddy's voice magically appear again, yet instead of heading for the tunnel through the thicket and home, she turned for the jagged-topped mountain on their right.

They clambered over rock formations and up grassy inclines, sometimes with Mia on all fours like him. The higher they climbed, the more she huffed and puffed, and droplets of moisture gathered on her unusually red face.

If his leg had been fully healed, it would've been wonderful fun, but as they clambered over a rock area, he panted with the effort, his tongue lolling out.

Mia tousled the fur on the top of his head. "Not far now, Kai. Don't worry. But we can take a quick break, if you're tired."

Having retrieved the water bottle from her backpack, she cupped one hand, poured in some water, and offered it to him. He gulped it down, then they set off again.

After a further short climb, they reached a grassy hollow that looked as if a giant had bitten a chunk out of the mountainside. Mia wiped her brow with her forearm and slung her backpack on the ground.

"Wasn't that bad, was it?" She slumped down on the grass, breathing hard.

Kai lay down too and gazed around. They were much closer to the jagged peaks stabbing the sky, but apart from that, he couldn't see why it was so much better up here. He stared down at the lake, the water shimmering with golds and reds as the sun sank behind the far mountains. Pretty, yes, but not worth the struggle.

Mia pointed at the vanishing sun. "Not long now, Kai."

The crimson smears across the sky slowly faded and the heavens became an inky-blue blackness.

Kai wondered what they were waiting for. Everything seemed the same, except that now everything was bathed in milky moonlight instead of sharp sunlight.

His stomach rumbled, the climb having taken a lot out of him, so he nuzzled Mia's backpack. How did this thing open?

"You hungry, boy?" She pulled the pack to her. "Let's see what we have left, shall we?"

They finished off the sandwiches, Kai wolfing his, Mia nibbling hers, then she took a drink from the bottle before cupping her hand for him to sate his thirst.

As she repacked the backpack, Mia whispered, "Look" — she pointed to a grassy plateau below them —"there's a fox."

Kai looked down. A creature with a bushy tail trotted across the hillside. It stopped, sniffed the ground, then looked in the direction from which Kai and Mia had come, then in the direction in which they'd continued up the mountain.

A breeze wafted toward them, bringing a strange yet familiar scent with it. Kai twitched his nose, sniffing the air. It was the dog-not-a-dog that had peed on the gnarled tree he'd found yesterday.

He watched the animal scour the area for food before disappearing amid the rocks.

Was that what all the fuss was about?

It was marginally interesting to solve the mystery of the pee on the tree, but it really wasn't worth all the struggle of climbing when he had a bad leg, especially when they had to go all the way back down again.

"It's starting." Mia nudged him. Even though she whispered, an intense thrill filled her voice.

Kai looked at her. She had an expression he hadn't seen before: her eyes were wide and her mouth curled up at the corners, as if she was going to do happy-teeth, yet her teeth remained hidden. Just when he thought he understood her, this happened. If it wasn't genuine happy-teeth, was she happy or not? It was only moments ago he'd solved the mystery of the gnarled tree pee, and yet here he was with another unfathomable puzzle. Maybe this was another version of the cruel cookie trick — not torturing his body, but torturing his mind.

What was she seeing that he wasn't? What was he missing?

He looked at the mountains. Exactly the same.

He looked at the lake. Exactly the same.

He looked at the sky. Exactly the — what the...?

Chapter 15

Far, far away in the inky blackness of the sky, something moved. Kai squinted. Had he really seen that? He stared, waiting for whatever it was to reappear. It didn't.

He could see well in the dark. With the dim light from the nighttime sky, or the illumination created by people's machines, his eyes had never struggled in the dark. So why were they fooling him now?

He sighed. Another mystery.

How long was he going to have to wait before this one was solved? The answer came a second later.

A wave of green light twisted out of the blackness. Kai's eyes popped wider at the most mysterious thing he'd ever seen.

Expanding, it snaked across the sky, while also reaching upward, becoming fainter and fainter until it disappeared into the heavens. It shimmered and writhed, like a bejeweled green curtain blowing in a summer's breeze.

As if the spectacle in the sky wasn't magnificent enough, the lake mirrored the action, like a partner dancing with the love of their life.

Mia draped her arm around his shoulders and rested the side of her head against his. Together, they watched the heavenly display, as if it had been choreographed by the gods just for them.

Time lost itself while the light played, as if everything in the world had stopped to watch its splendor.

"It's called an aurora," Mia said in the gentlest of voices. "Mommy loved snuggling up here to watch it."

She clawed her fingers into his flesh, gripping him tightly, and drew a deep breath, as if she was in sudden pain. But how could she be when they were watching something so beautiful and nothing had changed?

"It's the first time I've seen it since," she said. Once again, it sounded like she'd started a story she never intended to finish.

As easily as the light snaked into the world, it snaked back out and faded, faded, faded... Gone.

Her grip relaxing, she blew a breath out noisily and ruffled his fur. "Okay, time to go."

Mia took a flashlight from her backpack and they carefully picked their way back down the mountainside. Kai couldn't stop thinking about the green sky-light as they made their way down and through the darkened woods. There really was magic in this place. Strong magic. What other wonders was he going to encounter during his stay here? He was so deep in thought that the return journey flew by, and in what felt like no time, the lights from the house windows beckoned through the shadowy trees.

Daddy had some food waiting for them. Kai's brown gunk lasted just a few seconds, then he went to sit in his protective space between the two blue chairs. Mia, however, never finished her meal — she fell asleep on the sofa, with a plate of half-eaten food in her lap.

After removing the plate, Daddy carried her upstairs without waking her, Kai padding along behind. Easing up one of Mia's limbs after another, Daddy removed her clothes, put on her pajamas, and then tucked her into bed. He kissed her on the forehead, then left, clicking off the light as he shut the door.

While Daddy's footfalls faded, Kai turned around three times in his fluffy-bowl and then settled down. The day had been crammed with mysteries and magical moments, all of which begged for his attention, but his eyelids drooped, and in no time, sleep stole him from his thoughts.

In the middle of the night, darkness cocooning the room, a noise woke Kai.

He peered into the shadows, scanning the shapes and shades of black for changes. What had woken him?

He saw nothing.

He sniffed. Nothing. Pricked his ears to listen for the tiniest sound. Nothing.

Everything was the same, just as it should be, so he settled back down and closed his eyes.

A barely audible moan slipped through the darkness, sounding like a small animal in distress.

He jerked upright. There *was* something there. Again, he squinted into the dark and sniffed. The sound came again. Not so much a moan, but a whimper. A whimper coming from Mia's bed.

He padded over.

The bulge facing the wall under the comforter was the right shape to be Mia, and it smelled like her, which meant there was nothing else there, so what could be making the noise?

Another whimper.

Kai frowned.

Was it... her? Why would she be making a noise like she was hurt?

He looked back at his fluffy-bowl, then looked at Mia. What should he do?

If a member of a pack was suffering, it was a good dog's duty to help, if they could. However, Kai had lost his pack; he had a duty to no one.

He crept back to his fluffy-bowl. And behind him, the whimpering continued.

He put a paw into his fluffy-bowl but hesitated, one paw in, three out. He glanced at the whimpering bulge in Mia's bed — the bulge that had given him heaven, the bulge that had healed his wounds, the bulge that had shown him nothing but kindness, especially when the demons in the night had done all they could to torment him.

It might be the cookie trick all over again, and he might get hurt more than he'd ever been, but maybe it was worth risking it if Mia really was in pain and he could take it away to see happy-teeth once more.

He padded back to the bed. Resting his head on the covers, he nuzzled the girl.

She whimpered again, so he nuzzled her again. And let out a little whimper too, to show she wasn't in pain alone.

Mia rolled over, her cheeks glistening wet. She flung her arms around him and hugged him, the wetness brushing off on his nose. Without thinking, he licked it. Salty-water.

Mia sobbed, her breathing coming in shuddered gasps, her body jerking with each one. Kai did what any good dog would do when one of its pack was in pain: he licked Mia. Licking healed wounds and cured pain. Licking was a dog's superpower.

"I m-miss her s-so much," said Mia.

She gripped Kai, her fingers relaxing and then clawing, relaxing and then clawing again.

There was something broken inside her. A deep dark pain. So dark it had the power to overwhelm her and smother the joy for life that glowed from within her like a beacon — the very thing that made her *her*.

She clutched him, as if trying to pull closer and closer, as if no matter how close she was, she felt completely lost and alone.

Though he could be way off the mark, Kai thought he'd solved another mystery: this wasn't another version of the cruel cookie trick. No, Mia was as broken as he was. And now, they'd found each other. Two broken pieces falling into each other to make a whole. He'd wondered why he was here, so maybe now he knew — he was here because here was precisely where he was always meant to be.

He nuzzled Mia. Licked her so she'd know she was not alone but that he was there with her, guiding her through the darkness and back into the light. She buried her face in his fur, hugging him as if they were long-lost friends who had been reunited after a momentous struggle. Gradually, her sobbing subsided.

Kai climbed onto her bed. Mia had saved him, and now she was the one needing to be saved. For the second night, she curled around him so they fit together to form a circle. Two parts making a whole.

Kai's magic obviously worked, so he used more of it and licked the little girl again.

This had to be how the world worked — everyone wandered around aimlessly until they stumbled into that special someone who was broken in just the right way so they fit together to make each other whole. That certainly explained why so many of the people he'd met seemed to be so unhappy: they were broken and hadn't yet found that one person able to fix them.

He snuggled next to Mia, feeling her chest rising and falling, her warm breath on his ear.

He'd never dreamed of being with anyone but his mother and brothers, but now...? Now he couldn't dream of being anywhere but here with his little girl. In that instant, he solved a mystery he hadn't even known existed — he understood love.

Chapter 16

Over breakfast, Mia was her usual bright self, as if she'd found some form of release and let go of some of the darkness that had been trapped inside her. Kai was pleased. Not least because it meant his licking had worked. In fact, it had worked better than he'd hoped for.

While it was still too early to say for sure, he now believed he knew why they'd brought him here — he might not be the only one pining for something. Mia didn't merely *want* someone to be with, to walk with, to play with; she *needed* someone on a far more primal level, something far more instinctual. She needed the kind of belonging and unconditional love found in a pack.

To make her feel this way, maybe she'd lost someone too, and like he had, she'd been hunting for someone to fill that void.

He sat on the floor beside his little girl in case she needed his tongue again.

Daddy said, "So what have you got planned for your last day of freedom?"

Mia frowned. "Shhh. I haven't told Kai yet."

Daddy arched an eyebrow. "Because you think he'll understand you?"

"He understands more than you think. He's a very clever dog."

"I'm sure he is."

Mia spread fruity red gloop onto a piece of warm singed bread. "I thought we might take a trip into town so I can show him around." The bread crunched as she bit it.

"Show him around? He used to live there. And from the state he was in, I doubt he'll enjoy being reminded of it."

"But he's never seen it in a nice way."

Daddy shrugged. "Maybe. You're not intending to stop by to see how my new office is coming along, are you?"

"Don't you want us to?"

"No, it's not that, but what if Kai thinks he's going to be taken out the back and abandoned in his box again?"

She gasped. "Oh, poor, Kai... no, we'll stay away from that part of town."

He finished chewing a piece of heaven. "Don't forget we've got to take him back to the vet today to make sure everything is healing properly."

"I thought..." Mia shoved a sausage back and forth across her plate. "I thought I could take him."

"You?"

"Uh-huh."

"On your own?"

"Uh-huh."

Daddy grimaced. "I don't know if that's a good idea."

"But I told you I'd look after him so you wouldn't have to."

"Taking him for a walk in the woods is a lot different from taking him into the city for medical care."

"But if I'm going to help around the house now and have grown-up responsibilities, I have to do grown-up things."

Daddy blew out a long, slow breath.

"I'm not a little kid, Daddy. I can do stuff." She reached over and held his hand. "Let me help you."

Daddy was quiet and tiny pools of water formed in the bottoms of his eyes. He cupped her hand. "Do you want to do it because it will help me, or do you want to do it because it will help you?"

Mia thought for a moment. "Both."

"Well..." Daddy rubbed the back of his neck. "I suppose if I call and arrange it, then call again after the visit to clarify everything..." He shrugged.

"So, I can take him?"

Daddy nodded.

Mia did happy-teeth, then popped a chunk of sausage in her mouth.

"Mommy would be so proud." Daddy leaned over and kissed her on the forehead. "You're sure you'll be able to handle him on your own? Maybe I should drive you and just let you take him in."

"Nah-huh." Finishing chewing, she shook her head, then swallowed. "That's not me taking him, that's you taking me. We'll get the bus. He was so good yesterday, it'll be fun."

"Yes, but he wasn't on a leash, was he?" Daddy poured hot dark brown liquid into his cup from a white pot.

"So I'll try him outside first," said Mia. "But before we go, we're going to have a bath, aren't we, Kai?"

"Thank goodness for that."

"Don't say that." She cupped her hands over Kai's ears. "You'll hurt his feelings."

"Well, despite the vet cleaning him up, he is a bit funky, don't you think?" He added white powder to his cup.

"Not funky. Earthy."

"Oh, earthy, is it?" he said, stirring his drink.

"It means natural."

"I know what it means. I'm just surprised you do."

"Google." Mia tapped her magic-board on the table.

Daddy nodded, raising his eyebrows. "So, if he's funky now, what's he going to be after his bath?"

"Aromatic," said Mia with a cheeky sparkle in her eyes.

"Google again?"

"A coffee commercial." Mia cut another piece of a sausage. "Anyway, it's not his fault, is it? The vet said he couldn't get his wound wet for three days, and you'd be funky if you'd been sleeping on the street."

"Here" — Daddy raised his arm nearest her and shoved his armpit

94

toward her — "I'm funky without sleeping on the street."

Mia made hacking sounds, pinching her nose and scrunching up her face. "Ewww. Yes, you are."

Kai gazed up at his little girl. She was hacking again. Hacking! That was such a good sign. His licking had worked better than he'd ever imagined it could, yet it meant something else too. Even though he hadn't wanted it, hadn't even known it was possible, he'd become part of something bigger than he was. Bigger even than a pack. He'd thought nothing could be bigger than a pack, but he now knew how wrong that was.

His connection to Mia was somehow different. He didn't just live with her, didn't just walk with her, didn't just eat, sleep, play — do literally everything with her — there was something more. Something he couldn't put his paw on. It was as if he was somehow joined to the girl, somehow linked by an invisible thread. One end reached up inside her, extending into that special part that was "Mia," while the other extended down into him — deep, deep down — where everything that made him *him* lived.

He'd seen people with their dogs on the streets, in the park, and even in cars. He'd seen a kind of joy in their behavior, which he never understood because it wasn't only unnatural, it was illogical. After all, how could a person and an animal be so happy simply by being with one another? Didn't they each have separate lives, separate needs, separate wants? What kind of a bond held them together like that?

Now he figured he was beginning to grasp it.

Daddy said, "Don't forget Mrs. Paget's going to be looking in on you while I'm out."

"She doesn't have to. We'll be fine, won't we, Kai?" She patted Kai on the shoulder.

"That may be, but she's looking in anyway. And if you change your plans and end up on one of your mammoth hikes, what are you going to do?"

Mia stared, her hanging mouth open. "Errr..."

Daddy leaned over and tapped her magic-board.

"Ohhh." Mia nodded. "Call you. Yes, I remember."

"And...?"

"And...?"

"And Mrs. Paget."

"Oh, yeah. And call Mrs. Paget."

Daddy kissed her on the head. "That's my girl."

They continued chatting while they finished their breakfast, then after clearing the dishes to the counter, Mia fastened a blue cord to Kai's blue-neck-band and led him to the back door. The second the door opened, Kai bolted, desperate to get to his new peeing-post.

Staggering after him, Mia shouted, "Kai, stop. Stop!"

Kai kept going, pleased they had the cord connecting them. Now he could decide where they went, how quickly they went there, and most importantly, how long they spent sniffing things on the way, safe in the knowledge that Mia couldn't wander off and get lost either. It was an excellent device with which to start her survival skills training.

He scampered down the steps, dragging the little girl behind him, who squawked all the way to the bottom. When he stopped next to his peeing-post and cocked his leg, she squawked even more.

She heaved on the cord. "Kai, not there. Not there!"

She caused such a fuss, it almost put him off peeing, yet he managed. The poor thing just didn't understand marking territory at all. It wasn't the best start to the day's lessons. However, as it was her first proper day of training, he'd go easy on her.

Once he'd relieved himself, he ambled away toward the wood, hauling along Mia, who was still squawking and squawking.

For her second lesson, he took Mia for a walk in the woods. It was much easier going at his pace than at hers thanks to the cord, but he wasn't sure she agreed. It was as if she didn't want to go anywhere, because no matter how hard he pulled, she seemed to go even slower. She made it almost impossible to go anywhere. And the look on her face...

Every time he turned around, she scowled more and more. Didn't she appreciate she was not just failing this lesson too, but ruining the walk? If he wasn't so strong and his bad leg so much better, this walk would be a disaster.

He stopped, sat on the ground, and looked at her, hoping she'd explain her behavior.

Mia wagged a finger at him. "Bad dog. You're supposed to stop when I tell you. How are we supposed to go into town if you won't walk properly?"

Kai tilted his head to one side and wagged his tail.

"That was very bad, Kai. Very bad." Mia put her hands on her hips and blew out a noisy breath. "What am I going to do with you?"

There was no sign of an explanation for her behavior, or happy-teeth, so he gave an exasperated whimper.

Her shoulders slumped and her expression softened. She crouched in front of him and ruffled the fur on either side of his head.

"I'm sorry, Kai. I should have guessed you didn't know how to walk on a leash."

She shook her head, and Kai thought he almost saw happy-teeth.

"Never mind, you're a clever dog, so I'm sure you'll learn."

Mia stood back up, staring him in the eye while holding up one finger, and said, "Stay."

She took one step backward and stopped again.

Kai stayed where he was because he didn't see any point in going anywhere one tiny step at a time.

"Stay," she said, her finger still raised.

Another step back and another "stay."

It was so much more fun doing it his way, but if this was going to make her do happy-teeth... he stayed where he was, waiting for some signal that it was all right for him to resume leading their walk.

A third step back, followed by a fourth "stay."

She lowered her finger, waited a moment, then patted her thigh. "Come on, Kai. Come on."

It hardly seemed worth moving such a short distance — not what he'd call a walk — but he trundled over to her.

Finally, Mia did happy-teeth and scratched him under the chin.

"Good boy, Kai. I knew you were a clever dog. Good boy."

He wagged his tail, pleased she was happy, and to show he forgave her for walking so badly, he licked her cheek.

The licking made her do that hacking sound, which, for some mysterious reason, he'd grown to like. So, he licked her again, and again she hacked.

A crazy thought occurred to him — it appeared that the more he licked, the more she hacked, so could the two be connected? To test the theory, he licked her once more and got the same result. Had he just taught her to hack on command?

Finally, a successful lesson.

If she was clever enough to learn that, maybe she could learn to do other things properly too. Teaching her was going to be hard work, but ultimately rewarding when she mastered all the skills she needed to make it through life. Suddenly, getting her to pee on the peeing-post no longer seemed an impossible dream.

But if she was going to do things to please him, it was only fair he did things to please her, even if it would be a huge effort because it meant doing things the wrong way. Therefore, as a reward for learning today's lesson, Kai meandered along at the pace Mia set for the rest of their walk.

His cunning tactic worked because Mia did happy-teeth most of the way back to the house.

At the bottom of the steps up to the veranda, Kai hesitated, a strange smell wafting from above. It was kind of a people-smell, but stale and musty.

Mia tugged his walking-cord and climbed the steps. "Come on, Kai."

He padded up after her.

A scrawny woman with a face like scrunched paper lounged on the bench near the door. She didn't look dangerous, but an intruder was an intruder.

Kai hung back, glaring at Mia. This was what happened when she didn't let him pee properly on the peeing-post to mark their territory. The sooner she mastered the art of peeing on things, the better. That lesson couldn't come soon enough.

"Hello, Mrs. Paget," said Mia.

Despite this stranger's intrusion, his girl's tone suggested she

98

didn't feel threatened, and Kai's nose confirmed it because he couldn't smell fear on her. All the same, no way was he getting too close. He slunk back behind Mia.

"Hello, Mia." The woman did happy-teeth. "And this must be Kai."

He peeked around her legs so he could glimpse the intruder through one eye.

Mia stroked him. "It's okay, silly. I told you about Mrs. Paget from next door."

"Oh, bless him. If he lived on the street, it's not surprising he's wary of people."

"I found him in a moldy old box."

"Awww. Poor little thing." Mrs. Paget picked up a plastic bag from beside her. "No worries, your father warned me, so I came prepared."

Kai sniffed. Before she'd even removed it from the bag, he knew what it was. He leaned farther out sideways so he could see the woman with both eyes.

She held a warm sausage toward him.

"*Cookie trick! Danger! Danger!*" He jerked back to hide behind Mia.

Again, Mia stroked him. "It's okay, Kai. It's for you. Go on, boy."

Her touch was as reassuring as her tone, so he peeked out again.

Mrs. Paget wiggled the sausage. "Come on, Kai. Here, boy."

He looked up. Mia did happy-teeth, and Mrs. Paget did happy-teeth too.

He crept his right front paw out toward the woman, then stopped and looked at each of them again. Still happy-teeth.

He took another step. Still happy-teeth.

Another step and another.

The sausage smelled so meaty and fresh, he drooled, but again, he checked. Still happy-teeth.

Within reach, he leaned forward, eased his mouth open, and closed his jaws around the sausage.

Cringing, he shut his eyes and waited for the kicks he knew would come.

They didn't.

Mia petted him. "Good boy."

"Well, that's a first," said Mrs. Paget. "I've never known a dog to be so gentle where meat's concerned."

"Oh, he's really clever. And so good." Mia shrugged. "Most of the time."

Kai opened his eyes, the sausage still sticking out of his mouth. Was it really his? From a stranger?

Keeping his gaze fixed on the woman, he wolfed down his prize, half expecting her to pry his jaws apart and snatch the sausage back. But she didn't. How odd. Mia and Daddy had been nice to him, and now a complete stranger had given him a freshly cooked sausage. What was wrong with these people?

He eyed the woman, alert to any sudden movements that would reveal her true motive.

Mrs. Paget said, "Listen, dear, I have to get the bus to run some errands later, but if you have time now, I've got some of that mushroom soup you like and some bread fresh from the oven."

Mia's eyes popped wider. "That sounds nice." She looked at her magic-board and winced. "Oh, but I don't think we can. We're catching the two fifteen bus for Kai to see the vet."

"That's the bus I'm catching. Maybe we could have soup and travel in together."

"I'd love to, but I really don't think we have the time because before we go, I'm going to give Kai a bath."

"On your own?"

"Yes. Why?"

"I can help if you like."

"Thanks, but he's only small, so it should be easy."

The woman did happy-teeth and seemed to be stifling a little hacking. "I'll tell you what, dear, I'll wait here so you can holler if you need me. Okay?"

"Okay. Thanks, Mrs. Paget." Mia led Kai to the back door, and as they entered the house, he glanced back at the shriveled woman. She did happy-teeth at him.

Mrs. Paget behaved just as inexplicably as Mia and Daddy. Was it something in the water? Ohhh... no, he knew exactly what it was —

100

an advanced case of people-crazy. Had to be. The disease must have pushed them so far over the edge they just didn't know how to act like normal people anymore. It was the only logical answer.

Once inside, instead of Mia removing Kai's walking-cord, she used it to lead him upstairs and into the white-and-blue-tiled room. It reeked of chemicals. There was a fake smell of flowers, a fake smell of fruit, a fake smell of so many things from outside. His nostrils clogging up, he turned to leave, but Mia shut the door.

Why would she do that? He'd done what she wanted earlier, so wasn't it his turn to choose what they did now?

"Come on, Kai. This will be fun."

Mia guided him back around and pushed his butt down, so he sat on the pale blue tiles.

On the wall hung a cupboard with a picture of Mia on the front, but the moment she opened its door, the picture disappeared. It wasn't as impressive as making Daddy's voice appear from the magic-board, yet it was a fair trick.

He soon forgot about the magic, however, because with the cupboard open, the stink grew worse and enveloped him as if it were trying to glue itself to his fur.

Mia took out plastic bottle after plastic bottle, cradling them against her body with one arm, and then arranged them on the floor in front of him.

The stench. Was she trying to make him vomit?

"So what do you want to smell of, Kai?" She picked up a white bottle and a green one and studied the labels. "Rosehip and cactus fruit, or apple cider vinegar, or" — she picked up a third bottle — "coconut. Or maybe we forget the smell and have conditioner with vitamin E?" She picked up another bottle and shook it at him. "What you think?"

He looked at her. He didn't know what she intended to do with any of these bottles, but whatever it was, he was certain it was going to be absolutely horrifying.

"Oh, I know." Mia did happy-teeth and rubbed her hands together, then picked up yet another bottle. "My favorite: argan oil."

She patted the rim of a long white container that spanned a big part of one wall. "Up, Kai. Up."

Did she expect him to get into that thing and thus willingly increase his own discomfort?

He shuffled back.

She twisted him around, then lifted his front paws onto the rim.

While he was considering whether to take them off again, she lifted his back legs and tipped him into it.

He stood in the white container. From all the old flowery and fruity chemical smells festering in it, it had to be the dirtiest thing he'd ever had the misfortune to come across.

But what could he do? He glanced at the door, then pushed his front paws onto the rim, tensing his muscles to jump out.

"Nah-uh." Mia pushed his paws off the top. "You're going to be the cleanest dog in the world, Kai. The most aromatic ever." She did happy-teeth.

He had no defense against happy-teeth. He was trapped. No escape.

Okay, so it stank in this thing, but was it really that bad? He could stand it for a while to make her happy. It wasn't like it was going to get any worse.

Mia lifted a bendy silver tube above his head and it started to rain.

So just when he was starting to trust her, the torture began!

Chapter 17

The instant Mia opened the bathroom door a crack, Kai wiggled his nose into the gap, pried it wider, and shot out. He bolted into her bedroom, leapt onto her bed, across it, and down onto the floor. He hurtled around the bed, back out of the door, and down the stairs.

Mouth agape, Mia watched from the balcony as he tore through the living room, around the kitchen table, and back up the staircase.

He flew past her, back into her room, and dove into his fluffy-bowl. He rolled around and around and around.

He had to get the stink off him. Had to. He'd spent his whole life developing his dog smell, creating a unique scent so anyone who met him would recognize him and know to stay away from everything he'd marked. Now, underneath all the chemicals smothering him, there was a faint hint of a fruit, or a nut, or something that once grew naturally; however, it was so overwhelmed by heaven only knew what that even *his* nose struggled to identify it.

Why had she done this to him when he was just starting to trust her? Why?

He'd been good today. So good. He'd wanted to walk and play the way he wanted to, but he'd let Mia have her way. And this was how she repaid him? Treachery!

He squirmed in his fluffy-bowl, desperate to cover himself with his old smell.

Mia came in, yet instead of being sorry for what she'd done, she hacked and hacked. As if she hadn't tortured him enough!

He was never going to understand people. Never. There was simply no logic to them.

From the corner of his eye, he saw Mia busying herself with pulling clothes from a big cupboard, throwing them onto her bed, then putting them back, only to throw something else onto her comforter. More crazy.

He'd no idea how many items she messed with because he was far too busy cleaning the filth off his coat. He rolled and squirmed and wiggled and wriggled. He had to get the stink off. Had to.

In the midst of his struggle, a flash of bright color caught his attention as Mia pulled on a red jacket. She strolled over, crouched, and reattached his walking-cord.

"Come on, boy. Time to go." She tugged the walking-cord, but Kai glared at her through narrowed eyes as he rubbed and rubbed against the inside of his fluffy-bowl.

"Come on, Kai, or we're going to miss the bus." She heaved on the cord.

Kai ignored her.

Mia dropped the walking-cord and threw her arms in the air with a gruff, "Ohhh!"

She stomped from the room. Moments later, a smell caused Kai's nose to twitch. He glanced up while still cleaning.

Standing in the doorway, Mia held out a strip of heaven. "Coming now?"

Kai eyed the heaven. Was this more torture or a genuine apology? His mouth watered.

"Come on, Kai. Come on, boy." She wafted the strip through the air, even more of its aroma spreading throughout the room.

Kai couldn't take it — he jumped up and shot to the door.

Mia did happy-teeth and gave him his treat. It vanished instantly.

Holding a second strip above his head, she coaxed him down the stairs.

Kai couldn't take his eyes off the heaven, drool stringing from his mouth.

They exited through the back door and while Mia fumbled to lock it, Kai leapt up and snatched the strip from her hand.

Putting her key in her pocket, she wagged a finger of her free hand at him.

"Kai! That's not very polite, is it?"

That was the last strip of heaven she had — his nose was never wrong — so Kai bolted, hauling Mia along the veranda past Mrs. Paget, whose pinched expression suggested she wanted to hack but was doing her best to resist doing so.

The moment Kai reached the bottom step down from the house, he dove onto the ground and writhed and writhed. The scent of fresh grass cleared his nostrils of the foul-smelling chemicals, so it had to be cleaning his coat as well.

Mia yanked on the cord. "Kai, you'll get all dirty again."

He continued to writhe in the muck.

Mia heaved with both hands to pull him to his feet. "Kai!"

Mrs. Paget leaned over the balcony. "Yep, that's dogs for you — never happy unless they're covered in their own stink."

Relatively content he'd scraped as much of the stench off as he could, Kai scrambled up.

"Good boy. Now stop all that and walk nicely." Mia waved up at the veranda. "We're going, Mrs. Paget."

"Okay, Mia. Just give me a moment." The old lady shuffled down the steps to join them.

A path they hadn't taken before led to a narrow road that snaked upward through the trees. Side by side, they strolled to the end where it joined a much wider road with traffic going both ways. They turned left and walked for a minute or two before stopping at a tiny metal building that had only one wall and a roof. Its blue paint was chipped and pitted, with rust crawling over various areas.

Mia sat with Mrs. Paget on the metal bench against the wall, while Kai lay near the road to watch the world zooming by.

Soon after, a blue bus thundered over the hill, heading straight for them. Kai jumped up and shuffled away from the road. He glanced at Mia, hoping she'd know the best place to hide, but instead of appearing fearful that they were going to be crushed, Mia did happy-teeth and stepped closer to the road.

"Oh, good, it's on time," said Mia.

Kai slunk under the bench and cowered against the wall, scrunching himself up to be as small as he could be. The bus was going to squash them if they didn't get far enough away.

Instead of hiding to save herself, Mia stepped onto the very edge of the road, almost into the path of the marauding blue beast.

He barked to warn her and heaved on the cord to yank her back.

But Mia stood firm. She flung out one arm.

Kai tried to shrink even farther back. Mia was too small to stop it from hitting them, especially using just one hand. It was going to smash them into the ground.

Kai screwed his eyes shut, pictured his mother, and longed for her to rescue him.

But then the thundering noise quietened.

He dared to peek.

The blue beast was going slower and slower. Before he knew it, it had stopped completely, right next to Mia's hand.

He gazed up at her. She looked so small, so much smaller than nearly all the other people he'd ever met, and yet she was unbelievably powerful.

A door folded in half and banged to one side. Mia stepped into the bus as if it was perfectly normal, but the tension in the cord made her turn back to him still cowering.

She did happy-teeth. "Come on, Kai."

He glanced back.

Mrs. Paget stood behind him doing happy-teeth, too. "Go on, boy."

If Mia had the power to control this thing, maybe it was safe. He tottered forward, craned his neck, and peeked inside. He sniffed. Nothing smelled threatening, only different, and he was with Mia — possibly the most powerful being in the whole town.

He stepped in.

106

Mia handed some old scrunched-up paper to a man sitting at the front and he gave her some new smooth paper in return, which seemed a good trade. As the bus jerked and vibrated along the road, she led them along a central aisle between rows of maroon seats.

Kai shrank down and hung his head. There were people everywhere, and where there were people, there was pain and fear. Always.

His heart pounding, he pushed up against Mia's leg as close as he could as they walked.

In times of danger, the pack had to stay together, fight as one, and even have individuals sacrifice themselves for the greater good. It didn't matter about a single dog — the only thing that mattered was making sure the pack survived. He eyed the people warily, ready to snap at any hand that tried to grab them, or leap from a foot that tried to kick them.

Despite being surrounded by people, Mia didn't seem afraid. It wasn't just that she strode down the aisle with her head up and her shoulders back but that his nose could sense fear and he couldn't smell it on her.

Her courage boosted his, so he shuffled along beside her to a seat and they sat down, Mia letting him sit next to the window so he could look out. Mrs. Paget took the seat behind them.

Because it was a sunny day and Kai was now higher up, he had a magnificent view of grassy plains, forests, and hills. However, the journey quickly became a huge anticlimax. He could see everything, yes, but because of the glass barrier and the speed at which they were traveling, he couldn't smell a single one of the amazing sights. What should have been the highlight of the day was a complete flop. It was a pity the glass couldn't be removed so he could stick his head out. My, what a glorious way to travel that would be.

The lush woodlands and rolling hills were gradually replaced by bleak concrete and angular buildings. The bus rumbled to a stop in the center of the town and they got out at another tiny building with only one wall that sat next to a busy road. Kai winced: the assault on his senses...

The stench of chemicals clogged his nostrils while the cacophony of traffic clogged his ears. He missed their peaceful woods already. How had he ever lived with this unrelenting onslaught?

Mrs. Paget pointed away down the street. "I'm going this way, so I'll see you later, Mia."

"We're going that way, too."

Mrs. Paget raised her eyebrows. "Oh, good. So we can walk together."

A short stroll away, Mia stopped and slumped her shoulders. She gazed at a four-story brick building surrounded by an area of flat black ground, everything enclosed by high metal fence.

Standing by her side, Kai looked up at her, then to the building, and then back to her. Something was wrong, but what?

With but the barest of nods to the building, Mia said, "I have to go back there tomorrow."

The sparkle had vanished from her voice. It was like someone had drained all the joy out of her.

"School. Urgh."

Kai looked at the building. From the size of it and the number of windows suggesting it had endless rooms, he guessed it was very easy to get lost in there. He wouldn't want to go in if he didn't have to.

"But that's tomorrow," Mia said, sounding a little more like the upbeat girl he knew.

Mrs. Paget had strolled on a few steps but turned back. "Everything okay, Mia?"

"Fine." They rejoined the lady.

As they meandered farther along the sidewalk, Kai felt a confidence growing inside him he'd never known before. He wasn't alone now. And as if that wasn't enough, Mia had proven on the bus that she was so respected — or maybe feared — that no one dared to bother her. Probably because they knew she was powerful enough to stop a thundering vehicle with nothing but a wave of her hand. The dark buildings that had seemed so threatening only days before didn't seem so ominous anymore, the shadows no longer so foreboding.

He'd dreamed of having a pack for so long, yet because he'd

108

forgotten what it felt like to be in one, he hadn't realized he'd actually found one until now. He trotted past the monstrous buildings with his chest out.

Just like before, cars prowled the streets and people barged down the sidewalk, except now, everything was completely different. When he ambled along, people swerved around him instead of bulldozing over him, and when he crossed the street, cars stopped instead of trying to mow him down. On his own, he'd been invisible, but now... now it was like he'd become a respected member of the community.

Mia had to be an extremely important person to be revered so. Maybe that was why she didn't have to pee on things to claim them as hers — people knew her by reputation and were rightfully fearful of incurring her wrath. Maybe word had gotten around that those who displeased her were stuffed in a long white container and smothered in stinky oils, or had their noses trapped in a door and stretched down to their toes.

Yep, that would do the trick.

He'd bet they had an appropriate name for her too — Little Miss Nightmare or something.

His head held high, he sauntered along the sidewalk. It looked like he hadn't just found a pack but found one of the most powerful packs ever to exist.

Mia frowned. "Mrs. Paget?"

"Hmmm?"

"Errr... you do have, er, some errands, don't you? You're not just saying that?"

"Of course I do, dear. Why?"

"So Daddy didn't ask you to come to watch us?"

"Watch you what, dear?"

"You know," said Mia, "to watch that we're okay."

"That would be a little sneaky of him, wouldn't it?"

"It would, yes."

"And does Daddy often pull sneaky tricks like that?"

"I don't think so."

"Well, there you go, then." Mrs. Paget pointed to a one-story stone building with big square windows. "That's you, isn't it? Do you want me to come in with you?"

"Thanks, but Daddy called and arranged everything, so we'll be okay."

"Would you like me to wait? Maybe we could find a café after for a coffee and a cake? My treat."

"I would, but I've got a special treat planned for Kai already."

Mrs. Paget sighed. "Well, then, I'll, er, be off to run my errands."

"Okay. Bye, Mrs. Paget."

"So long, Mia. You take care now."

Mrs. Paget dawdled down the street while Mia led Kai toward the stone building.

After a short wait inside, they met the green-uniform man again. Kai sat on the metal table, quiet, unmoving, and obliging. He didn't take much notice of what the man was doing, being too focused on Mia. How wrong he'd been about her. This remarkable alpha. *His* alpha.

He was so deep in thought, he didn't even notice Mia had reattached his walking-cord until she tugged on it, coaxing him off the metal table. Outside again, Mia did one of the biggest happy-teeth he'd seen, then crouched and hugged him.

"He says everything's okay, Kai. You're going to be just fine." She squeezed him, then pulled back to look him in the eyes. "And you were so good in there. I'm so proud, I think you deserve a treat."

They set off again. Mia skipped down the sidewalk, humming to herself, while Kai trotted alongside.

They were untouchable.

But on turning a corner, Kai saw something he recognized. He froze. Stared. Then shuffled a step back.

Glowing brightly across the street hung a hot dog sign... And darkness bled from the alley nearby.

Chapter 18

Glowering at the alley, Kai pulled to go back the way they'd come. A scent hung on the air — a scent burned into his memory.

"No, this way, Kai." Mia yanked on the walking-cord.

No way was he crossing that road. He didn't want to upset his alpha, but he couldn't do what she wanted. Taking the easiest option, Kai sat on the cold, hard ground.

Mia frowned. "What's wrong, boy? Did something bad happen here when you were alone?"

She glanced around. He hoped her nose was as good as his so she'd realize the danger, because his was alerting him to one critically important thing: Hound had been in the area.

Mia crouched to him. "Kai, it's okay. There's nothing to be afraid of." She ruffled his fur. "Come on, I'm with you now, so nothing bad's going to happen."

Kai sniffed the air. The scent of Hound was there, but it was old. Maybe a day or so. His nose was never wrong, yet he couldn't afford to make any silly mistakes in such a dire situation. He sniffed long and hard, sucking in as much air as he could manage to give his nose every chance of uncovering the whole truth.

It was then he realized that there was something missing — a particular scent that was not on Mia.

He sniffed one last time, gazing up at her. No, not a trace. There wasn't the faintest hint of fear coming from her.

He'd already witnessed how powerful she was, so if she wasn't afraid, maybe he shouldn't be either.

He stood up.

"Are you okay now?" she asked.

He licked her cheek and she hacked like he knew she would, proving everything was going to be fine.

On the move again, Mia marched out into the road on a path of black and white stripes with Kai alongside. Partway across, a roaring bus hurtled straight at them. Mia didn't seem to care, moseying on regardless, so Kai lurched forward to drag her out of danger. Still she dawdled, without even glancing at the bus, while tugging back on his walking-cord to slow his pace.

To Kai's amazement, the vehicle slowed and halted to let them pass. She'd stopped it. Again. And this time, she hadn't even needed to use her hand.

Oh yes, his alpha was unbelievably powerful.

Reaching the safety of other sidewalk, they approached the food truck. The scent of warm pork was dizzying, yet Kai shrank behind when the skinny man draped in a white apron stared at them from the serving hatch. He was the man who'd once kicked him.

Kai pulled back on the leash, not enough to halt Mia's approach, but enough to slow it so he had time to monitor how events unfolded.

He glared at the aproned man, his muscles tensed, ready to bolt and drag Mia to safety.

But the man did happy-teeth. "What can I get you, little lady?"

"Two jumbo hot dogs, please," said Mia.

"Two jumbos coming up."

Oh my, to get a reaction like that from someone like him, people had to be terrified of displeasing her. Maybe he'd put the "peeing on things" lesson on indefinite hold.

The atmosphere was so thick with the smell of cooking hot dogs, burgers, and sausages, it was as if the air itself was made of pork, as if Kai could just take a bite out of it and eat it.

A string of saliva hung from his jaws. He couldn't believe his dream was coming true. Every single day of his life, he'd dreamed of standing in this very spot, enjoying these exotic smells, and munching on the cooked meats.

The aproned man handed Mia two jumbo hot dogs in exchange for some scrunched-up paper.

It was the second time Mia had given a man scrunched-up paper and the man seemed happy. Paper was obviously important. Maybe that was why Daddy used it for his art projects. But was paper more valuable before or after it had been used to mop up his pee? Probably after — it smelled way too boring before.

Ambling away from the food truck, Kai drooled from both sides of his mouth. He gazed up at Mia and the biggest hot dogs he'd ever seen. They were almost as big as the hot dog in the glowing sign. This had to be the best day of his life. Maybe the best day of anyone's life. This had to be how kings lived.

Mia ripped away a piece of the bread and meat and offered it to Kai. He trembled with excitement. This was really happening — he was having a warm, fresh hot dog. A fluttery feeling rose from his stomach and he tingled all over. A real hot dog. *For him!*

His immediate impulse was to snatch it and gobble it down before anyone else could steal it. However, he parted his jaws slowly, leaned forward, and let it all but tumble from Mia's fingers into his mouth. He held it there for a moment and closed his eyes to focus on the experience. The juices tantalized his tongue, the meaty scent teased his nose, and the warmth caressed his mouth. It wasn't heaven, but it was mighty close. A dream come true.

Mia munched on her other part of the hot dog and guided Kai away from the truck. She gestured to her left. "This way, Kai. It's a shortcut to the bus stop."

Kai froze. That was *the* alley. The alley in which Hound had nearly crippled him. Even on a sunny day with Mia, shadows devoured it and drenched it in gloom.

Mia ripped away another chunk of hot dog and offered it to him. He ignored it, unable to tear his gaze from the alley.

"Go on, Kai. It's for you." She held it closer.

Unable to resist the meaty scent, he took it.

Chomping the hot dog, he sniffed to confirm what his nose had already told him. Mia didn't smell afraid and the alley didn't smell of Hound — at least not a fresh scent. Maybe it was safe.

Mia strolled into the alley, so Kai slouched along at her heels, his ears pricked for the tiniest of sounds, his nose sifting through scents for the tiniest of dangers.

Maybe he was panicking for no reason.

Mia had already proven more than worthy to be their pack's alpha. She'd healed his wounds without licking them once, she'd stopped the thundering bus without even touching it, and she'd gotten them the biggest hot dogs in the entire world without having to do anything except give a man some scrappy little paper. It was as if she had magic powers. That was the only explanation. No one could do what she'd done and be an ordinary person. No, it had to be magic.

Trotting alongside her, Kai took another piece of hot dog from her. Fresh, warm hot dog tasted better than he had ever dreamed it could, and Mia had made it possible. Magic. It couldn't be anything else. However, the best part was, they still hadn't started on the second one.

Ahead at the far end of the alley, traffic tootled along in either direction. The rumbling cars meant Kai couldn't isolate sounds as well as he would've liked, and to compound the problem, the breeze was coming from behind them, blowing scents away instead of toward him. Uncaring, he gazed up at Mia — magical Mia. Nothing could possibly go wrong. Not with her powers.

Mia gave him the last bit of the first hot dog. "Shall we have the second now or save it for later?" Mia motioned to put the hot dog in her bag.

This again? She was willing to risk losing a real hot dog instead of stuffing it down as quickly as possible? So there was a limit to her magical powers.

A dark scent made the fur on Kai's back stand on end. He froze. Stopped chewing. Stared wide-eyed.

"What's wrong, Kai?" Mia frowned and glanced around the alley, but there was nothing to see.

Kai growled.

She crouched down in front of him and stroked his head.

"It's okay, boy. You're safe. There's nothing here. Everything's fine."

He ignored her, staring past her into the darkness. She was wrong. So very wrong.

Chapter 19

What's wrong, Kai? Huh? What's wrong, boy?" Mia stroked his neck and shoulders, trying to soothe him and convince him there was nothing to worry about.

There might have been nothing to see, but he could smell it lurking in the darkest shadows. Waiting. Hungry. Savage.

He peered into her face. Why didn't she know? Surely she could smell it.

She hugged him. "It's okay, silly. There's nothing to be afraid of. Come on."

A growl came from behind her. Deep. Guttural. Oozing malice.

Mia clawed at Kai's fur and her whole body tensed as she obviously realized she was wrong — nothing was fine; there was everything to be afraid of. Then his nose told him something he struggled to believe, but his nose was never wrong, so he had no choice but to believe it — Mia smelled of fear.

Oh, no. Oh please, no.

If the most powerful person he'd ever come across was afraid, boy were they in serious trouble.

With her breath coming in short, sharp pants, Mia turned around as she stood. She gasped.

Hound stood in the middle of the alley, blocking their way. Its head down, it curled its top lip to reveal fangs ready to rip and tear. It snarled.

Kai growled back. Hound had beaten him days earlier. Beaten him badly. However, that time, he'd been on his own. Today, he was with his pack, and his pack was more powerful than Hound could ever dare to imagine.

Kai looked up at Mia, willing her to magic it away, magic it away, magic it away!

But Mia didn't magic the monstrous dog away. She trembled and the walking-cord shook in her hand.

Kai's heart pounded. Something was wrong. Why hadn't Mia magicked it away?

He pressed up against her leg, so they stood side by side, making his pack look as big as possible. She had to magic it away. It was their only chance. Hound would rip them to pieces if she didn't.

Her hand shaking, Mia held the second hot dog out toward Hound.

The monstrous beast stalked closer. Though it was still a few strides away, it jerked forward and snapped at them, displaying its size, stating its dominance, promising violence.

Kai whimpered. Hound was so big, and though Kai was healing, he still wasn't as fit as he'd been when he'd faced Hound the other day. No way could Kai fight it. Not alone. He needed his pack to act as one, but his pack was faltering.

Hound prowled another step toward them with a big black paw, its huge claws scraping on the concrete.

Kai stepped forward. He didn't want to fight, yet he had no choice. He had to protect his alpha. A pack could survive without an individual dog, but it couldn't survive without its alpha. An alpha was more important than anything else — even him.

Mia gripped his walking-cord tighter, holding him by her. She twisted around, heaved her other arm back, and launched the second hot dog into the air. It sailed up the alley the way they'd come.

The massive black dog stormed straight at Kai and Mia. Kai thought it was going to grab him in its gigantic fangs, but Mia pulled him to one side.

Hound flew straight past them, fixated on the hot dog.

"Run, Kai. Run!"

They hurtled down the alley and out onto the crowded street, where people bustled to and fro, clutching boxes and bags filled with precious things. They ran and ran and didn't stop until a whole bunch of people stood between them and the entrance to the alley — people Hound would have to fight before reaching them.

Heaving a breath, Mia patted him with a shaking hand. "You were a good boy, Kai. So brave."

She glanced back, as did Kai. Hound wasn't following them.

"Poor thing. It must've been starving to do that."

Mia led them down a street lined with buildings, each of which had huge windows displaying all kinds of precious things — magic-boards, food, fake-people... he walked alongside her, regularly glancing up at her. She hadn't used her most powerful magic to escape Hound but performed a relatively simple trick. That wasn't just smart but wise because if she'd exhausted all her magic then, they'd be in even bigger trouble if they fell into another emergency.

Whenever he figured he'd fathomed what made her tick, she did something else to surprise him and set him right back to the start. How was he ever going to fully understand her?

They cut down another similar street, and at the next, Kai smelled their own scent; it was the street on which they'd arrived in the town. They passed the big red building, and again, Mia rolled her eyes and made a face that looked as if an interloper had pooped in her favorite pooping spot.

"School. Urgh."

Turning away, she gestured ahead. "The bus stop's just along here."

They strode on to another tiny building. This one was a little posher than the others, having four walls no less, all made of glass. Mia sat on the bench built into the back wall while Kai gazed around.

Farther down the road, traffic circled one of the tiniest parks he'd ever seen. A single tree sprouted from the middle, while a thorny bush curved around the back area. He couldn't imagine many people visited it because an endless stream of cars and trucks drove around and around it, almost without a break.

Why had Mia stopped here? Nothing seemed to be happening, and he'd already seen enough of the town's roads and traffic in his life, so he lay at Mia's feet and went to sleep.

When Mia shook him awake, a blue bus was heading toward them. Again, she held out her raised hand and her magic stopped it. Amazing!

They got on and the bus bumped and vibrated along the road. While it was nice to see things from a high vantage point, Kai was still upset he couldn't smell anything. Whoever designed buses must not have been able to use their nose properly. Or maybe they had a far better nose than he did and could smell through the glass barrier. Maybe one of those fat-long-noses Mia had a picture of on her wall. A nose that long would surely be able to smell through glass, and if it couldn't, what use was it?

While Kai contemplated if it might be worth trapping his nose in a door to stretch it and boost his sense of smell, a group of boys clambered on board. They did what boys always did — shoved each other around while being way too noisy for no reason.

He shrank away, squeezing closer to Mia, yet he couldn't smell fear on her. Didn't she know about cruel-boys?

A skinny one with brown curly hair who smelled of cheese and peppers spotted Mia, but instead of shouting or kicking, he did happy-teeth. He swung into the seat in front of them and twisted around to her.

"Hey, this the new dog, huh?" said the boy. "Fantastic!"

Before Kai had time to jump down and hide under the seat, the boy leaned over and ruffled the fur on his neck. What was happening? Boys were nasty, savage things. Was this another version of the cookie trick?

"Hey, Johnny." Mia did happy-teeth, too.

"Man, he's cool."

Kai shrank back to be safe, but the boy just went on scratching him.

"Yeah, we do everything together," said Mia. "He's the best dog ever."

"And he's gonna be big too — look at the size of those paws."

"You think?"

"Oh, yeah. That's how you can tell, according to my dad."

Kai stared at them. What was going on? Mia wasn't only not *afraid* but was actually *happy* to see this boy. And though Kai hated to admit it, the boy's scratching felt good. Kai twisted his head to the left to let the boy's fingers knead a different area, and the boy obliged.

Kai frowned. This boy was... being nice. That wasn't what boys did. Was this one ill?

While Mia talked with the boy, Kai allowed himself to be stroked and petted, yet he couldn't help but keep his muscles tensed, ready to either attack or run. Boys couldn't be trusted. He knew that. Except this one did nothing but make Mia do happy-teeth, scratch Kai's neck just how he liked it, and then leave the bus without doing anything even remotely threatening.

Another mystery — were there some boys who weren't complete monsters, or was it that they behaved well in Mia's presence because they were in such fear of her power?

While he was pondering the possibilities, the bus stopped, and Mia guided him off. They ambled back down the narrow road toward the house.

Back at home, Kai guzzled down his brown gunk. He hadn't realized how starving he was after the day's stresses and excitement until he stuck his snout in his silver bowl; then he wolfed his food down even quicker than usual. Empty, the bowl clunked across the wooden floor in a desperate bid to escape Kai's unforgiving tongue, but he shuffled along in hot pursuit, determined to lick out every last scrap.

The bowl gleaming once again, he looked at his safe place between the two chairs, then looked at Mia. He strolled over and sat at her side at the table. After they'd eaten, Daddy and Mia lounged on the sofa, so Kai slunk over to lay at the little girl's feet.

"Daddy, you should've seen it — so big and scary. And all it wanted was some food."

"It sounds like a real adventure. How was Kai with the other dog?"

Mia reached down and patted him. "Oh, you'd have been so proud. He was going to fight to protect me, until I told him not to."

Daddy nodded and glanced down at Kai. "Sounds like it's a good thing he was with you."

"He's my hero." She ruffled Kai's fur on top of his head. "Even though the other dog was a giant, Kai was still going to fight it for me."

"It was that big?"

Mia held her arms out and her eyes popped wide. "It was huge. Like Mr. Paget's old dog, Rocky, but even bigger and all black."

"A German shepherd?"

"It was so big you wouldn't believe." She scratched under Kai's chin. "That's why Kai was so brave."

"He already means the world to you, doesn't he?"

Mia's happy-teeth vanished. "Of course. Why? You aren't getting rid of him, are you? Because you can't, Daddy. You just can't!"

Daddy held up his hands, palms facing her. "Hey, hey, don't panic. Kai's not going anywhere." He slung his arm around her shoulders and pulled her to him to cuddle. "He's one of the family now. I can't believe what a difference he's made. It's wonderful to see you smiling again."

She snuggled into his chest. "I love him, Daddy. And I love you for letting me have him."

"Maybe it was destiny you found him in that box."

"What's destiny?"

"When something is supposed to happen for a reason, so there's no way it can *not* happen."

"Oh, definitely destiny, then. I can't imagine ever being without him now, and it's only been three days."

Daddy smoothed his hand down over her long black hair. "No, I can't either."

Mia reached down and ruffled the fur on Kai's neck. "We'll be together forever, won't we, boy? Forever."

Chapter 20

The next morning, Kai couldn't wait to gobble down his breakfast and dash outside with Mia to discover the adventure the new day had in store. However, from the get-go, things developed in an unexpected and disconcerting way.

Breakfast wasn't the normal leisurely affair. While he had two strips of heaven to go with his bowl of gunk, instead of being able to wolf it down and then relax at Mia's feet, for no apparent reason, Daddy and Mia kept rushing around. Mia wolfed down her breakfast at a truly impressive speed, which boded well for the day's lessons, but then things started to go wrong.

Instead of dashing out to use that saved time on their walk, she dashed around collecting things from upstairs and the living room. Kai followed her, having to jump out of the way twice, so he wouldn't get stepped on. Mia then packed, unpacked, and repacked her backpack, all the while glancing to the circle on the wall with the little sticks that moved around.

Meanwhile, Daddy bustled about preparing more food even though they'd only just eaten. He placed sandwiches, fruit, and a cookie in a white plastic box and handed it to Mia. Instead of being pleased with such a generous gift, she rolled her eyes, dragged things out of her backpack and again repacked it.

Mia then spun around so quickly she kicked Kai. He yelped, not because it hurt, but because of the shock that she'd done such a thing.

She crouched and hugged him. "Sorry, Kai."

He was just enjoying the attention when it ended and she went back to dashing around the house.

And then things got even worse.

Mia led him outside for his early-morning walk but barely gave him enough time to finish peeing on his peeing-post before hauling him back inside and shutting the door. It wasn't just disappointing but extremely impolite.

What was going on?

At the front door, Daddy and Mia talked in hushed voices.

"Do you think he knows what's happening?" Mia whispered, as if she didn't want Kai to know she was talking, which was pointless, considering how good his hearing was. If they wanted privacy, they should've gone outside and to at least the bottom step.

Daddy rubbed her upper arm. "Listen, he'll be okay. It's only for a few hours."

"A few hours? School's till three o'clock, Daddy. *Three o'clock!*"

"Sweetheart, if you think that's a long day, you're going to love your first full-time job."

Mia frowned. "Don't joke. I'm worried about him."

He crouched down to her level. "He'll be fine. Trust me. Just enjoy your first day back, and he'll be waiting for you when you come home."

She heaved a breath.

Daddy said, "Are you sure you don't want to travel in with me?"

"I can't." She glanced over at Kai, her face lined in ways Kai had never seen before. "That would mean he'd be on his own even longer. Anyway, I want to go on the bus like always."

Daddy sighed. "Okay." He stood up and kissed her on the top of her head. "Love you. Have a great day back."

"I love you too. Bye, Daddy."

Daddy left through the front door, Mia standing in the open doorway for a moment to wave. She then led Kai up to her room, where she spent what felt like forever moving her hair around while looking at a picture of herself on the wall that twisted and turned the way she did.

Unfortunately, no matter how she moved her flowing black locks, she never seemed happy with the outcome. The strange thing was that she repeatedly moved it into the exact same shape, then, looking very upset at it, shook it all into a big mess, only to start over and move it exactly the same way yet again. Kai tried to spot a difference, but the outcome always looked the same to him. People. He was never going to understand them.

Mia glanced to her bedside table and the small rectangular box with glowing red marks on the front that changed throughout the day. She clutched her mouth and squealed.

"Look at the time!"

She raced into the bathroom, leaving the door ajar. Kai trundled along and nosed it open to find her sitting on the small white platform that had a hole filled with water in the middle.

His jaw dropped.

She wasn't...?

He sniffed.

She was! She was peeing in his secret water bowl!

That was outrageous. He had to drink out of that. How would she like it if he peed in her pink cup?

Mia finished, stood up, and flipped a silver lever behind the platform. A torrent of water whooshed down and swirled around and around before disappearing through a hole.

Kai watched all the pee disappear, then turned and stared at Mia as she washed her hands. That was good pee, that was. It could have marked countless things, announced to the whole neighborhood Mia was around, and claimed the peeing-post as theirs once and for all. What a waste. Even with all her magic, there was no excuse for wasting good pee.

However, on the plus side, he could cross off one more mystery on his "To Solve" list — people did pee, only in the strangest of places.

Scurrying back into her room, Mia grabbed her bag and a jacket, then raced out and down the stairs. Kai trotted behind her.

At the back door, she bent down to him and enveloped him with her arms. "Don't worry, I promise I'll come back as quickly as I can, then we'll have a nice long walk." She hugged him tighter. "I miss you already, Kai."

When she stood up, she flung the door open and dashed out, shouting over her shoulder as the door slammed shut in Kai's face, "Bye, Kai."

Her footsteps clomped along the wooden veranda as she ran, and Kai stared at the door. The closed door. The closed door separating him from Mia, who was getting farther and farther away from him.

What was happening?

He whimpered.

Seriously. What was happening? Why was everyone abandoning him?

He pawed at the door, raking his claws down it, desperate to find a crack to pry wider.

No good.

He ran around into the living area and jumped onto a chair, resting his front paws on the windowsill. Mia scampered up one of the paths through the trees as the bright sunlight cast long shadows across the ground.

Why was she going without him? It was the duty of every good dog to protect the pack, especially the alpha. He had to be with her.

He clawed at the window. Barked. Barked again. But Mia still got farther and farther away.

He dashed back to the door and nuzzled and pawed at it, but there was no way out.

Back around to the window, his eyes widened — Mia had vanished.

He barked and barked and barked.

He'd only just found his new pack, yet already it was falling to pieces.

Kai ran upstairs and into Mia's room, then the bathroom, everywhere he could get. There had to be something he could do to reach her. But there wasn't. He was alone. Again.

Kai prowled around the house endlessly, walking and walking, but never arriving anywhere he wanted to be. What could he do?

What could he do? With no answer coming, he sat before the back door and stared at it.

He whined. It felt like Mia had been gone forever. Where was she? The alpha couldn't desert the pack.

He slunk around to the window again, hoping he would see her coming back. However, though he looked and looked, she never did.

The sun had hidden behind lumpy gray clouds, and the wind crashed the trees' branches from side to side. A horrible day. He would've been pleased to be inside, if he hadn't been abandoned.

He whimpered.

Then he sensed it. Something coming from behind him. That meant it was coming not from outside, but inside.

He turned and sniffed, then gasped. If his nose was right, he'd soon be with Mia.

Chapter 21

There was a new scent in the house, which should have been impossible *if* all the doors and windows were closed. It meant only one thing...

Kai followed his nose across the living room, up the stairs, along the balcony, and to the one room into which he hadn't yet been allowed: Daddy's room.

He sniffed the gap at the bottom of the door. The smell from the world outside was far stronger than it should have been, but more, a cold draft blew against the tip of his nose. Inside, there had to be a hole to the outside. He prayed it was big enough for him to squeeze through.

He jabbed the door with his nose, but it held solid.

Rising onto his hind legs, he pushed against the door with his front paws. Still solid.

Pushing his snout into the corner of the door where the floor met the frame, he shoved with all his might. His paws skidded on the polished wood floor, so he bent forward and heaved with his shoulder.

Solid.

This was a nightmare. If he could just get through this door, he could reach Mia, yet it seemed impossible.

Having tried everything else, he had only one option left. Only one possible solution.

He barked at the door.

Growled at the door.

Snapped at the door.

But the door ignored him, as if gloating he couldn't get through it.

Kai wasn't a huge monster of a dog like Hound, but he wasn't a powerless puppy anymore either. This door was not going to beat him.

Backing up against the banister spindles, he made as much space between him and the door as he could, then leapt at it.

He smacked into the door but bounced off and smashed into the floor so hard he yelped.

Scrambling up, he glared at the door and snarled.

He shunted back again, taking a huge breath to fill his muscles with all the power he could muster, then launched himself.

Kai slammed against the wood once more. Hitting higher than before, he raked his front paws down the door and over a piece of silver metal jutting out. It twisted downward, the door swung open, and Kai fell into Daddy's room.

His head held high, he barked at the door. He'd beaten it and now the horrible thing would know he could do it anytime, so it was best not to mess with him.

In the room, though most of the furnishings were white, beige, or chocolate brown, exotic sights and scents bombarded Kai: a small gold pot filled with shriveled flowers and leaves laced the air with a heady perfumed smell, while on the walls hung pictures of landscapes. These weren't realistic representations of any countryside he'd ever seen but instead hinted at what they were supposed to be, with vibrant reds, blacks, yellows, and blues of such a rippled texture, they looked as if they'd been layered on with a knife.

Kai would've loved to explore the room and nose into all its nooks and crannies, especially as the scent of the mysterious third person — the "like-Mia" person — was so much stronger, but he didn't have time for such trivial puzzles when Mia was out in the cruel world alone.

A draft blew through the inch-wide gap of a partially open window, wafting outside smells to him. He raced over and leapt onto the sill, his tail thrashing a second gold pot that he hadn't seen into the air.

It crashed to the floor, spewing smelly crumpled plant bits across a fawn rug.

Ignoring the accident, Kai nuzzled his snout into the gap in the window and pried it wider. In an instant, he was through and dashing over the veranda roof, the red tiles clattering under his paws.

When he peeked over the edge, a queasiness gripped him. Oh boy, he was high off the ground. So, so high. His legs trembled at the thought of jumping. So many things could go wrong, and if even the tiniest one did, he'd break his leg, or his neck, or his back, or... well, everything. No way could he jump.

He tottered to the far end of the roof, his claws tip-tapping on the tiles. Even jumping to the steps leading to the grass was too far. He'd never make it without crippling himself. It was useless. He'd lost her.

Wait!

He gasped as a possibility clawed at him.

Maybe...

He checked the angles again.

Yes, he could do it. He could break his fall using the banister rail running up either side of the staircase. If he timed his leap to perfection, he could kick off the rail and spring safely onto the steps.

Tensing his muscles, he readied himself to leap before the terrifying height changed his mind.

He gulped a last breath and kicked away from the roof. But one of the tiles under his left hind leg twisted and his paw lost traction at the vital moment.

Kai soared through the air in a downward arc, his angle completely wrong.

The rock-hard wooden steps hurtled toward him, so he twisted in midair, desperate to realign his flight to be able to kick off the rail and save himself.

But he was already too close. Already out of time.

He crunched into the steps and tumbled, head over tail, head over tail, all the way down the staircase. At the bottom, he splattered face-first into the ground.

Clambering to his feet, he expected pain to stab him from

countless places, but apart from a few twinges, he seemed fine.

He eyed the house. He'd managed it; he'd escaped and was going to be able to reach Mia. Oh, she was going to be thrilled to see him.

Trees and bushes zipped by as he raced up the narrow path to the road, using Mia's scent as his guide. At the top, he dashed out of the trees and onto the sidewalk of the wide road.

He sniffed. Mia had gone left, the same way they'd gone together the day before.

Following her trail, he trotted down the road. He couldn't believe he'd managed it. His heart pounded, only this time with joy rather than fear. Mia. Mia. Mia. He was going to see Mia.

He skidded to a halt and glanced up the road, then down it. Something was wrong.

He sniffed. Sniffed and sniffed with all his might.

Mia had vanished.

All trace of her had disappeared as if she'd been picked up and whisked away somewhere without ever touching the ground again.

He looked back and forth along the road. What now? How could he find her if he couldn't see or smell her?

His stomach clenched. He had to find her. But how?

He whined.

Behind him stood the one-wall building. He studied it as thoughts crashed through his mind. He sniffed, then ambled over to the bench and sniffed again.

Mia had been there. Her smell was still fresh.

He followed her scent across the ground, all but scraping the gray flagstones with his nose until he reached the black of the road. That was where she disappeared.

He took a step to his left and smelled the black ground there. Mia was there as well, but a fainter Mia — the Mia from yesterday.

Kai looked at the stream of traffic coming over the hill and zipping down past him, then at the other lane crawling up. In the middle of the vehicles heading up, a blue bus grumbled along, people's faces peering out from the windows.

From over the hill, a familiar roar raced toward him. Another bus.

Remembering Mia's magic, he sat politely at the curb and raised his paw. The bus would take him to Mia, he was sure. He just had to believe — believe in Mia's magic and the power it had to stop the monstrous vehicle.

The bus thundered closer and closer.

Kai cringed. It was so close, so fast, so terrifying. He ached to run out of its path, but he stayed, paw out. Mia's power would stop it. It had to.

Instead of stopping, the bus careered straight past him and continued on down the hillside.

Kai watched it disappear into the distance.

How stupid he'd been to think he could stop it with his paw. He didn't have magic like Mia in his paws. Stupid. Stupid. Stupid. Now he'd never get to her.

Skulking over to where the sidewalk turned to grass, Kai hung his head. Now what? He couldn't see Mia, couldn't smell her, couldn't hear her. It was impossible. He'd lost his beloved pack again.

Shoulders slumped, Kai stared at the black ground of the road. There was nothing here for him, especially with that stench — like something had been burned to a crisp and then burned even more.

He whimpered. He'd lost her. Maybe forever, like his mother. There'd been nothing he could do about losing her, so there was obviously nothing he could...

No!

Yes, he was stupid, but not because he thought he could stop the bus.

He didn't have magic in his paws — of course he didn't. His magic was in his nose.

He jerked his head up and gazed in the direction the bus had disappeared. That stench was the key. He couldn't smell Mia, but he didn't have to because he could smell that stench. It would lead him to exactly where he needed to go.

Kai hurtled down the hillside, his nostrils clogged by the acrid stink.

Mia. He was going to see Mia. Mia. Mia. Mia!

Chapter 22

The reek belching from the bus led Kai right into the center of the town. His paws ached from all the running, though it was going to be worth it to see Mia.

Keeping to the safety of the sidewalk, he passed the tiniest park in the world that had only a single tree and a bush. Just as much traffic circled it as the last time he'd seen it. He trotted along another road and by the tiny glass-walled building in which he'd sat with Mia, waiting for the bus to take them home.

He strode on but stopped. What was that drifting on the air?

Turning his head in a wide arc, he sniffed, searching. There! It was Mia's smell.

He scampered along the sidewalk, following his nose. She was close.

A fence of black metal bars rose out of the ground. Kai ran alongside it, Mia's scent growing stronger and stronger with each step — so strong he knew he was almost there.

His stomach fluttering with anticipation, he felt sure he must be doing happy-teeth the way Mia did.

Halfway along the fence, Mia's scent turned, yet there was nowhere to go next: the metal bars rose up in front of him, to his right and to his left. They were way too high for Mia to have gotten over by herself, and even though there was a gap under one particular spot, it didn't look big enough for Mia to squeeze through.

Kai hunkered down and stuck his head through the gap. Mia's scent was indeed stronger on that side.

Shuffling forward, he wiggled under and leapt up. He was in. But in where?

A four-story red-brick building loomed before him, surrounded by flat black ground.

It was *that* building — the one Mia had been unhappy about seeing — and her scent disappeared inside the massive, dark complex. How was he ever going to find her in such a gigantic place?

Well, he'd do the only thing he could do: whatever his nose said.

He followed Mia's smell across the black ground to where two glass doors were shut side by side. He pushed the first one with his snout. Solid. He pushed the second. Solid.

He peered through the glass. A cream-walled hallway led into the depths of the building, gray metal cupboards lining either side of the gray speckled floor.

With no way in from the front, the only solution was to go in another way.

Kai trotted around the building's perimeter, looking for an open door or window, but there wasn't a single one.

At the front of the dark building again, Kai sat on the ground and glared up at it. He'd come so far, yet he was still alone because Mia was still beyond his reach.

There was only one thing left to try — only one thing a dog could do when its pack was lost and needed to be guided back home. Kai raised his face to the sky and howled.

And he howled.

And he howled.

Faces appeared at the windows on all the levels of the complex. Not long after, children and adults appeared in the corridor.

He scoured the faces gawking at him, searching for that one special one, yet she wasn't there.

He howled again, as loud and for as long as he could.

The front doors opened and two men dashed through while a woman struggled to hold the children inside, a few leaking out.

One of the men dashed over to confront Kai as a gust of wind blew. The hair combed over the top of his head flapped in the breeze, revealing bare skin underneath. Brandishing a flat stick with markings on it, he lunged at Kai.

"Get out of here, stupid dog!"

Kai dodged with ease and took a deep breath for another howl.

The flappy-hair man jabbed the stick at him again, so Kai growled. This man was not going to keep him away from Mia.

"Kai!"

Kai gasped. Spinning around, he searched the faces staring at him.

His heart raced and his eyes popped wider when he saw his little girl running around the left-hand side of the building. Mia!

He bolted, running as quick as his legs would let him. And Mia ran to him with her arms wide.

Flappy Man scowled at her like his worst enemy had peed on his favorite peeing-post. "Please don't tell me this is your dog, Mia Dubanowski. You do know it's against regulations to bring pets to school, don't you?"

Mia! Mia! Mia! Kai wagged his tail so hard it wagged his whole body.

Mia knelt on the ground and flung her arms around him. He licked and licked her face while she was doing the biggest happy-teeth he'd ever seen.

"I'm sorry, Mr. Wat—" Mia hacked, struggling to talk. "Mr. Watkins. He must have" — more hacking — "escaped."

She twisted her head this way and that, but there was no way Kai was going to let her get away from his licking.

"So, what do you intend to do with him now?" Flappy Man jabbed his stick at Kai. "Because that animal cannot stay on school grounds."

Standing up, Mia gripped Kai's blue-neck-band to hold him by her side, but he jumped and jumped to lick anything he could reach.

"I'm sorry, Mr. Watkins. I'll call my daddy and see what he can do."

Flappy Man frowned. "Well, he better do something quick, young lady, because that beast has caused enough disruption for one day."

Flappy Man turned toward the building. "Okay, everyone back

134

inside, please. The show's over." He opened his arms, herding the children toward the doors, then looked up at the windows and pointed. "Away from the windows, please. Yes, that means you, Timothy Armstrong."

"Yo!" One boy punched the air. "Nice one, Kai!"

Flappy Man stabbed the stick toward the boy. "My office, now, John Sanger."

In just a few seconds, everyone disappeared, leaving only Kai licking Mia while she talked into her magic-board.

Soon after, Daddy arrived. He was scowling almost as much as Flappy Man had. He wagged his finger at Mia. "We'll be talking about this when you get home tonight, young lady."

Daddy then carried Kai toward the car parked at the other side of the fence. Kai was thrilled to see his other pack member, so he lashed Daddy's cheek with his tongue. Daddy gripped him by the scruff of the neck and pulled him away so he couldn't reach an inch of skin anywhere to lick. Anyone would have thought Kai had done something wrong with the way he was being treated. Couldn't people grasp what he'd been through to get there and the scale of his accomplishment? It was a crazy world where genius didn't only go unrecognized but was actually punished. Although, why was he surprised? People-crazy was everywhere.

All the way home in the car, there was no happy-teeth or hacking. When Daddy opened the door to the house and they both went in, Kai jumped and tried to lick him again.

Daddy held him away and wagged a finger like he had at Mia. "If you're going to live here, you're going to follow the rules like everyone else."

Daddy locked the door behind them, then stomped around the ground floor and yanked on all the windows so hard they rattled, but not one of them opened. All the while he muttered under his breath.

Wanting to be good, Kai sat on the rug in the middle of the floor and quietly watched Daddy.

When Daddy trudged upstairs, Kai couldn't see him, but he could hear the man rattling more things to test how sturdy they were.

The noises moved from Mia's room, to the bathroom, and finally, to Daddy's bedroom.

"Oh, for the love of..."

Daddy's footsteps clomped back onto the balcony, and he slumped over the rail. Staring down at Kai, he shook his head and hacked. "You little devil."

That was all the invitation Kai needed. He bolted up the stairs to Daddy and leapt up, licking his hand. This time, Daddy let him and ruffled the thick fur on Kai's neck.

"It looks like we've all got things to learn if we're going to live together, doesn't it, boy, huh?"

Kai licked him again. He didn't know what had caused all the upset, but thank heaven he was there to use his magic to lick away Daddy's problems and put everything right. It certainly was tough work being the voice of reason in such a crazy world.

While Daddy busied himself cleaning up the shriveled plants off his bedroom floor from Kai's accident, Kai toddled downstairs to lie on the floor in front of the back door. Part of his pack was home, which was reassuring, but the alpha was still out doing whatever alphas had to do — probably hunting for food and secretly peeing on things.

So, at the door, Kai waited. And waited. Until the faintest hint of Mia's scent drifted in through the gaps around the door. Lifting his head off his front paws, he pricked his ears, straining to hear her footsteps crunching on the gravel path. He heard them. As they grew closer, he leapt up and paced back and forth, wagging his tail frantically.

The silver metal thing jutting out halfway up the door twisted and the door swung open. Mia waltzed in.

He jumped up at his girl, lashing her with his tongue.

Hacking, Mia crouched down, so Kai planted his front paws on her shoulders and pushed forward to lick her face. Off-balance, Mia toppled onto the floor to lie on her back. Standing over her, Kai licked and licked and licked, while she rolled left and right, trying to avoid his magic tongue, but failing, and all the while hacking and hacking and hacking.

"Kai—" She fought to shield her face, but he nuzzled his way in to lick again and again.

"Kai, I-I—" Mia hacked. "Let me—" She twisted left, but he nuzzled and licked. She twisted right, but he broke through her defenses again. "I—" Hack, hack, hack. "Kai—"

Joy bubbled up from his stomach to envelop his whole body in a warm glow. This was such a marvelous game — Mia turning her head this way and that so he could lick almost every tiny little bit of her to show how he'd missed her. She should turn like this every day for a good licking.

When he was sure there was no part of her face he hadn't licked at least three times, Kai eased up. Mia grabbed the chance to clutch him and hug him tight, holding him so her head was alongside his and out of the licking zone.

"I missed you so much." She buried her face in his fur.

With the pack reunited, they enjoyed a meal together, after which he and Mia went for a walk in the wood. It was as if nothing had changed. Kai went to bed that night happy everything was back to normal and that he'd never be left alone again.

But then morning came. Daddy left. Then Mia left. And again, he was alone. Completely alone.

He searched the house, trying all the doors, checking all the windows, but this time, there was no escape.

With no other option, Kai lay staring at the door. Waiting.

Yet again, Mia came home late in the day. After the licking and hacking, they enjoyed a meal together, went for a walk together, then went to bed together.

The next day, the same thing happened. It was like a pattern.

The days stretched into weeks, and Kai realized if he waited what he thought was long enough, and then waited even longer, Mia always came back. They had a couple of days together at regular intervals, but she always left again, so most of his time he spent at home, waiting. He didn't like the waiting and being apart from each other, but he loved their daily reunion, when he'd leap and lick, and she'd do happy-teeth and hack. It almost made all the waiting worthwhile. Almost.

Chapter 23

As time passed, it grew colder outside and weird things started happening in their woods. On one early-morning walk, while shafts of sunlight beamed through the trees like heavenly searchlights, Kai wandered down the path ahead of Mia. He sniffed all his favorite spots to check for changes, but a strange smell clogged his nostrils. It had been blanketing the area for weeks, growing stronger and stronger. No matter where he sniffed, the smell was always there, yet, he couldn't work out what was causing it. A smell... like life was leaving.

Initially, he'd added it to his list of mysteries to be solved and gone about enjoying their walks as best he could with his impaired nasal fun, but things were going from bad to worse — it wasn't only the smells that were changing but the colors, too. Around the same time the smell had appeared, the leaves on the trees had developed yellow or brown tinges, with their weird new colors becoming more vivid every day.

He meandered along their usual path, the trees now almost unrecognizable — what few leaves remained drifting to the ground in a gentle shower of reds and browns and golds, while bare branches towered overhead like the gangly limbs of some malnourished beast.

Kai wandered over to one trunk, its bark a peeling skin of silver. He leaned closer and pushed the tip of his nose against the damp, cold bark to draw in the biggest, longest breath he could. Hmmm, that was interesting. Were all the trees like that?

He ambled over to the next one.

Behind him, Mia moseyed over to a big pile of leaves and kicked it. She hacked as the mass of red and brown exploded upward and cascaded back down like a slow-motion fountain.

Kai sniffed the second trunk, then strolled over to the next.

It was the same story with each one. They smelled as if they were stopping living. Like the very force of life that coursed through them was retreating to their core, draining away as if all the trees had decided they no longer wanted to live and breathe and grow. How odd.

Despite solving the mystery of what was producing the strange smell, it only created an even bigger one: why were they doing it? Why would something choose to stop living?

There could only be one reason: all the trees were broken.

Content he'd solved his latest mystery, Kai dawdled after Mia as she kicked another pile of leaves into the air.

Wait...

He froze midstride.

No, he hadn't solved a mystery but done quite the reverse. He'd uncovered the greatest mystery he'd ever encountered. If something broke and stopped living, what happened to it next? What came after life?

Kai trudged over to the gnarled tree that sometimes smelled of the dog-not-a-dog. Standing and staring up at it, he pondered this great new mystery of life. There was an answer. There had to be. There was an answer to everything if it was investigated properly and enough information gathered.

From every experience he'd had and every observation he'd ever made, he'd assumed the world was the way it was and always would be. Except it obviously wasn't: the world changed. The trees were the proof. And if it happened to the trees, maybe it happened to other things, which meant he had to be prepared. But prepared for what? What could possibly come after life?

He sniffed the gnarled tree, studied its bare branches, and watched one of its brown leaves lilting this way and that as it fluttered down toward him.

Maybe...

He sniffed the leaf as it danced past his snout.

Maybe...

In the deepest, darkest corner of his mind, the tiniest spark flickered as an idea struggled to be born. He frowned. Concentrated as hard as he could. Fought to mold the pieces of a fractured idea into a form he could grasp.

As slowly as a leaf falling, a concept crawled toward the light and the jigsaw mystery pieced itself together. Yes, he was onto something; he almost had the answer.

He closed his eyes and focused his full attention on fitting together all the pieces to reveal the answer to this great puzzle.

Kai gasped, his eyes popping wide open. Maybe the answer was—

A wet wad of leaves slapped into the side of his face.

Mia hacked. "Come on, goofball. This is called a walk because that's what we do — walk!"

He barked.

Mia hacked again and threw another handful of soggy leaves at him.

Again, he barked, then sprang toward her. She shrieked and ran away.

Kai gave chase, splashing through a puddle, muddy water splattering his belly — when he caught his girl, he'd shake that off on her as his revenge.

His tongue lolling out of his mouth, Kai bounded through the woods as Mia dodged around trees and shrubs. He could have easily run her down, but where would be the fun in that?

As she ran around a bush, instead of following her, he spun and darted around it in the opposite direction. Unfortunately, Mia was ready for him. She jumped out and hurled another fistful of soggy leaves at him. The wet brown mess burst in his face.

He shook the decaying debris off and barked, so Mia hacked and fled back the way she'd come. To surprise her, he ran back the way he'd come too to cut her off.

When she saw him tearing toward her, she squealed and kicked a pile of leaves into the air in front of him. As the leaves cascaded back to the ground, Kai leapt and snapped at them, tearing leaf after leaf from the air.

Mia kicked more leaves, over and over, so Kai spun around and around, snapping at anything that drifted close to him. He didn't catch many because they came so thick and so fast, but he couldn't remember a day he'd had more fun. It was one of the best times of his life.

On their way home, Kai thought there was some significant puzzle he was supposed to have solved, but he was sure there couldn't be a solution to any puzzle that could compare to the day he'd shared with Mia, so he didn't dwell on it. If he'd already forgotten it, whatever it was obviously couldn't have been that important.

From that day on, the days grew colder and the early-morning light grew sharper, until one morning, Mia opened the door and Kai froze at what he saw.

Outside had vanished.

His mouth agape, he stood in the doorway, gazing out at an alien landscape.

White stuff.

Everywhere.

White stuff covering the grass.

White stuff covering the trees.

White stuff covering the hills.

White stuff... everywhere!

It was the weirdest thing he'd ever seen, so of course, he had to investigate.

He bounded down the steps, which were the only things partially scraped clear, and leaped into the ocean of white. He stuck his snout into it. So cold! He flinched and whipped his face out of the white stuff, then shook his head to dislodge the clumps that had stuck up his nostrils and in his fur. Yes, this stuff was very odd.

And it smelled watery.

He frowned. Water was runny and clear, not powdery and white. It definitely wasn't water, so why did it smell like it?

Well, there was one way to check. He licked a big lump of white stuff covering one of his favorite bushes. The lump vanished, but as if things couldn't get even weirder, it didn't only vanish, but water appeared in its place.

Magic! The white stuff was magic!

A ball of white stuff slapped into the side of his head just like with the wad of soggy leaves weeks earlier, leaving Mia hacking and hacking. Again, he barked, and again she shrieked and took off running away.

She would not get away with the 'flinging-in-the-face' trick a second time.

Kai darted after her but immediately toppled face-first into the deep white stuff, his paws getting stuck. Mia hacked while he struggled up. Lifting his paws up higher to run, he bounced through the white stuff after her as she fled, kicking white powder up behind her.

Mia scooped up more white stuff and turned, raising her arm to hurl it. But Kai was already on her — he leapt, his front paws landing on her chest. She wailed as she toppled backward into the deep white with a crunch, Kai on top of her.

To claim his victory, Kai stood on her chest and licked and licked and licked.

Mia hacked and hacked, throwing her arms up to protect herself, but she couldn't hide from his tongue. Reaching over her head, she scooped up a great handful of white and flung it in his face. The stuff got in his nose, in his eyes, in his mouth. He stumbled back and shook his head, then sneezed, and sneezed again.

His nose finally clear, he barked, hunkering down ready to pounce and renew his assault. Mia was still lying on her back but was now repeatedly opening and closing her legs and moving her arms in an arc at her sides.

He frowned. Was she having some sort of mental breakdown?

"Look, Kai, it's a snow angel." Mia did happy-teeth.

He tilted his head to one side and studied her. Happy-teeth suggested everything was okay, so what was going on? Instead of diving on her, he dove into the white and rolled and rolled, clumps of the stuff plastering his body. Mia was right to do happy-teeth — this was fun. Fun, but oh so cold.

He clambered up, splayed his feet, and shook himself, white stuff flying everywhere, much of it showering Mia with her own personal little white stuff storm.

Mia squealed and shielded her face with her arms. When the air cleared, she clambered up too and gazed down at the imprint she'd made in the snow, then at the one he'd made.

"We need to sign them."

Crouching down, she ran her hand through the white stuff and scratched a few marks, then looked to Kai. "Your turn."

He looked back at her, then at her mark, then at her again. Was she expecting him to do something?

"Let me help." Mia took his right front paw and placed it in the white stuff next to her mark. When she removed it, a paw print was left behind.

"Perfect," said Mia, standing up and gazing down with her hands on her hips. "Now, I don't know about you, but I'm dying for some hot chocolate. Shall we go get warm, huh, boy?"

Mia led them back to the house, Kai bouncing through the white stuff and thinking what a magical time they'd had. Unfortunately, it seemed not everyone appreciated the magic of white stuff.

As they tramped along the veranda to the back door, exhausted from all their fun, Kai heard the lanky, gray-haired man who lived with Mrs. Paget next door. The man's voice was not a happy one and came through gasped breaths as he heaved another shovel of white stuff onto a big pile he'd created nearby, a narrow path, clear of white, snaking to his house behind him. Panting, the man jammed his shovel into the white and leaned against it, then wiped the moisture off his bright red face with his sleeve.

Kai couldn't understand why the man was suffering such backbreaking work by shoveling the white stuff instead of licking it until it disappeared. Typical people-crazy — struggling to make the world the way they thought it should be instead of reveling in the way it was.

That evening, Kai lay on the living room floor while Mia and Daddy lounged on the sofa, watching the rectangular black board in the corner of the room. Like a huge version of Mia's magic-board, it showed moving pictures and made all manner of sounds that regularly fascinated Mia and Daddy for hours. Kai couldn't understand why because none of the people or animals ever had any smell, so it was obviously all fake. It was clever, yes — like those fake-people who never moved, yet managed to change their clothes — but trickery nonetheless.

Of course, there was the odd exception. Like the classic "dog catches a ball," "dog eats food," or the moving picture that defined the genre: "dog barks at a noise." Oh, yeah, he never tired of watching that one. So much suspense and action. Incredibly, these masterpieces were rarely shown, and even when they were, they never lasted more than a few seconds. The people who made all the moving pictures obviously had little concept of what constituted true art.

With her feet up on the sofa, her back leaning against Daddy, Mia said, "When I get my guitar for Christmas—"

"Don't you mean 'if'?" he said.

"If what?"

"*If* you get a guitar for Christmas."

She twisted around, frowning. "Why 'if'?"

"You didn't hear the news?"

Mia shook her head.

Daddy said, "Santa can't give away musical instruments anymore. It seems the elves signed a petition because the reindeer wouldn't stop blowing trumpets."

"Oh, ha-ha." Mia rolled her eyes. "Santa, Daddy? Santa? How old do you think I am?"

"Old enough that you should know without having to ask me." He pushed to get up off the sofa. "But we can check your birth certificate, if you like."

"Stop changing the subject."

"You asked a perfectly reasonable question, so I'm just trying to give you a perfectly reasonable answer."

Mia frowned. "Don't you want me to have a guitar?"

"Of course I want you to have a guitar. Much more than I want you to have bagpipes, but not quite as much as I want you to have spiritual enlightenment."

"What's spiritual enlightenment?"

"Quiet. Wonderful quiet."

She shuffled away from him and folded her arms. "You don't think I'll be any good on guitar, do you?"

He pulled her closer. "Sweetheart, if you want to be, I think you'll be an absolute rock star."

Mia grinned and settled back down beside him. "Did you hear, Kai? I'm going to be a rock star."

She twisted back to look at Daddy again. "Can Kai be my groupie?"

"Do you know what a groupie is?"

"Someone who handles the band's equipment."

"Kind of." Daddy grimaced. "But I think you mean a roadie."

"So, what's a groupie?"

"Someone who handles the band's equipment in a very special way."

"Kai's special."

"Yes, but unless you want to perform solely to your fellow inmates in a psychiatric prison, it might be best *not* to make him *that* special."

Kai looked at Mia and Daddy. He couldn't help wonder why they were so different from all the other people he'd encountered. They had the basic people shape and people smell — not to mention their fair share of people-crazy — yet they were so different. It was like they weren't people at all but were almost — *almost* — animals. He'd thought briefly about this before, but as time went on, it was proving more and more obvious: Mia and Daddy didn't fight against the world to bend it to their will but embraced the wildness of it all. They were animals. Or as close as people came to being animals.

How was that possible? How could one thing be another thing, yet still stay the first thing? How could a thing change, but not change?

Well, puppies changed into adult dogs and children changed into adult people. Those were both change and not-change.

Maybe he was onto something.

Was that where all the changing stopped, or did adult dogs and adult people go on changing, and if so, what did they become?

Dogs were pretty much perfect as they were, so Kai couldn't imagine why they would change any further. The evidence was irrefutable: they could smell better than people, see better, hear better, run better, jump better, and of course, pee better. The list was endless; dogs simply did everything that mattered better. It still confounded him that people were in charge of the world. How the devil that had happened, he had no idea.

So, dogs couldn't really be improved upon, but people?

He glanced at Mia. The highest compliment he could pay her was that she was the closest a person could get to being a dog without actually being one.

Daddy? A little behind Mia, yet still on the way to being a fine example of a canine.

However, everybody else had plenty of scope for improvement, but if things could change, how far could such changes go?

Could it be that the best people, those who loved the world the way it was, not the way it "should" be, continued changing? But into what? Well, if Mia was almost a dog, then maybe that was the answer, and the sequence went children into adults, then into puppies, and finally, into dogs. If that was the case, what a wonderful world it was going to be one day when every person had changed and the world was full of dogs!

Kai gasped. So, had he once been a person? A shiver ran down his spine at the horrendous proposition of having a useless people nose that couldn't even smell poop when a pile was right in front of him. What a dismal world that would have been. Still, he wasn't surprised. That stubby little thing they had in the middle of their faces didn't look like a proper snout, so it was no surprise it didn't function like one either.

He gazed at Mia and Daddy, his chest aching for them. The poor noseless creatures.

Chapter 24

Shortly after the white stuff arrived, for no logical reason, Daddy put a tree in the house. An outside tree *inside*! If that wasn't crazy enough right there in the living room, Mia hung colored balls on its branches and draped flickering lights around it, then stood back and gazed at it as if it was the most beautiful thing she'd ever seen. It was obviously far more special than all the other trees outside and, as such, needed protecting, so to claim it as theirs so no one would steal it, Kai peed on it.

It was a while before he saw happy-teeth that day.

Colored packages appeared under the tree a few days later. The next morning, Mia was possibly the most excited he'd ever seen her. She flew downstairs in her pajamas, shouting to him over her shoulder.

"It's Christmas! It's Christmas! Run, Kai. It's Christmas!"

Holding on to the end of the banister, Mia flung herself around into the living room and raced past the blue sofa. Kai stumbled behind her, wondering why he wasn't still warm and cozy in his fluffy-bowl. No light filtered through the drapes. These days it was often gloomy first thing, but not dark. Was it morning yet?

At the foot of the tree, she sat on the floor and grabbed a shoebox-shaped package swathed in silver paper. She shook it next to her ear.

He sat beside Mia as Daddy clomped down the stairs in his pajamas, his mouth gaping, arms stretching up into the air.

Mia did the biggest happy-teeth Kai had ever seen as she lifted a flat limp package wrapped in white-and-gold striped paper, her eyes sparkling. She squished it with her fingertips, her brow knitted. "What do you think it is, Kai?"

"Uh-uh," said Daddy, "you know the rules: no touching."

"But it's for me."

Daddy shuffled toward the kitchen. "And it will still be for you if you wait until after breakfast." He looked at the metal band with a disk on the front strapped to his wrist. His mouth dropped open and he rubbed his brow. "Oh, boy." Yawning again, he trudged back toward the stairs. "Or maybe at least wait until after sunup."

"Aww, but it's Christmas."

"It is. All day," said Daddy. "See you in the morning."

Mia slumped, face angled down, big eyes gazing at him.

Nothing interesting seemed to be happening, so Kai padded over to his silver bowls. If he was up, it was obviously breakfast time.

Arching an eyebrow at Mia, Daddy heaved a breath, then slouched over and collapsed in a heap beside her. He selected a book-shaped red package from under the tree and offered it.

She did happy-teeth again. "I can open it?" She reached toward it.

Daddy pulled it a few inches back toward him. "Unless you'd rather wait for a civilized hour, like, oh, I don't know, six o'clock."

Her happy-teeth was so wide, her eyes scrunched up. Mia grabbed the package and, like a rabid beast, savaged the wrapping, shredding the paper and tossing it into the air over her shoulders.

Kai nudged his empty bowl with his snout, making it clatter against a cupboard door. No one noticed.

Mia gasped. "*Animals of the World* DVDs." She turned to him, cradling the unwrapped package to her chest. "How did you know?"

"I have my secret sources." He handed her the silver package she'd picked up first.

She pointed to a lumpy blue one. "That's a special one."

"For me?"

She shrugged, squeezing her lips together to stifle happy-teeth.

While Mia ripped away the paper from her package, Daddy tore open his to reveal something blue inside made of wool. Mia watched

148

him out of the corner of her eye. He did happy-teeth, so she did too.

He leaned over and kissed her on the forehead. "It's lovely, sweetheart. Thank you."

"Mrs. Paget helped me choose it. But it was my idea."

"And an excellent idea it was. Couldn't have been better." He pulled on a blue sweater over his pajamas. "What do you think?"

She hacked. "You can't wear it with pajamas."

"I can. I'll start a new craze. By March, it'll be the height of fashion, just in time for the red carpet at the Oscars, you'll see."

She pushed him on the shoulder playfully, then tore the last paper off her gift. "My hiking boots!" Again, she pushed him. "You said they were too expensive."

"They were. You have to promise never to wear them if the police are around."

She took one shoe out of the box and pulled her right leg up so her knee was under her chin, then slipped the shoe on her bare foot. "I've got new shoes for our walks, Kai." She twisted to where Kai had been sitting, then scanned the room and spotted him in the kitchen.

"Kai!" Mia beckoned him. "Come on, Kai. We haven't forgotten about you!"

With a final glance at his still-empty bowl, he toddled over.

Mia slid a huge cube swathed in shiny gold paper across the floor to him. "Merry Christmas, Kai."

He looked at the cube, then at Mia.

"Do you want me to help?"

With her fingernail, she teased up one edge of the gold paper, tore a strip away, and threw it on the floor.

He still stared at her.

"Look." She teased up another chunk of the paper. "You can open it. Just stick your nose in."

The cube obviously meant something to her, but what? He sniffed it, hoping to discover what was so fascinating.

The moment he put his nose near it, Mia said, "That's it. Just take it in your teeth." In an exaggerated fashion, she chomped with her teeth.

Hoping for some sort of direction, he gazed at her.

She lifted another bit of the paper. "Here. Bite it."

It was right in front of his mouth, and he was tired of this game, so he bit it and ripped it away.

"Good boy."

Mia clapped, so he ripped away another piece, tossed his head back, and threw into the air.

Mia patted him on the back. "Good boy, Kai."

He tore off another strip and tossed it in the air too, then another, and another. Mia and Daddy were right — it was fun.

He shredded enough of the paper to reveal a brown box underneath the gold. Mia opened the flaps for him and pulled out a fake, fluffy creature with floppy arms and legs.

Mia said, "It's a little friend to play with so you never feel alone." She squeezed its middle and it squeaked.

Kai looked at it, then at the empty discarded box.

It was wonderful. Everything he could have wished for.

He stuck his head in the box, poked his snout into each corner, and sniffed. Yes, it was possibly the greatest thing anyone had ever given him. Barring strips of heaven.

He tried to lift his head out, but the flaps stuck in the thick fur on his neck and the box lifted up with him.

Unable to see, he shook his head, but the box held firm.

He pawed it, yet his claws slipped off the cardboard.

Instead of helping, Daddy and Mia hacked and hacked.

He walked backward, but that didn't help, so he shook his head again. The box was glued to him.

Finally, Mia pulled it off him. Kai clamped his teeth around one of the flaps that had grabbed him and jerked his head from side to side, then flung the box. It hurtled through the air and crashed near the staircase. He ran over, snatched it up again, and once more savaged it.

"Kai, *this* is your present," called Mia. She waved the fake-fluffy-thing at him.

He ignored her. He was having way too much fun with his box to bother with something as silly as that. He hurled the box again, then chased after it across the room before grabbing it and once more tossing it into the air. Every time he threw it, he set off racing after it before it had crashed to the floor.

While Kai played, Mia and Daddy destroyed so many colored packages that when Kai threw his box and it landed next to them, they were surrounded by a rainbow of ripped-up paper. Mia was sitting cross-legged on the floor, wearing both new shoes and a pink wool cap and matching scarf, while studying a large book with pictures of animals inside.

Kneeling beside her, Daddy said, "Well, that's it for another year." He started picking up all the scraps of paper.

"Thank you, Daddy," said Mia. "They're the most wonderful presents ever."

"Really?"

"Of course. I love them all."

Stretching, he reached over the back of the sofa. "So you won't want this one, then."

"What?"

Daddy lifted out a strange object wrapped in gold — a long "arm" jutted out from a flat, curved body.

Mia gasped and clutched her mouth.

"I can take it back to the store," said Daddy. "It's not a problem."

Her mouth agape, eyes wide, Mia reached for it without a word.

Doing happy-teeth, Daddy handed it to her. "Merry Christmas, sweetheart."

Instead of frenziedly tearing at the paper, Mia eased up one edge and peeked inside. She gasped again.

"It is," she said, peering at Daddy. "It's a guitar."

"Did you think I'd forgotten?"

"I... I..." Pools of water formed in the bottoms of her eyes. "I didn't think I'd ever get one."

He slung his arms around her and hugged her, stroking a hand over her flowing black locks. "I wanted it to be a surprise." He kissed her on the head and pulled away.

"Thank you, Daddy. Thank you a million times."

He winked at her and resumed picking up the paper.

"Look, Kai. A guitar. I've got a guitar."

Peeling back the gold paper, she revealed a piece of hollow wood that had a narrow plank sticking out at one side, along which were stretched six metal wires.

Mia gazed at it wide-eyed. She caressed the wires, then ran her hand over the polished wood, fingertips barely touching it. Finally, she picked it up. Holding it against her chest, she pressed the fingertips of her left hand onto the long plank part to hold the wires down and scratched across them. The most horrendous collection of noises screeched through the house, as if each sound was fighting with all the others — and all of them were losing.

She looked at Daddy with a sparkle in her eyes as if proud she'd made the hollow-wood-machine scream in pain. Daddy did happy-teeth, though Kai could tell it wasn't genuine. Strangely, it was like Mia didn't see that. She scratched the metal wires again, and again the sounds battled. Time and again the jarring jangling filled the house.

Repositioning her left fingers, she scratched again but did something wrong and a harmonious sound drifted through the air, as beautiful as their green-sky-light dancing over the lake.

She stared at Daddy, open-mouthed, eyes wide.

This time, Daddy did genuine happy-teeth, but that quickly vanished when Mia moved her left hand and the screeching returned.

Mia spent the day torturing her hollow-wood-machine. Occasionally, she made a mistake and the machine sang, but most times, she preferred to do the other sound, the one that made Kai's teeth itch.

While Mia was busy, Kai played with his box. Hour after hour. By bedtime, it wasn't very box-shaped anymore and had big chunks missing, but he carried it upstairs to his fluffy-bowl nonetheless and curled around it to keep it safe.

It had been a wonderful day. He drifted off to sleep dreaming of a future filled with such times.

Chapter 25

The white outside lasted for weeks, then magically disappeared and everything warmed up again. To Kai's amazement, the trees fixed themselves and burst back to life. As if that wasn't astonishing enough, the weather got hotter and hotter, and when it got really hot, Mia abandoned "School. Urgh" and they spent what felt like forever playing in the wood all day every day.

Just when he thought life couldn't get any better, Mia started doing "School. Urgh" yet again and he was back to endless hours of waiting and waiting at the door. To make things worse, the days once more grew colder and colder, and for a second time, all the trees developed brown-leaf and broke.

Kai wondered if the white stuff would come again. He didn't have to wait long for the answer. Shortly after, he got another box. This one was even better than the first because it was circular, so when he took it to his fluffy-bowl, it was much easier to curl around. Boy, he loved Box Day.

For the next week, his box went everywhere with him, even on one of their walks where the white stuff made it soggy. Unfortunately, it quickly became apparent that his box didn't like the wet because bits of it started falling off and soon, there was little left except the bottom and a small piece of the side. Then even that disappeared. Kai hunted everywhere, but even his nose couldn't solve that mystery, so he suspected foul play, maybe a box thief. He didn't know where his box had gone, but he hoped it was somewhere it would be happy. Somewhere dry.

As the weeks went by, the white stuff disappeared and as if by magic, all the trees fought off brown-leaf and erupted with fresh greenery, just like before.

The world had gone crazy. Crazy!

Or had it?

There did seem to be some sort of pattern to the craziness, even if there was no logic as to why it was happening. Although, since people were in charge, it wasn't surprising everything was always messed up. But surely if people made it happen, presumably because they enjoyed a change, it would have been much nicer if it was all random and each morning was a wonderful surprise. Or better yet, have it all on the same day — the leaves falling off in the morning, everything white by lunchtime, midafternoon would be scorching hot, and the trees would be green again by bedtime. Boy, what a day that would be. And of course, if there was white stuff every day, logic dictated he'd also get a new box. Every day! Wow! He wagged his tail at the thought of that.

The hot-cold-green-leaf-brown-leaf pattern outside continued, but it wasn't the only thing changing. There were some very odd, utterly mystifying changes inside too — even to a dog who was a genius at solving mysteries.

Chapter 26

One morning Kai lay in his fluffy-bowl, half-watching Mia getting up. The sun shone through the window and birds sang in the nearby tree, which was recovering from brown-leaf, since tiny green buds erupted from the ends of its branches. Everything suggested it was going to be another beautiful day. A perfectly *ordinary*, beautiful day.

Dreaming about his breakfast, Kai wasn't really paying attention to Mia flitting about naked. He'd witnessed the scene so often, he rarely took much notice anymore. However, when he glanced over, his eyes popped wide open.

What the devil was that?

He squinted, focusing on the area in question.

Was that...? It was! It really was.

He scrambled to sit up for a better angle.

Yes, Mia appeared to have a light covering of fur developing near her pee-machine.

Was this the moment he'd been dreaming of for so long – the moment Mia finally changed into the dog she truly was?

Kai toddled over and stood before her, his head cocked to one side, as she busied herself with a selection of clothes laid on her bed.

Yes, it was definitely fur. It seemed an odd place for it to start growing, yet he was sure once it spread to give an all-over silky black coat, it would look wonderful. Assuming he was correct and it was fur and not a small creature that had crawled onto her in the night. He couldn't smell an animal in the room, but some of the critters in the wood sure were sneaky — he often smelled the dog-not-a-dog, yet he seldom saw it.

With her back to him to put on her panties, Mia bent over, as if presenting herself for inspection. Being the good dog Kai was, it would have been rude for him to decline, so he thrust his snout up between her thighs to sniff out what was going on.

Instead of being happy that he was looking out for her, Mia shrieked and jerked upright like his nose was on fire. Standing on only one leg, and with her panties caught on her other foot, she toppled forward and crashed onto her bed.

Well, that wasn't the reaction he'd expected.

Mia spun around to him. "What the heck, Kai? Bad dog!"

She swung her arm out to the side, stabbing a finger at his fluffy-bowl. "In your bed. Now. Bad dog. Bad dog!"

He stared at her, widening his big brown eyes. Why was she using her unhappy voice? It was as if he'd done something wrong, yet that made no sense. If she sniffed his butt, he'd be delighted. It was unlike Mia to take a compliment so badly.

"Bed!"

His head hanging and tail down, Kai trudged toward his fluffy-bowl. Halfway across the room, he turned back, hoping she'd relented.

She glowered at him. "Bed."

He slunk to his fluffy-bowl and curled into a ball as small as he could manage.

Mia's bedroom door opened, and Daddy poked his head in. "Everything okay?"

Mia squawked again, grabbing her comforter and whipping it over herself. "Get out!"

Daddy covered his eyes with his hand. "Sorry, sorry!" He ducked out.

Mia glared at Kai and shook her head. "Bad dog."

Kai whimpered. She'd attacked him and then Daddy, completely unprovoked. *Someone* had woken up in a bad mood.

156

For the first time in his life with Mia, a full day passed and he didn't see happy-teeth once.

The next morning, he didn't approach her while she was dressing. However, he did scrutinize her as closely as he could from the safety of his fluffy-bowl. It was definitely fur growing down there. Not very long and not very thick, but fur nonetheless.

As she was bending to put on her panties, Mia turned and looked straight at him, as if she didn't trust him.

Kai shut his eyes. He waited a few seconds, then peeked from just one. She was still staring, so he shut it again. When he next dared to peek, her panties were up, putting an end to that day's investigation.

Over the next few months, Kai monitored the developing situation as closely as he could from the confines of his fluffy-bowl. Unfortunately, no matter how hard he willed it to be different, his initial joy at Mia changing into the dog she was deep down gradually dissipated because the fur didn't spread or grow any denser. Instead, it remained a pathetic little patch that was too small and nowhere near thick enough to offer any layer of protection or insulation. Utterly pointless.

He sighed. Maybe it hadn't developed further because her outburst had stalled her change. After all, if a dog didn't find joy in sniffing a butt and having its butt sniffed, it really wasn't a dog. Mia had sabotaged herself!

Still, he'd waited this long for her to change, so he could wait longer. Waiting was one of his superpowers.

However, the patch of fur wasn't the only change.

Despite the fact she didn't seem to be eating more than usual, Mia was getting fatter — considerably fatter. However, it was in the strangest of places. Two mounds of fat were developing on her chest, one on either side, and every day she strapped them up.

With his propensity for solving mysteries, Kai had pondered on these fat mounds and why Mia imprisoned them every day. He'd narrowed it down to two scenarios: the mounds were either at risk of dropping off or so delicate, they'd bruise if prodded. In either scenario, no way would a bit of flimsy lace solve the problem. On numerous occasions, he'd nudged his two silver bowls toward her as a means to secure the mounds in place and protect them, but Mia hadn't seemed to get it, so he'd given up on trying to help.

But that wasn't the end of the changes. Mia's scent was changing. She was growing into one of the adult kinds of people, and they always had a harsher scent than the young. Mixed in with that was something else too, something he couldn't put his paw on. Something small. Tiny. Almost hidden under all the major elements of her smell. Something... not quite right. Like a piece of heaven that had been left out of the cold-making-machine overnight: still good enough to eat, but not if it was left much longer. It was probably meaningless, yet he wished he knew what it was because he hated unsolved mysteries.

Her scent also developed a pattern like the trees and temperature. It changed every few weeks, and for a few days Kai didn't see happy-teeth as often. She and Daddy often talked louder during these periods too — much louder, and for much less time than normal. These conversations usually ended with Daddy banging around downstairs and Mia slamming her bedroom door and banging around upstairs. Kai didn't like all the banging, but he liked the hugs and happy-teeth that invariably came later.

Compared to Mia, Daddy had only changed a tiny, tiny bit. He'd changed from Daddy to Dad, but Kai struggled to tell the difference because he looked and smelled the same, except that the little patch of fur he had over his top lip had spread downward to cover his chin too. After the fur disaster with Mia, Kai was not holding his breath hoping the fur was going to spread anytime soon.

Even the house was different. One day Kai had woken up in a pink bedroom, gone for a long walk with Mia, and at bedtime found the room a pale cream. Mia had even replaced the pictures of the fat-long-nose-creature and all his friends with pictures of young men with their mouths open, wider than if they were talking but not so wide it looked like they were shouting, each holding a metal cylinder in front of their face. Those changes were mildly interesting, but some were utterly stupefying: his beloved fluffy-bowl had changed too, somehow shrinking. It used to be so big he could roll around

158

inside it, but nowadays, he had to squeeze into a tight ball or lie over it, flattening its spongy sides.

Crazier and crazier. Heaven only knew what other insane changes might have come about if he hadn't been there to be the voice of reason.

Kai didn't like all these changes. They weren't normal. Things had been the way they were supposed to be and that was how they were supposed to continue. He was sure that nothing good ever came from change. Not least because his theory of good people changing into animals didn't seem to be working out as logic dictated it should. No, changes were bad. He was going to make sure nothing else changed. Ever. They had a perfect life together and that was how it was going to continue.

Chapter 27

The sun beamed down on their special place as Kai and Mia lay on the grass, she resting her head on his side, her hollow-wood-machine lying across her stomach.

Neither of them made so much as a sound for a long time as they basked in the warmth of sharing the day with each other.

Kai often thought the sign of true friendship was the capacity to be with someone without having to do or say anything, yet still feel completely at ease. Most people filled the world with needless noise that never actually said anything worthwhile, but only served to soothe their own discomfort. Kai enjoyed the quiet times. The deafening silence spoke volumes.

Without shifting her position, Mia fractured the quiet. "I'm thinking of joining a band."

She scratched on the metal wires of her hollow-wood-machine. Over the years, she'd scratched it so often she'd worn away most of the original sounds, so the only ones left were the harmonious ones she only ever used to find by accident. Kai was pleased his teeth no longer itched, but sad she'd lost her unique gift for making wood and metal scream in pain.

"What do you think?"

Another harmonious scratch. She just couldn't find that old sound.

"Johnny Sanger plays drums in a band and they play gigs and

everything. I mean, it's only kids' birthday parties and school dances and stuff like that, but, man, that's just so cool."

She craned her neck around so she could look at him.

"So? What do you think? Can you see me as a rock god?" She did happy-teeth. "We could play that little ballad you like."

Settling back, Mia scratched her wires and did the talking-not-talking thing at the same time.

"You once lived in a moldy box,
With no one to take you out for walks."

Kai lifted his head and pricked his ears. Gazing at his girl, he wagged his tail.

"But now I'll be your true best friend,
And love you till time meets its end.
Then as the stars fall from the sky,
I'll sing to you this lullaby.
Sweet Kai, little Kai, me and you,
Little Kai, sweet Kai, one not two.
Sweet Kai, little Kai, me and you,
Little Kai, sweet Kai, one not two."

As he lay in the sun, a warm glow welled up from within Kai to fill his body with joy. He was with Mia, in their special place, listening to the special sound she created just for him. He couldn't imagine any moment could possibly be better than this one.

When he was with Mia, the world was in perfect harmony, with everything in its place, just where it was supposed to be. When she was missing, it was like a part of him was missing too. Yes, that was it; she was a part of him. He could feel it — not in his stomach like hunger, nor in his head like a thought. It wasn't even in his heart like a feeling. No, it was all of that and none of that — it was simply the thing that made him *him*. A spark. A light. A thing he couldn't see, touch, or hear, and unbelievably couldn't even smell, though he tried and tried and tried. It was as if it didn't exist, but he knew beyond question it did. It was real, and it was joined to Mia. Forever. A bond that could never be broken.

He gazed at the girl. *His* girl. Did she have this nonexistent-existent thing inside her too? Could she feel their bond?

She laid her hollow-wood-machine down, then rolled over onto her stomach and hugged him.

He basked in the warmth of her embrace. They lay together, entwined, silent, breathing in unison. Oh, yes, she had that thing, too.

Kai closed his eyes. This was his life now. Perfect. Forever.

He dozed for a while, then woke when Mia stretched.

Mia checked her magic-board. It used to have a picture of a kitten on it, but these days it regularly changed to anything from a picture of a very handsome dog to a man with his mouth open, to Mia with people he didn't know — though one looked like an older version of the boy who'd petted him in the bus years ago.

"Oh, look at the time. We should be making tracks."

Clambering to her feet, Mia picked up the hollow-wood-machine and slung the strap across her chest so it hung down her back.

They set off up the mountain to watch the green-sky-light dancing over the lake.

They'd been there so many times Kai knew the way, so he'd run ahead, have a good sniff around, and then run back to her, before running off again. He never strayed too far, though occasionally, Mia obviously thought he had because she called him back. The pack was nothing without its alpha, so whenever she called, he always dashed back as quickly as he could.

Kai left Mia clambering over a rocky outcropping and scooted up a grass slope, nose to the ground, investigating the scents. A hint of something he recognized grabbed his attention. He scrambled over rocks and around a small bush, then his nose led him over the brow of a small incline. There, he smelled the spot where someone had been rummaging around looking for food within the last couple days — the dog-not-a-dog. It was good to know their old friend was still enjoying mountain life. Good to know that some things never changed.

"Kai!"

He pricked his ears.

162

"Kai!" Mia shrieked.

The fur on his neck stood on end. It was Mia, but like he'd never heard her before. His pulse raced, the tone of her voice making him quake inside.

He bolted back the way he'd come.

Rounding the bush, he pulled up. Where was she? He hadn't gotten so far ahead so she should have caught up to him already, yet he couldn't see her. He sniffed, but he couldn't smell her either because the wind was blowing scents in the wrong direction. He raced farther down the mountainside.

Skidding over the rocks, he dashed ahead, scanning the area for any sign of her. He leapt to the grassy slope and careered down toward the last place he'd seen her.

Clambering over the rocky outcropping, a flash of color caught his eye. He whipped his head around.

Slumped against a boulder, Mia clutched her stomach, legs splayed out on the ground.

Kai shot over.

"I don't feel so good." Her voice was strained, not bright like it usually was.

He nuzzled her with a whimper.

"I don't think I can make it today." Still clutching her gut with one arm, she lifted the other and ruffled his fur. "Sorry, boy."

Beads of moisture dotted her face, and her breath came in sharp pants.

He didn't like change, and this was one of the worst he'd seen, so he did the only thing he could do to help the situation — he licked her.

Instead of happy-teeth, Mia grimaced, her face scrunching up with more lines than even Dad's did.

"We better head back, Kai. I really don't feel good."

Holding on to the boulder, Mia heaved herself to her feet with a groan. She grabbed her hollow-wood-machine from the grass with her free hand, her other remaining pressed to her stomach, and then they began their descent. Instead of running on ahead, Kai stayed by her side, constantly looking up to check how she was doing as she

163

lurched back down the mountainside.

When they reached their special place, Mia's face was bright red and droplets of moisture dripped off it. She slumped to sit on the grass, panting for breath. Kai sat and pressed as close as he could against her. He whimpered.

Her voice raspy with the effort of talking, she said, "It's okay, boy. Not far now." She patted his shoulder.

She clambered to her feet with a groan and they set off again.

It took them twice as long to get back to the house as it usually did and when they finally opened the door, Dad's jaw dropped and he dashed over.

"What's wrong, sweetheart?" He slung his arm around Mia's back and guided her toward the sofa.

"I don't know. I thought it was something I'd eaten, but..." Her face screwed up and she clutched her stomach with both hands.

"So it's your stomach?"

Mia collapsed onto the sofa. She blew out a huge breath at the relief of getting off her feet, and her whole body slumped.

"I don't know," she said, her head back, eyes closed. "Kind of. That's how it started."

Dad dashed to the kitchen and brought back a glass of water and some tiny white pebbles that she swallowed.

Kai sat before her. Watching. Worrying. Whimpering.

Dad stroked Kai's shoulders. "It's okay, boy. She'll be fine."

Kai scrutinized her, resting his chin on her thigh. He wondered why Dad didn't rush her to sit on the metal table for the man in the green uniform to jab a sharp thing in the back of her neck — it had worked for him and taken the hurt away. But maybe the white pebbles were Dad's magic. Kai hoped so. If anything happened to his alpha, he didn't know what he'd do.

Chapter 28

One afternoon, Kai was lying in his usual spot at the front door waiting for Mia and Dad to return. Whenever they went out together, they used this door, not the back one to the woods, so he knew this would be where he'd be reunited with them. They'd left after breakfast, so they were later than usual. Kai whined. It wasn't good they were so late. Unless it was because they'd found someone able to help Mia.

Even though Dad used his magic on her every day, it hadn't worked. She still did happy-teeth and hacked, but not as regularly as she used to, and when they went walking, she shuffled instead of scampered, often lurching back to collapse on the sofa.

Sure enough, after a lengthy wait, he smelled both Mia and Dad walking toward the house. But there was another smell too. He shuddered. It was the kind of scent he'd smelled so very long ago in the alley when monstrous Hound had threatened to rip them both apart: fear. Except this time, it wasn't coming from Mia. No, for the first time ever, Dad was afraid.

Even though Kai's stomach quaked, he jumped to his feet and wagged his tail as his pack got closer and closer to the house. He walked around in a circle and then once more stared at the door, but he couldn't settle, so he circled again and looked back to the door. It was always the same — once he knew Mia was coming, she could never come quickly enough.

When they finally came in, Dad's eyes were red and puffy. Before Mia had a chance to bend down to Kai, Dad wrapped his arms around her and squeezed her. She hugged him too, patting him on the back.

Kai jumped up, resting his front paws on them, and licked Mia's arm.

She dropped one hand to Kai's shoulder and massaged it.

She still smelled like Mia, but there was something different. Kai had believed her scent was changing, that it was somehow mingling with something else lurking inside her. Something hidden. At first, it had been almost imperceptible, and for the first time in his life, he'd seriously doubted his nose, thinking he was imagining it. Except his nose was never wrong, and now that hidden thing was stronger, bigger, bolder, as if it was tired of being where it was and wanted to spread and get out. It reminded him of a smell from the streets — like a hot dog lying in the gutter, too old to be fresh, but not quite old enough to be rotten. That "in-between" smell.

Mia kissed Dad on the cheek. "It's going to be okay. It might not seem like it now, but it's going to be. Trust me."

Dad's voice wavered. "I-I hope you're right, sweetheart. I don't know what I'd do if..." He squeezed her tighter.

They hugged a moment longer, then separated.

Dad headed for the kitchen. "Well, I don't know about anyone else, but my stomach thinks the cook's been shot."

Mia bent down to Kai and dug her fingers deep into his thick fur. "We'd love some bacon and eggs, wouldn't we, boy, huh?"

Daddy turned back. "We?"

"He's been neglected all day. He deserves a treat." Mia stood and ambled toward Dad. "I'll give you a hand."

"No, you won't." He pointed to the sofa. "You'll do nothing but sit there and take it easy."

"Dad, I'm not an invalid." She picked up Kai's silver bowls and pulled the bag of meaty pebbles along the countertop.

"You know, I remember a time when it was always *Daddy*, and you always did what *Daddy* said." He took a plastic pack of strips of heaven from the cold-making-machine.

166

"I could call you *my old man*, if you'd prefer."

He arched an eyebrow at her as he laid out strips of heaven ready to put in the hot-making-machine.

Mia stroked her chin. "Or *Pops*. Or *Pappy*."

She hacked, leaving Kai's filled bowls on the counter so he could eat with the pack as usual. However, when she did happy-teeth and turned to Dad, he'd frozen. He stared at the strips of heaven on the counter, his hand hovering over them. It trembled.

"Hey," said Mia.

Dad gulped and looked the opposite way.

She touched his arm. "Hey."

When he turned to her, his face was contorted and salty-water streamed down his cheeks.

Mia held her arms open, and he fell into them, burying his head in her shoulder, his own shuddering. His breath came in horrible judders — like hacking, but in reverse. It was the most mournful sound Kai had ever heard.

Cradling Dad, Mia said, "It's going to be okay, I promise. I can feel it."

Kai didn't know what to do. The sounds of heartache, the scents of fear, the knowledge that something was lurking to tear their pack apart... the situation seemed hopeless. And yet, they had their strength, their love, their bond. He stared. They were a strong pack and Mia was an incredible alpha. It would be okay, he just knew it.

Sniffling, but breathing easier, Dad broke away from Mia, dragging the back of his right hand across his eyes. "I'm sorry. Sometimes it gets..."

"I know." She made a face like happy-teeth but without the teeth. "But there's a bigger problem."

Dad slumped. "Oh, good grief, no. What haven't you told me?"

"Not me." She nodded at Kai staring up at them. "Someone knows the bacon is out of the refrigerator."

Daddy hacked. It was a tiny one, but still a hack.

Yes, everything was going to be fine. Kai would bet on it.

Mia did proper happy-teeth. "Oh, I know" — she pointed at Dad — "*he who must be obeyed.*"

"Now that one, I like." Dad did a kind of happy-teeth that looked almost real, but water still pooled in his eyes.

"Hey, it really is going to be okay." She rubbed his arm. "I can feel it."

Dad went to return the heaven to the cold-making-machine, yet Mia held her arm out in front of him.

"I think we need more than that, don't we?" she said.

Dad shot her a sideways glance, then did the same to Kai.

"Do you know the price of bacon?" said Dad, turning back to the hot-making-machine.

"Well, it's not like you can take it with you."

Dad arched an eyebrow at her. "Seriously?"

"Too soon?"

Daddy looked at the tiny machine strapped to his wrist. "It's been one hour and... sixteen minutes."

Mia nodded. "Too soon."

She meandered over to the sofa. Kicking off her shoes, she sighed, then fell back onto the seat and swung her legs up to lounge along it.

"I could get used to this," she said.

"Well, see that you don't. The dishes will still need doing later."

Mia gasped and spun around to him, frowning.

Dad did happy-teeth — genuine happy-teeth. "You're not the only one who can make bad jokes at a time like this."

With the smell of fear fading, and hacking and happy-teeth once more filling the house, it felt more like home again, so Kai snuggled down on the floor beside Mia. Maybe all this upset was a temporary thing like the hot-cold-green-leaf-brown-leaf pattern outside. Things changed and then went back to normal, so while the pack was distressed, confused, and frightened for now, soon everything would be fine again. Just like tonight — things started off badly, but now everyone was back to normal doing happy-teeth.

Kai's mouth watered as the heaven cooked, the scent of its juicy meatiness drifting through the room growing stronger and stronger.

A few minutes later, Dad placed two plates of food on the table and his silver bowls on the floor.

"It's ready," said Dad.

Mia heaved herself off the sofa and slouched over to her pink stool at the table, Kai strolling over with her.

Kai gobbled down two strips of heaven followed by a bowl of meaty pebbles, then ambled over to sit at Mia's feet. Tension filled the air again.

Dad said, "You said you'd love some bacon and eggs, sweetheart? That wasn't just for Kai's benefit, was it? Because it isn't Kai who needs—"

"No, no, I did want that. Really." Mia scraped her knife against her plate to cut something, yet didn't lift anything toward her mouth.

"So..." Dad gestured to her plate.

Mia pushed her food around.

Dad raised his eyebrows and gave a little nod to her food.

Mia rolled her eyes but sliced off a tiny piece of heaven, stabbed it with her fork, and moved it slowly in a wide arc to put it in her gaping mouth.

She looked at Dad as she chewed. "Mmmm."

"One tiny piece? What's that going to do? Come on" — Dad gestured to her food — "a proper mouthful this time."

Instead of digging in, Mia shoved her meal away, her silverware clattering off the plate.

Dad stared down at the table for a moment and drew in a long breath.

"Please, Mia. Can we take this seriously?" He looked at her.

She did hacking that sounded strange — angry. "You think I'm not taking it seriously? You think I want to be sick?"

"Of course not, but—"

"Do you know what it's like to have something growing inside you — inside *your own body* — that's slowly killing you and there's not a thing you can do about it? Not one freaking thing? Huh? Because I sure do."

"I'm sorry, sweetheart. I just meant" — Dad reached out to hold her hand, but she whipped it away — "I'm trying to be encouraging. Especially because we're hoping you'll be fit enough to go back to school soon."

"I don't need 'encouraging.' I need supporting."

Dad nodded. "Okay. Then that's what you'll get."

"That means if I can't eat, I can't eat."

"Okay."

"I'm going to fight this, and I'm going to beat it. But you have to let me do it my way. Promise me."

Dad reached farther and grasped her hand. Salty-water ran down his cheeks again. "Okay, I promise, Mia. Your way, all the way."

Mia sliced another bit of heaven and ate it, and though she remained at the table with Dad until he finished eating, she gave the rest of her food to Kai before going to join Dad on the sofa. Barely another word was said as she and Dad sat glued to the giant magic-board, watching the moving pictures without really watching them.

By the time they got to bed that night, Kai knew something was seriously wrong because the pack dynamic had gone haywire. Instead of making three circles of his fluffy-bowl and then settling down to sleep, he padded over to Mia's bed and climbed on. She hugged him. He gave her a good lick, so his magic could heal whatever ailed her, then closed his eyes.

They fell asleep together, Kai knowing that tomorrow would bring more change and that as everything went in a pattern to balance out eventually, that change was bound to be for the better. How could it be anything else?

Chapter 29

The next morning, Mia was much more like her normal, bright self. She had breakfast with Dad, where she polished off a bowl of white liquid and yellow flakes, plus a slice of warm singed bread, which made Dad much brighter, too.

When she opened the back door for her and Kai to head out for their morning walk, Dad called out, standing at the kitchen sink. "Make sure you take—"

"My phone." She patted her pocket. "I know. And don't go too far in case I have problems. Anything else?"

Dad turned from the sink, soapy water dripping from his hands. "Just one thing."

Mia's shoulders slumped and she rolled her eyes. "What now?"

Dad tapped his cheek with a wet finger.

Mia did a tiny happy-teeth and shook her head. She strolled over and kissed him.

"Can we go now?" she asked, arching an eyebrow.

He turned and thrust his hands back in the sink. "Geez Louise, what's with all the questions? Can't a guy get a bit of peace and quiet around here?"

With another tiny happy-teeth, she slapped his arm, then headed back for the door.

Outside, Kai headed straight for his favorite peeing-post and cocked his leg while Mia sauntered by without a word. Things were already changing for the better if she wasn't complaining — it was going to be a grand day.

Birds chirped in the trees, a breeze blew refreshing cool air up from the lake, and flowers speckled the grass with a rainbow of color. Kai zigzagged across the path into the woods, so he could capture and process as many scents as possible, while Mia ambled behind, picking small white flowers that sat on the end of slender green stalks. Every time he turned back to check on her, she was fiddling with more of them.

When they reached the archway through the thicket and Mia called him, he scampered back.

"Here you go, Kai." She crouched down, eased a loop of the white flowers that had somehow become chained together over his snout, and draped it around his neck.

"Oh, such a handsome boy."

She'd slotted some of the stalks through her long flowing locks too, so it looked like flowers were growing out of her hair. The white of the petals was so vibrant against her luscious black hair, the blooms almost glowed.

Kai hunkered down and crawled into the archway, sunlight bathing the grass at the far end in a golden glow.

Halfway through, a noise like someone coughing and choking at the same time made him freeze. He turned and looked for Mia. She wasn't there.

The strained guttural cough came again.

He barked and waited.

Mia always replied when he barked. Always.

He pricked his ears. Nothing.

Something was wrong. Kai twisted around, the thorny bush stabbing all over his body. He darted back along the archway and burst out of the other side.

Bent over, Mia supported herself with one hand on a tree trunk while making the horrible strained cough sound. What smelled like white liquid and yellow flakes erupted from her mouth to splatter the grass.

172

Kai dashed to her side and whimpered.

Mia wiped her mouth with a paper tissue while patting him with her free hand.

"We can't tell Dad, okay? He can't know. He's already been through too much."

She took a bottle from her backpack, swished water around her mouth, then spat it on the ground.

Kai nuzzled her thigh, and when she put her hand down to him, he licked it. His magic would work. It had to work. He couldn't allow something bad to happen to his alpha. Not again. He couldn't save his mother because he'd been too small, but now he was much bigger and stronger.

With a groan, Mia heaved herself away from the tree but then wobbled on her feet, so Kai turned back for the house. However, Mia pointed ahead, deeper into the woods.

"This way, Kai. This disease might be trying to kill me, but it sure as hell isn't going to control my life."

Tottering instead of strolling confidently, Mia started down the path. Kai faced the house and barked. He wanted to go home and see her lying on her bed, resting and healing.

Without turning, Mia beckoned over her shoulder. "Come on, boy. Come on."

They'd only walked for a few more minutes when Mia slumped down onto a boulder, gasping for air. The sun had crawled higher than the treetops but was nowhere near overhead, so they hadn't been out any time compared to walks from the past.

She raised her left arm and dragged her forehead across it to wipe the droplets from her face, then jerked her T-shirt in and out, wafting warm stale air out and cool fresh air in. Dark stains hugged her T-shirt's armpits.

Without any warning, Mia lurched sideways and made the guttural coughing sound again. This time nothing jetted out, but she strained and strained, her face becoming redder and redder.

Kai whimpered. He didn't know what else to do.

Mia sat upright again, panting for air, droplets covering her face.

"I think..." She gasped for breath. "I think we'd better head home."

She raised her arm to stroke him, her hand shaking, but before she reached him, her arm flopped down again.

"In a minute." More gasping. "Just give me a minute."

It took them more than twice as long to get back. Not least because Mia spent half of the time slumped against a tree or a rock.

When they finally made it home, she collapsed on the sofa and didn't leave it for the rest of the day. Kai spent the entire time at her side in case she needed him.

As the hours crawled by, Kai never left her side, but he stared at her, licking her hand every so often for his magic to do its work.

In the evening, Dad came home. Mia pushed off the sofa to greet him.

She said, "I was going to start dinner, but I must've fallen asleep."

"Why, are you hungry? That's a good sign, if you are."

"I could eat a little something, yeah. But not too much. I had a big sandwich for lunch, so I'm still pretty full."

He kissed her on the cheek. "That's excellent, sweetheart. You sit down and rest. Leave dinner to me."

Dad slung his jacket on one of the chairs while heading for the kitchen. "How was your walk with Kai? Go far?"

Mia flopped back down on the sofa. "Good, thanks. We were out for ages, weren't we, boy?" She scratched Kai under the chin.

Rooting in the cold-making-machine, Dad said, "Don't forget we have that appointment at ten tomorrow."

"I remember."

"This doctor is supposed to be one of the best in the field" — Dad turned and held up a packet in each hand — "so he should get things back on track, shouldn't he?"

Pointing to the packet on the left, Mia said, "Let's hope so."

"Okay, pork chops it is." He returned one packet to the cold-making-machine and took the other one over to the counter.

Mia leaned down and hugged Kai, squeezing him like she never wanted to let go. She whispered, "The doctor might be good, but he better be fast."

174

Chapter 30

As the sun dragged the day's shadows across the living room floor, Kai stared at the front door. Mia and Dad now went out regularly together, each time full of hope laced with dread. Could it be a good sign that they had been gone longer than usual today?

Gaze fixed on the door, Kai sifted the scents in the air and strained to hear the tiniest of sounds. If the wind blew onto the front of the house, his nose was always the first to discover Mia and Dad were coming, but if the wind was blowing away, it was his ears that let him know.

Kai whimpered. He didn't know exactly what was wrong with Mia, yet he knew it was bad. He licked her every opportunity he got, and he knew she used her own magic, but she seemed to be getting weaker and weaker.

His nose alerted him to something outside. He jumped to his feet and smelled the tiny gap across the bottom of the door.

Mia was coming.

Tail wagging, he stepped back and stared at the door. Waiting. As he always did. As he always would.

The scent got closer and closer, and he wagged his tail harder and harder until his whole body shook.

Mia. It was Mia. Mia. Mia!

The door swung open and Mia and Dad trudged in. Kai jumped up and licked her.

"Hello, boy." Mia patted him. "Did you think we'd run away?"

He padded around to the sofa with her, pressing against her leg to be as close as possible.

Mia slumped down, sighing heavily.

As usual, Dad headed for the kitchen. "Do you think you can manage something?"

Mia shrugged. "Maybe. But not too much."

She did a double take at something on her shoulder, then picked strands of her long black hair off her jacket.

"What do you call too much?" Dad turned to Mia as she raked her fingers through her hair. A clump of it came away in her hand.

Her face scrunched up and her voice wavered. "Dad." She opened her arms toward him.

He took one glance at the hair between her fingers and raced over. He dove onto his knees in front of the sofa, flinging his arms around her, and cradled her head against his shoulder.

Kai whimpered. He didn't know why, but this wasn't good. He could smell fear — more fear than he'd ever smelled his entire life.

* * *

The next day, Mia tied a red bandanna around her head, tucking all her hair up inside it. However, over the next few weeks, even securing her hair under this cloth didn't stop it from falling out. It got to the point where, when she took the bandanna off to go to bed, her head was a hodgepodge of clumps of wispy hair and patches of sallow skin.

She smelled different too. The "in-between" smell had been replaced by something he'd never sensed before. The closest he could think of was how the grass in their wood smelled compared to the grass in the town's park — one was wild, fresh, and exhilarating, while the other was synthetic, stale, and laced with chemicals.

But it was still Mia. Underneath all the chemicals, the bandannas, and the weakness, it was still his vibrant, full-of-life Mia. Despite the strained coughs that came far too regularly from the bathroom and how she sometimes struggled to talk, let alone walk, she always had happy-teeth for him.

176

Kai watched her water the plant on her windowsill that had often had pink flowers but now lay a withering mass. She sighed, stroking one of its limp leaves, then plonked down on her bed, picked her bandanna off her comforter, and tied it around her head, tucking her remaining wisps of hair under it.

In a flash, it dawned on Kai what was happening: Mia didn't have leaves to lose, so she was losing the only thing she could — her hair — while her arms and legs were so spindly, they looked like bony branches. The answer was obvious. Mia had caught brown-leaf! Probably on one of their countless walks in the woods. How stupid he'd been not to have realized earlier. All that worry for nothing.

His stress drained away in an instant at the good news. If brown-leaf was causing all of this, then he just had to wait long enough, and like the trees, Mia would fix herself and burst back into life.

Except, the trees took ages to heal themselves. He didn't want to see Mia suffering for months and months. No, he had to help her fix herself far quicker than that. The trees could take their pretty time, but Mia would be fixed as soon as he could manage it.

Kai would lick his girl at every opportunity. He didn't care if he got brown-leaf too and all his fur fell out. All that mattered was that she got better. Quickly.

And if his licking wasn't enough to fix her, Dad would use all the magic he had, too. And of course, Mia had the strongest magic of all. Kai was sure that with so much magic working for them, things were bound to change, and they'd beat brown-leaf far faster than anyone thought possible. He just had to be patient and wait. And if there was one thing he was good at, it was waiting.

Besides, he and Mia were going to be together forever, so a little waiting was nothing in the grand scheme of things. Yes, change was coming. He could feel it.

Chapter 31

With the most strained coughing Kai had heard, Mia hunched forward in her bed to lean over the white plastic bowl Dad held while sitting beside her. It sounded like her insides were bursting out through her mouth. She coughed and retched and coughed and retched, as if the two were feeding off each other.

Holding the bowl with one hand, Dad draped his other arm around her shoulders. Her skinny, skinny shoulders. Mia had always been slim, but now there was hardly anything to her.

Mia swept back a few strands of hair, her hand trembling with the effort, as she lifted her face, her head now bald except for the odd wisp. She gasped for breath.

Kai cringed. Mia was in such pain, and he ached to take it away for her. He whimpered, desperate to help, but lost as to what he could do.

The room smelled of illness. Of decay. Even Mia's cherished pink-flowering plant couldn't help disguise the smell with its leaves dry, brown, and brittle.

Outside, the wind howled through the blackness as it whipped the house. With each hellish gust, something scraped over the walls as if a demon was trying to claw its way in to snatch children from the unwary.

Mia jumped. Her face so drawn it looked as if she had too little skin to cover it, she stared at the window, one hand gripping her bedsheet, the other Dad's arm.

"It's okay, honey." Dad stroked her head and the few wisps of hair clinging to life. "It's okay. It's just the wind blowing the tree."

Dad put down the bowl and dabbed her mouth with a white paper tissue, then used a fresh one to wipe her brow and sunken cheeks.

Her eyelids drooping as if she didn't have the strength to hold them up, she glanced at Kai sitting in his fluffy-bowl. She raised her shaking hand toward him. For a second, the tiniest of happy-teeth flickered across her face. Genuine happy-teeth.

Her voice weak and hoarse, she said, "Good boy."

For a moment, Kai saw the real Mia again. *His* Mia. The Mia who loved him more than anything else in the world. In that instant, it felt like everything might be okay again, as if the brown-leaf might finally be beaten.

However, Dad turned his face away from her and it twisted into more pain than Kai had ever seen on any living thing. Salty-water ran down his cheeks, and silently, he brushed it away.

Mia jerked forward. Strained coughing erupted once more.

Dad spun back and grabbed the bowl for her, then continued stroking her head.

"Hold on, sweetheart. The ambulance is on its way."

Soon after, blue flashing lights bled in through the drapes, smearing the room with an eerie glow.

Dad dashed downstairs, then brought two men and a woman up to Mia's room, each dressed in a dark blue uniform.

Kai barked. This wasn't a time for strangers to disturb his girl. Why the devil were they here?

A dark-skinned man with a beard said, "Can you remove the dog, please? It'll be easier for us to work."

"Of course," said Dad. "Sorry, I should've thought."

Dad dragged Kai toward the door by his blue-neck-band. Kai bucked and jerked. He had to stay with Mia. Had to protect her and help her heal. Dad gripped harder and hauled him out and along the balcony, Kai's claws scraping on the floor. Opening his bedroom door, Dad shoved Kai inside, then slammed it shut.

Kai whined. He shoved the door with his snout, raked the bottom with his claws to try to dig his way out, then barked for help. Nothing worked. He was trapped.

Beyond the door was lots of movement, lots of noise, and lots of scents. He'd no idea what was happening, so it was vital he got to Mia to protect her and be there if she needed him, just like he always had been.

He barked again and again and again, but no one came to help him.

And all the while, the wind whipped the house and that demon scratched and scraped to claw its way in.

Kai whined again and then finally, Dad opened the door. Kai raced out and into Mia's room, but she'd disappeared. He shot out and down the stairs, but she wasn't there either. His nose said she'd gone through the front door, so he jumped up at it again and again, and barked and barked. But the door stood firm, taunting him.

Dad hauled Kai away from the door with one hand while opening it with the other.

"I'm sorry, Kai," said Dad, his eyes puffy and red. "This is one time you can't go with her."

He dashed out and slammed the door behind him.

Kai stared at it.

Mia.

He howled.

Chapter 32

The sun came up and shafts of light fell on Kai from the living room window. Unblinking, he stared at the front door as he lay on his stomach, chin on his front paws. Though his legs ached from being in the same position all night, he couldn't move – if he moved, even the tiniest fraction, he might miss the very instant Mia came back.

So, he waited.

And waited.

And waited.

But Mia didn't come.

As the sun sank behind the trees, creeping long shadows in through the living room windows, Kai smelled something coming from outside, heading toward the house. Something he recognized.

Kai pushed up to stand, but his leg muscles screamed after the inactivity, and he slumped back to the floor. He heaved himself up again, and this time, stood, legs trembling. His heart pounding, he sniffed the air seeping in from outside, filtering the countless scents, confirming what his nose had discovered.

He whined, padded right up to the door, and sniffed again.

They were coming. They were coming. *Dad and Mia were coming!*

Again, he whined. The scent was getting closer and closer, but way, way too slowly. Whenever Mia was coming home, she always – *always* – came too slowly.

Kai trotted around in a tight circle. They were coming!

After so much upset, this had to be the greatest day in the history of the world. He pictured Dad and Mia ambling along the path to the house.

He leapt, imagining licking Mia over and over, licking her so much his tongue stuck to her so they could never be parted. The light after the dark flooding his body with joy, he leapt again.

But then he stopped. Stared at the door. What was that?

He sniffed.

Sniffed harder.

Something was wrong.

He barked. His nose had never let him down — never — so why was it telling him something that couldn't possibly be true? He barked again. His nose was wrong. It had to be.

However, when he sniffed, his nose told him the same thing — Dad was almost here, yes, but Mia?

Every time Mia and Dad went out together, they always came back together, so what was happening now? Mia was way too sick to be left on her own.

When Dad opened the door, Kai stuck his snout in the gap to wiggle his way through, but Dad blocked him with his leg.

Kai sniffed the air gushing in, scouring the scents for that special one. It wasn't there.

Dad shut the door and, without saying a word, lurched past Kai and across the room, where he collapsed on the sofa. Resting his elbows on his knees and his head in his hands, his shoulders trembled. Droplets of salty-water splashed the wood floor.

Kai looked back to the door. Mia would come. What else was she going to do? This was her home, her pack. It was where she belonged.

He lay down, chin on his front paws, and stared at the door.

Gloom gradually enveloped the despair-laden room, a murky moonlight struggling in through clouds that hung unmoving, as if nailed to the sky. The salty-water had stopped falling on the floor, so the small pool had dried, but Dad still sat with his head in his hands. It was as if he didn't know what to do, as if he'd always been "Dad" for Mia and didn't know how to be anything else.

Kai knew how Dad felt. Their home didn't feel like a home anymore. A home was filled with love, companionship, and sharing. Now...? Now it was just a building in which they both happened to be at the same time. It wasn't just the feelings that had vanished; it was like the house itself had transformed. Their house had always been so full of life, so full of activity, so full of happiness, so... *full*. Now it was empty. Eerily silent. And with no movement, so vast.

Neither Dad nor Kai moved for the rest of the night. Though they were only feet apart, each of them was imprisoned in their own isolated cell, each tortured by their thoughts.

Kai did nothing except stare at the door. It wasn't just Mia that was missing, it was part of him — the part of him forever joined to her. It was as if it had been ripped away, leaving nothing but a gaping hole, and every moment, more was ripped out, so the aching emptiness got bigger and bigger and bigger.

As the hours passed, the emptiness gnawed at all that made him *him*. He was a shadow at dusk, a tear in a hurricane, a name no one called. He was nothing. Lost. Purposeless.

Darkness bled in from outside, yet the only movement in the house was from the shadows cast by the moonlight.

When the sun finally came back up, Dad got out of his seat and stumbled upstairs without a word. Kai barely even noticed, hearing the plodded footsteps make their way across the room but not turning to investigate. All he saw was the door.

As the day's shadows crept across the living room once more, Kai still didn't move. There was no hunger, no thirst; there wasn't anything except the one thing that gave his life purpose: Mia.

He lay in front of the door all through the day. At some point, a bowl of meaty pebbles appeared beside him; however, Kai was so focused on the door that no sights or sounds had registered, so he had no idea how they'd gotten there or when. Time was nonexistent when it had nothing to give it meaning, so Kai waited and waited. That was all he had left.

A new mystery plagued him, gnawing away at his thoughts as he stared at the door. It didn't make any sense that Mia wasn't there. When the trees had brown-leaf, no one took them away. So why had they taken his girl? If she was going to beat brown-leaf quickly, she needed him and his magic. It was ridiculous they were being kept apart. How was Mia supposed to beat brown-leaf without him? It could take her months alone. Months!

That night, Dad knelt on the floor and pushed a bowl of water right up to Kai's snout.

"You've got to drink, boy. Mia wouldn't want this."

Ignoring it, Kai continued staring and waiting.

* * *

On the third day, Dad fastened Mia's walking-cord to Kai's blue-neck-band, then opened the front door. Kai could've tried to run past him to hunt for Mia, but he had no idea where she was. His best option was to stay where she knew she could find him.

"Kai. Come on, boy." Dad pushed the door wide open and tugged on the cord. "Come on. You need to move. You'll hurt yourself just lying there. I'm sure you need to pee, at least."

Kai stared out at the world beyond the door, the world he loved to explore so much with Mia. There was little point in venturing out without her, and as he hadn't eaten or drunk anything, he didn't even have to visit his peeing-post.

Dad hung his head with a heavy sigh. He dropped the walking-cord, shut the door, and trudged back to the sofa. They both sat: Dad staring into space, Kai staring at the door.

When it got dark again, Dad clomped upstairs and started rummaging around. Kai stayed where he was, but the clattering and banging about was so loud, he couldn't help but hear it. Then it all went quiet again.

The moonlight crept shadows across Kai, while the sound of silence was like a rushing noise in his ears. He dreamed of hearing Mia scratching the metal wires on her hollow-wood-machine again; he ached to hear her voice. He knew if he waited long enough, his dream would come true.

184

And, as if by magic, it did.

Kai gasped and pricked his ears. That was Mia's voice. She was home. For the first time in days, he looked around the room instead of at the door. There was no one else there.

Had he imagined it? Had he wanted it so much his mind was playing tricks on him?

Resigned to what he knew was his fate, he settled back down to wait at the door.

But he heard it again. Mia! That was Mia!

He jumped up, leapt around, and raced up the steps toward Mia's room.

It was Mia. She'd finally come back. Mia!

He shot into her bedroom, ready to jump on her and lick her to pieces...

He froze. Where was she?

Dad sat slumped on her bed, his face drenched in salty-water. Holding his thin silver-board, which seemed to be like Mia's magic-board, he did something with his thumb.

Mia's voice said, "Hey, it's me. You know what to do. See you later."

Kai looked at the silver-board, then at Dad, then back to the board. What did this mean? What was going on?

Mia said the same thing in exactly the same way. Again. And again. And again.

Except, it wasn't Mia. There wasn't even the tiniest trace of fresh scent. She hadn't come back. Yet.

Kai tramped back to his spot at the door. Everything changed, so maybe tomorrow's change would be a good one.

Chapter 33

The new day brought only more waiting, with the only thing to change being Dad. The usually well-groomed fur on his chin had spread across his cheeks and down his throat over the last few days, while his scent no longer smelled of man-flowers but increasingly of staleness, grime, and despair.

Around lunchtime, Dad gave Kai fresh water and meaty pebbles, pushing the bowls right up against Kai's snout.

Grudgingly, he lapped a few drops of water, then munched a few pebbles. Mia would be aching to go for a long walk when she came back, and if he didn't eat, he'd ruin their grand reunion because he wouldn't have energy to go.

He ate some more, and though he didn't like to think it, it did make him feel a tiny bit better. His bowl clean, he resumed his waiting.

Dad trudged upstairs. Kai didn't register how long he was gone, but when he came back, the extra fur on his face had gone and he once more smelled of man-flowers. He was dressed all in black.

Dad opened the front door. Kai lifted his head off his paws to watch. Mia was having difficulty getting home alone, so maybe Dad was going to search for her. Kai scrambled up to help Dad, but Dad opened the door only enough for him to squeeze through, then yanked it shut behind him. His footsteps clomped away and disappeared.

Kai sat back down. The crushing emptiness in his chest eased for the first time in days. Dad had finally gone to bring Mia home!

Later that day, Dad slouched back, his eyes redder and puffier than ever. Kai waited for Mia to come in, but she didn't.

Without saying a word, Dad stumbled over to the sofa and fell in a heap upon it, head back, staring at the ceiling.

Kai looked over at Dad, then back to the door, hoping it would reopen and Mia would appear. But she didn't. He looked back at Dad. Dad was a part of his pack, too, and he was hurting so, so much. A good dog would help anyone in its pack, not just the alpha.

Wincing with the effort of standing after not moving for so long, Kai pushed to his feet. He swayed to one side and thought he was going to fall but caught himself. He tottered over to Dad, his claws tap-tap-tapping on the wooden floor.

It wasn't like Dad to be so quiet for so long. He had to be in such pain, but that was fine, because Kai knew what to do to ease suffering.

Kai licked Dad's hand.

No reaction.

He licked again. Then again. His magic would work, it just needed time because the hurt was so deep.

Instead of doing happy-teeth or giving Kai a pat, Dad jerked his hand away.

Kai nuzzled Dad's knee.

No reaction again.

He nuzzled once more. Harder.

Dad didn't move, didn't even look at him.

Kai barked. Going back on his hind legs, he put his front paws on Dad's thigh.

"No, Kai. No." Dad shoved him off.

Kai stared up, heart aching.

"I'm sorry, boy, but I can't. Every time I look at you, I see her."

Kai tried one last time to nuzzled him, but Dad twisted away.

With no other option, Kai shuffled back to his door.

The world had patterns, so Kai knew things couldn't continue like this. Hot and cold, light and dark, good and bad. There had been so much bad recently, the time for good was long overdue. That meant when it came, it wouldn't just be good, but amazing. Kai just had to be patient.

* * *

The next morning, Dad talked a lot to his silver-board in the living room. Lots of voices talked back, but unusually, none of them were Mia's.

Dad shuffled across the room, rubbing his brow. "And you can get someone in by the weekend?"

A woman's voice said, "If that's what you want, I can make it happen. But it'll be reflected in the price I can get."

"I don't care."

"Then it's not a problem. You're in a very desirable location, so if it's cheap enough, someone will snatch your hand off, even on such short notice."

Dad paced back across the living room. "And you collect the rent, sort out utility bills, maintenance issues, everything?"

"Everything. It's all included in our price."

"So, I won't have to be here to do anything?"

The woman said, "No. As long as you can get online to authorize us to act on any issues that crop up with an e-signature, you can be anywhere you want."

"Then send me everything, please. I need to move on this immediately."

Dad stopped talking and threw the silver-board on the sofa. He ran his hands through his hair and heaved a breath.

The silver-board buzzed, so Dad grabbed it.

"Just finished arranging it all, Mom," he said. "The flight gets in around nine, so we'll see you around eleven tonight."

Another woman said in a gravelly voice, "We? You're still bringing the dog?"

"Well, I'm not going to leave him here, am I?"

"I thought kennels might be an idea."

Dad grimaced, pinching the bridge of his nose. "Mom, it's me and the dog. Period. Mia would never forgive me if anything happened to him."

188

"Okay, okay, I was just saying."

"Well, don't, please. I've already paid for the tickets and arranged to pick up a pet carrier on the way."

"It would've been easier if you'd come with us straight after the funeral, or let us come back to help you organize things. You know we're here for you, Ben."

Dad rubbed his eyes. "Thanks, Mom, but I couldn't face having anyone else here."

They finished talking and then Dad became more active than he'd been in days: searching cupboards and drawers, scurrying around collecting bits and pieces, creating piles of various items. He even took Kai's fluffy-bowl down from upstairs. He then crammed everything into two black duffel bags, which he shoved next to the front door. Kai glared at them. They were blocking his view. Luckily, Dad opened the door and carried the bags away.

When he returned, Dad tramped over to the back door and held it wide open. "Kai, pee time. Come on, boy."

Fresh air wafted across to Kai, tantalizing him with all the scents he'd loved to investigate with Mia. He could even smell his peeing-post. Wow, he'd done a good job marking that. Mia would be proud when she came back and learned she could smell his post from so far away.

Kai looked over at Dad and the world outside.

After drinking that water, visiting his peeing-post seemed like a good idea.

He trotted out, relieved himself, and went back up the steps. However, he froze at the top.

What was happening? Why was Dad standing outside and locking the back door?

Kai whined. He needed to get inside to his spot. The spot where he waited for Mia.

Dad hurried along the veranda to the steps. "Come on, Kai. To the car, boy."

Kai sat down outside the door.

When Dad turned and saw, his voice grew gruffer. "Kai. Come here."

Kai didn't move.

"Now, Kai. Come here. Now!"

Dad stomped back up the steps and grabbed him by the scruff of the neck. He dragged Kai along the veranda, farther and farther away from his spot.

Kai whimpered. He couldn't leave. Mia would never find him again.

Kai sat down and pushed with his front legs to stop him moving.

"We need to get away from here for a while. Trust me, Kai, it's best for both of us."

Dad was too strong. Kai's claws scraped on the wood as Dad hauled him toward the steps, then Kai thumped all the way down.

At the bottom, Kai lay on the grass and refused to get up. He couldn't leave this place. His duty was to wait until Mia came for him.

Dad's voice became the loudest it had ever been. "Get the hell off the ground, you stupid animal! I'm trying to help you."

He crouched, shoved his hands under Kai's body, and scooped him up. Carrying Kai, Dad turned and lurched for the path to the flat black ground where their car was parked.

No! Kai couldn't let this happen. He had to get away.

Kai twisted and writhed to break free. He wasn't the small puppy Dad had picked up in the alley a lifetime ago; now he was a big, muscular dog. No way was Dad going to take him away from Mia.

Dad clung tighter, squashing Kai, his fingers clawing into Kai's sides to grip him.

Kai bucked and bucked. He had to escape. Had to.

Breaking Dad's grip, Kai crashed to the ground. He scrambled up as Dad lunged to grab him.

Dodging to one side, Kai bolted. He flew for the cover of the trees and ran and ran and ran until the shadows swallowed him.

Chapter 34

A flashlight beam sliced through the dense shadows shrouding wood.

"Kai!" shouted Dad, his voice no longer filled with anger but desperation. "Kai! Here, boy."

Kai hid in the safest place he knew: the archway underneath the thorny bush. No one could see him there from the path, and even if someone tried to get in, the spikes would stab and stab until they retreated. Hopefully.

"Kai! Come on, boy. Please!"

Dad's silver-board buzzed, but from where Kai was, he couldn't hear everything said.

"Mom, I'll have to call you back. ... Yes, I'm still looking. What do you expect me to do? ... No, I had to buy another. It's tomorrow afternoon, three thirty. ... No, I don't know what I'll do if I don't find him in time. We'll have to cross that bridge if we come to it. ... Yeah, all signed and sealed. They'll be here the day after tomorrow, so I've no choice. Look, I have to go. I'll see you tomorrow."

The beam from the flashlight panned across the entrance to the archway. Dad was close. Too close.

Kai held his breath and prayed he was as invisible as he believed.

Twigs crunched underfoot as Dad neared. The beam scanned the thorny bush and fractured light bled onto Kai. A crazed pattern of bright streaks swept over him.

Kai cringed, a ball of dread eating away inside his stomach worse than any hunger he'd known on the streets. The tunnel was safe as long as he wasn't seen, but if he was, his sanctuary would transform into a trap because it was too narrow for him to turn around quickly, giving someone determined the chance to grab him.

He screwed his eyes shut. Hunkered down. Tried to squash himself into the ground so it swallowed him up to hide him.

Dad couldn't be trusted not to take Kai away, so the only option was to stay away from the man.

The beam of light arced back. Jagged shadows stalked over Kai's back and stopped. Kai dared not move — not even to breathe.

But no arm snaked in, and no fingers clawed into his flesh.

The light crawled over another bush and Dad's footsteps crunched leaves and twigs farther and farther away.

Once Kai could barely hear Dad, he shuffled out of the thicket and crept back to a bush on the edge of the grassland from where he could see their home.

If he couldn't wait in the house for Mia, he'd watch for her from there, while keeping track of Dad to ensure he didn't get too close.

For hours, Dad called Kai's name as he wandered through the wood, across the expanse of grass, and back through the wood.

Long after all the windows in the other houses had gone dark, Dad trudged home and their house was engulfed by blackness too.

In the morning, when sunlight glinted on droplets of dew clinging to the grass, Dad wandered out onto the veranda.

"Kai! ... Kai!"

Under the bush, Kai shrank as small as he could and watched Dad march down the steps and trail into the wood again, calling all the while.

Kai's chest hurt at abandoning Dad, but the pack's hierarchy was not just clear, it was crucial: everything revolved around the alpha. The alpha was indispensable, unlike any other pack member. If it was a choice between Mia and Dad, then there was no choice.

Dad scoured the woods until the sun was high overhead, then tramped back. However, instead of going home, he slouched over to the next house and chatted outside with gray-haired Mr. Paget. When Dad pointed to the woods, both of them looked over, then he handed the man a piece of paper and something Kai couldn't make out.

Talking on his silver-board, Dad trudged home. He spent a few minutes in the house before emerging to stand on the veranda. Shielding his eyes from the sun with his hand, he gazed out over the landscape.

He cupped his hands around his mouth and shouted, "Kai!"

Scouring the scene before him, he waited.

Dad's shoulders slumped. He locked the house door and shuffled down the steps and out of sight. Their car's engine revved, then disappeared into the distance.

Wary of it being a trick, Kai stayed under the bush, watching the house from a safe distance.

Nothing happened for hours, so he crept out to move closer just as a strange yellow car pulled onto the black ground where Dad's car usually parked. A frumpy woman dressed all in blue waltzed up the steps to their home and fumbled with some jangly bits of metal. The wind blew the smell of the fake-flowers she'd bathed in toward him.

What in heaven's name was she doing?

Kai's mouth dropped open when the woman unlocked their door and sauntered straight into *his* home!

Kai growled. He couldn't have been clearer when marking his peeing-post. What the devil did this woman think she was playing at?

He slunk out from under the bush, prowled to the steps, and stalked up them. With Mia and Dad gone, the pack was depending on him to defend its territory. He would not let Mia down.

The fake-flowers clogging his nostrils, he snarled as he approached the closed door. He shoved it with his snout, but it wouldn't budge. Standing on his hind legs, he pushed it with his front paws and barked.

From somewhere below the veranda, Mr. Paget shouted, "He's here. Call Ben, Mary. The dog's here."

The man bustled toward the house, while behind him, Mrs. Paget stared over.

She called out, "He'll be on his flight already."

"So leave a voicemail. Just tell him the dog's here."

Heading to the bottom of the steps, Mr. Paget held up an open palm. "Good dog, Kai. Stay there, boy. Good dog."

Kai had gotten to know the neighbors over the years: Mrs. Paget sometimes gave him warm sausages, while Mr. Paget had a knack for finding the best sticks for Mia to throw.

Kai wagged his tail. Thank heaven. Mr. Paget would help get the frumpy woman out of their house.

The gray-haired man stalked along the veranda, one hand toward Kai, palm out, the other behind his back.

Kai frowned. Why was the man moving like that, especially with one hand out of sight? Was he hiding something?

Doing happy-teeth, Mr. Paget crept closer. "Good dog, Kai."

Then Kai saw it. Dangling behind Mr. Paget's legs hung Kai's walking-cord.

Kai gasped. The man wanted to put that on him, to control him, to take him away from here.

Snarling, Kai glared and backed away. He didn't want to hurt Mr. Paget, but he couldn't let anything stop him from getting to Mia.

The window above him opened a crack and the frumpy woman shouted, "Can you get your dog away from my door, please?"

Kai spun, leapt at the window, and snapped, but the woman slammed it shut, so he hit the glass and fell back to the veranda.

Mr. Paget shuffled closer, one hand reaching out toward Kai, the other still hidden. "Be a good dog now, Kai. Be good."

Glowering, Kai faced him, head down, teeth bared.

An intruder had moved into their home, a man who'd seemed nice was trying to catch him, and Dad had abandoned their pack. What should he do? What should he do?

Kai's heart pounded so hard he thought it would explode.

The man got closer and closer, and the frumpy woman glared at him from the safety of *his* home.

What should he do?

Mr. Paget lunged to grab him, but Kai dodged. He leapt to his right, twisting in the air, and pounded his paws into the side of the house, his legs flexing to absorb the impact. Using the wall as a springboard, Kai sprang away and landed on the floor behind the man.

His head down, legs pumping, he shot along the veranda, down the steps, and deep into the darkening wood.

He ran and ran. Ran to the only sanctuary he knew.

Without a care for the stabbing spikes, Kai dove into the archway through the thorny bush to Mia's special place. He scrambled further into the shadows, thorns biting into his back, and cowered in the cold darkness.

All was lost.

What was he going to do now?

He hunkered down and there, amid the crunchy brown leaves and decaying twigs, he found old traces of Mia's scent.

It calmed him, gave him hope, and told him everything was going to be okay, because part of her was still there with him.

But how could he reach the real Mia?

As the cold night air bit at his bones and the nighttime creatures crept and hooted and stalked around him, Kai worked on the problem. He was an expert at solving mysteries. In fact, his entire life had obviously been building to this one moment — the solving of the greatest mystery ever. All of the other mysteries he'd solved had been preparing him for this huge one. The only one that truly mattered. There hadn't been a mystery yet that had beaten him, so he'd crack this one like he had all the others.

He went around and around in circles, studying the problem from different angles, struggling to understand what was happening and why, working to fit all the pieces into place to see the possible outcomes... Hour after hour after hour.

Shivering after spending a second night outside, Kai crawled out from the archway and into the morning sun. He shook himself and droplets of dew sprayed from his coat.

It had taken all night, but he'd solved the mystery, reaching a terrifying conclusion: if Mia could come home, she would have by now, therefore, the reason she hadn't was that something was stopping her. Mia would never abandon him, so something had to have trapped her to stop her from getting back to him.

That meant it was up to her pack to rescue her.

Other than their home, there was only one other place Mia had regularly gone. Kai shot away through the trees, knowing exactly where he was going and how to get there.

Chapter 35

Kai glared at the monstrous red-brick building, its four floors rearing over him.

This place had trapped Mia in the past. Almost every day, she'd been imprisoned there. For years. Maybe she'd gone in one day, gotten turned around in the warren of hallways and dead-end rooms, and been unable to find her way back out.

Luckily, when a member of the pack was lost, there was an easy way to guide them home.

Kai raised his head to the sky and howled.

He howled and howled and howled.

Like before, young faces appeared at the windows, then small and big people milled in the hallway behind the closed glass doors at the front of the building.

A warm glow filled Kai's heart. This was exactly how it had happened last time. And last time, Mia had come running to him.

Hope giving him strength, he howled louder.

Flappy Man raced out of the building, waving his arms. He shouted, "Away, dog. Away!"

Yes, it was working. Exactly like before. All Kai had to do was keep howling and his dream would come true.

He howled again, but Flappy Man lunged at him. "Get away, you mangy animal."

Kai dodged, scampered beyond reach, then turned and howled once more.

He peered down the left-hand side of the building — the side from which Mia had run to him the last time.

Flappy Man ran at him, anger creasing his face, arms stretched wide. "Out! Get out, you mangy mutt. Out!"

When the man was close enough, he pulled his foot back and let fly a kick at Kai.

Ducking under the man's foot, Kai darted away, then howled from a safe distance.

He stared down the side of the building and frowned. Something was wrong. Mia should've been there by now.

He scoured the faces at the windows. She wasn't there. He bounded around to the other side of the building, in case she'd come that way instead, yet she wasn't there either.

All the while, Flappy Man chased him, his cries getting more and more frantic, his face more and more red.

Kai ran down the side, barking for Mia. She had to hear him. Had to come.

He barreled along the back of the building, but when he turned the corner and sprinted along the left-hand side to the front, two other men appeared, one brandishing a bat. With their arms out wide, they tried to block Kai's path. He peered back as Flappy Man raced around the rear corner and hurtled at him.

Kai skidded to a halt on the hard black ground, glancing at the men blocking his path, then back at the one coming up behind him, then back to the two ahead. He didn't know what to do. He needed to rescue Mia, but he couldn't let himself be captured and imprisoned, because then they'd both be trapped with no one left to rescue them.

He had only one choice.

In the hope Mia might hear him and know he hadn't abandoned her, he barked one last time, then snarled and lurched forward.

Of the two men in front of him, the one on the left who smelled of bananas blocked the most direct route to the hole under the fence.

Kai careered straight at him, a gravelly growl coming from his throat, lips curling to show his fangs.

Bananas Man had two choices: move to let Kai pass, or see a part of his flesh ripped away.

Kai shot straight at the man, muscles pumping, teeth bared.

The man looked to his comrade, his eyes wide and mouth agape, yet it was too late. Kai was upon him.

Kai leapt at Bananas Man. He soared through the air, teeth gnashing and claws ready to rip.

Screaming, Bananas Man dove out of the way and crashed to the ground.

Kai bolted for the hole under the fence, snaked through, and rocketed down the sidewalk.

He'd escaped. But what was he going to do now?

Chapter 36

Kai prowled along the sidewalk to the tiny glass-walled building where the bus stopped. Waiting a moment, he listened. All was once more quiet farther along the street. That was good.

Creeping down the sidewalk, he slunk low to stay as far out of sight as possible. As the black metal fence appeared, everything was still quiet.

Excellent. His plan was going to work.

Kai wriggled under the fence and once more stood before the red-brick building.

There were no faces at the windows, no people in the hallway, no one outside.

Yes, it was a masterful plan.

He sat in the middle of the black ground, looked to the heavens, and howled.

Failing once was not a reason to give up. A good dog never gave up on his pack, just like his pack would never give up on him.

Kai howled again and again.

Faces appeared at the windows like before and Flappy Man lurched out of the building with the reddest face Kai had ever seen. Other adults joined Flappy Man, then a group of children streamed out from around the back of the building.

"Get back inside. All of you," shouted Flappy Man as he stalked toward Kai.

The children backed away but were too fascinated to leave.

Kai howled again, then studied the faces in the windows.

Bananas Man said, "We'll never catch him, Harry. I'm sure if we ignore him, he'll get bored and go back to wherever he came from."

Kai couldn't see Mia anywhere, so he howled again.

"Can you concentrate with that racket?" said Flappy Man. "We have to get rid of him one way or another. Now spread out."

Flappy Man, Bananas Man, and two others closed in on Kai from different angles.

Kai ran at Bananas Man, then at the last instant twisted, dove through Flappy Man's legs, and shot away to safety.

The goggle-eyed children laughed and clapped.

Running around the black ground, Kai dodged Flappy Man and anyone else who tried to stop him time and again. When he had the chance, he howled and barked, so Mia would hear and know he was rescuing her.

As Kai waged his war, the children cheered every time he successfully evaded capture. He even heard his name called, but it was a boy's voice, not Mia's, so he ignored it. Then, more and more children started chanting, "Kai! Kai! Kai!"

He'd never liked children. Too often, they'd caused him nothing but pain and misery. However, hearing them calling his name gave him a boost.

Kai swerved and dodged and barked and howled. But as more and more people closed in, it became more and more difficult. Finally, there were too many, so it was inevitable they'd catch him. If he stayed.

Just like before, he growled and bolted. If anything stood in his way, he'd rip it limb from limb. And just like before, the people cleared a path, flinging themselves out of his way as he hurtled at them.

Back on the street, Kai tore down the sidewalk and into the first alley he found. Hunkering down behind a dumpster, he panted, tongue lolling out. Once it got dark, he'd venture out to find food. Until then, he'd save his energy for his next rescue attempt.

The following morning, Kai again sneaked under the fence and trotted into the middle of the flat black ground, glowering at his red-brick nemesis as it towered over him. This thing would not beat him.

He howled.

Faces gazed out at him, the small ones doing happy-teeth and even one or two of the big faces too. But not Flappy Man when he came dashing out with Bananas Man and the rest of his gang. They shouted and formed an arc, holding their arms out wide to try to force Kai back against the fence.

Kai was used to their tricks now. He ran around the outside of them, his speed greater than anything they could muster. Next to him, they were so slow, clumsy, and uncoordinated they may as well have been standing still. It was only a matter of time before he was reunited with Mia. He barked again.

With one of the doors unguarded, a group of children streamed out and cheered as he ran past.

Kai sprinted toward the back of the building, glancing back as he rounded the corner. Flappy Man and two men chased after him. Others would be coming down the far side to trap him, but they had no chance because he was too fast. He'd proven that so many times, he was surprised they were even trying anymore. Frankly, it was embarrassing.

As he tore down the left-hand side, Bananas Man and some others blocked his way as usual. Kai glared at them. Seriously? Hadn't they learned yet? Wherever Mia was, he hoped she could see him outwitting all these fools who were trying to keep them apart. He was going to rescue her, and no one was going to stop him.

Nearing the front of the building, Kai swerved to his right, drawing the people over to that side, then cut sharply to his left. Paws pounding into the black ground, he sped past them.

It was so easy. So easy.

From out of nowhere, something looped over his head and snagged around his neck. It pulled tight and ripped him off his feet.

Kai smashed into the unforgiving black ground.

Shaken, Kai scrambled up. He looked back and gasped as his world crashed down around him.

"Got you!" shouted the Gray Man.

Chapter 37

In gray overalls, the Gray Man clutched a metal pole, at the end of which was a noose that constricted around Kai's neck.

Kai bucked and twisted to break free, wrenching on the pole, yanking it this way and that. He'd never seen his mother and brothers again after the Gray Man had taken them, so he had to escape or he'd never see Mia again.

Snarling, Kai lowered his head and bared his teeth at the Gray Man. He'd never bitten a person, but at that second, he couldn't think of anything he wanted more than to see the man's blood splatter the ground and hear his screams fill the air.

He leapt to rip a chunk out of him, but the Gray Man gripped the pole tight. Its loop cut into Kai's throat, jerking him back. Once again, he crunched into the ground.

Kai twisted to bite the pole, yet it merely turned with him, restricting his movements, so he couldn't get an angle to attack it.

He couldn't escape it, couldn't fight it. He was trapped.

Kai's hope drained away, taking all his energy with it. He slumped to the ground. Empty. Defeated. Alone.

Kai whimpered. He'd lost his one chance of ever seeing Mia again.

The Gray Man talked into a small black box strapped to his chest. "Bring the van around. I've got him."

A teenage boy with brown curly hair ran forward. He heaved his arm back and hurled a stone at the Gray Man. The stone bounced off the man's shoulder, making him flinch, but not enough to drop the pole.

The boy shouted, "That's Mia's dog. Leave him alone."

Flappy Man pointed to the main doors. "Get to my office, John Sanger!"

The boy threw another stone. "Leave Mia's dog alone."

The Gray Man twisted away, cowering behind his upraised shoulder and flinching when the stone smacked him on the back.

Flappy Man raced over and stood in front of the boy, rearing over him. "I hope you enjoy detention, Sanger, because you've just got yourself a month of it!"

A girl with a yellow hair ribbon shouted, "Leave Mia's dog alone."

She picked up a stone and hurled it at the Gray Man too.

The group of children that had cheered him dashed forward, snatching up stones. They formed an arc around the Gray Man, shouting, "Leave Mia's dog alone."

They pelted the Gray Man. He tried to dodge, but with so many projectiles firing at him, stones bit at his arms, head, legs, and body.

With a shriek, he threw his hands up to shield his head, dropping the metal pole imprisoning Kai.

One of the girls ran over and grabbed it. She clicked a button, and the noose around Kai's throat slackened.

He was free.

Kai leapt up and flew for the fence. Diving at the hole underneath it, he scraped the skin on his belly on the ground, but he wriggled through in an instant.

Without looking back, he darted down the sidewalk. He had to get away. Far, far away. Where it was safe. Where he could plan. But where?

People stood around the tiny glass-walled building, blocking his path.

His heart thumping for fear of what he might see, he dared to glance back.

The Gray Man raced down the street toward him.

With the sidewalk ahead blocked and danger behind him, Kai

204

bolted in the only direction he could — straight into the road.

A blue car's brakes screeched and honking blared.

Kai shot in front of it.

A silver car charged toward him from the other direction. He wouldn't make it across in time.

Kai careered straight down the center of the road with cars zooming past on either side of him. Ahead lay the tiny park with only one tree and a long thorny bush, around which traffic circled all day every day.

He was trapped again: fast cars on his left, fast cars on his right, fast cars in front, and the Gray Man behind.

Danger! Everywhere. What was he going to do?

There seemed no way out, but he had to find one, or he'd never find Mia.

He glanced back again and gasped. The Gray Man had crossed to the middle of the road and was dashing toward him.

Kai glared at the blur of speeding cars all around him — thundering, bone-crushing cars.

He gazed at the tiny park. He knew what he had to do.

Sickness rose from his stomach, and his legs wobbled at the thought of what could happen if he got it wrong, yet he had to risk it. For Mia.

Cars whipped around the tiny park. Fast, fast, fast.

However, *if* he was fast — faster than he'd ever been — he could make it. Once he was there, he'd be safe because the ring of endlessly circling cars would protect him.

His head down, Kai tore toward the tiny one-tree park: an island sanctuary in a sea of terrifying noise and pulverizing speed.

Yes, it was an excellent plan. It was bound to work. It had to work.

His legs pumping, paws pounding into the black road, he shot toward the tiny island.

A yellow car stormed around the island sanctuary toward him.

Kai saw it but knew he could beat it. He was fast. Unbelievably fast.

He shot farther across the circular road, his goal of reaching the lone tree the only thing that mattered.

But the yellow car roared.

It was coming fast.

Incredibly fast.

Too fast!

With all his strength, Kai leapt. He had to reach the island, had to reach safety. It was the only way to find Mia.

He soared through the air. The grassy ground reared toward him to greet him. He was going to make it. He could almost feel his paws thumping into the soft earth.

Almost.

The yellow car clipped Kai's hind legs.

Spinning, Kai hurtled through the air. He crashed down onto the island's tiny patch of grass and tumbled over and over, his legs flailing in the air and the ground pummeling his body.

He slammed into the lone tree, yelped, and crumpled at the foot of the trunk.

When he tried to stand, he yelped again; red-hot pain stabbed his right hind leg.

But that didn't matter. The only thing that did was that he'd made it and was now safe.

He glanced around to double-check.

The Gray Man glowered from the middle of the road, unable to reach the island for the traffic.

Kai heaved a great sigh of relief. He waited to watch the Gray Man leaving but frowned.

Why wasn't the Gray Man leaving?

The man watched the cars, then stepped onto the circular road with one foot before jerking it back when a silver car didn't slow.

Kai gasped. The Gray Man wasn't leaving because he hadn't given up — he was coming!

Pushing up, Kai tried to stand yet writhed in agony as red-hot pain once more speared his body. He reached forward with his front legs and hauled himself farther onto the tiny island. He had to get away.

Twisting around, Kai checked on the Gray Man — still standing in the road.

Kai dragged himself farther and farther. He needed to run. Desperately needed to run. But he couldn't. That left him only one choice — one slim chance to escape capture.

Pain slicing through his hindquarters, Kai pulled with his front paws and kicked with his one good back leg. Slowly, so slowly, he inched forward toward the thorny bush.

He clawed at the brown leaves and broken twigs underneath it, hauling himself on.

Just a little farther.

He glanced back and gasped again.

The Gray Man stepped out into the road, holding up his hand to a car thundering toward him. Instead of crushing him, the car slowed and let him pass.

The Gray Man ran toward the island.

Raking at the earth with his claws, Kai heaved himself closer to the spiky plant. It was his only chance.

He glanced over his shoulder. The Gray Man dashed the last few steps, and then he was on the island too. He was going to catch Kai and stop him from ever seeing Mia again.

Kai summoned the last of his strength. His back legs trembling with the effort, he stood and leapt as high and as far as he could. Thorns stabbed into his flesh as Kai crashed through the bush and slammed into the ground beneath it.

He fought to drag himself still farther as thorns ripped his body, but like a spreading fire, the searing pain from his back legs engulfed him.

He collapsed.

Kai lay. Unmoving.

Chapter 38

Kai's eyes flickered half-open, then popped wide as he remembered where he was and the impending threat. He thrust his paws into the ground to haul himself farther under the bush but yelped when pain shot through him as if his back leg had been crushed by a giant rock.

Gasping for air, he slumped into the mass of brown leaves and brittle twigs covering the ground.

As he glanced back, thorns scratched his head. He expected to see the Gray Man's hand grabbing for him and to be dragged out, yet the man wasn't there. Ignoring the bush's tearing spikes, Kai twisted one way, then the other. Moonlight filtered through the branches, and beyond, the lights of cars.

He yelped when he tried to move again. Thorns stabbed into him as he twisted around to lick his right hind leg, and the shadows and branches started to swirl as if he was being spun, though he was sure he wasn't moving. Darkness crept in from the edges of his vision and everything became blurry. He fought to keep his head up, but it slumped to the ground.

When Kai groggily came to and opened his eyes, the sun was shining, casting dappled shadows over him.

Again, he reached around to his injured leg. He stopped and stared.

Was that...?

It disappeared behind something white, but he was sure he'd seen it. He squinted, craning his neck forward and bobbing his head for a better angle through the branches.

Yes, there.

No... gone again.

Oh, wait...

Was it...?

It disappeared yet again behind something big and black.

Kai kept watching. A bus, then a truck circled his island, blocking his view until a stream of ordinary small cars came.

He gasped.

Yes, that was it!

A warmth lit up his heart, and for an instant, the searing pain in his leg vanished. He could see the black fence and part of the red-brick building, as well as the tiny glass-walled building.

His plan to howl and guide Mia home hadn't worked. In fact, he was lucky it hadn't ended in disaster. However, that he was still on the island meant the Gray Man couldn't reach him in his thorny bush. It was a safe place, so maybe the best plan was to wait here. One day Mia was sure to look out of one of the windows in the brick building or go to wait for a bus, then he'd howl until she saw him.

Yes, waiting was a good plan. After all, he was an expert at waiting, and the thorny bush was a superb lookout post from which to do it until his leg healed enough to out-run the Gray Man once more.

Kai watched the street for as long as he could, but his eyelids started to droop from exhaustion and lack of food. No matter how much he forced them open, they kept on fighting to close until he no longer had the strength to struggle. He slept.

The next day, the pain had eased enough for Kai to haul himself from under the thorny bush. With room to move, he twisted and licked all the gashes the thorns had slashed into his flesh, yet all the while, he watched the street.

By the time the sun was high in the sky, his stomach rumbled. He'd searched for food back in the old days, so he could find something if he needed to, but it would mean leaving his lookout post. That was not an option.

While the burning smell the cars spewed out overpowered many of the other smells on the island, something worthy of investigation caught his attention.

Swaying, he pushed up to stand on three legs, then achingly slowly lowered his right hind leg until the tips of his claws touched the ground. Easing down onto the pads of his paw, he put a little weight on that leg. His leg held firm.

That was good. Maybe his injury wasn't that bad after all.

He rested more heavily on that leg. A burning pain shot through his hindquarters like it was on fire. He yelped and whipped his paw back off the ground.

Holding his hurt leg off the ground, he hobbled to the far left of his tiny island.

He poked his snout into the dead leaves and sniffed as he nuzzled about. Snagging something between his jaws, he pulled it out of the dirt, then gingerly lay back down. He dropped a black-and-yellow wrapper on the ground, sandwiched it between his front paws and nibbled away at something brown and sweet that smelled like the stuff Mia sometimes enjoyed but would never share with him.

Constantly glancing through the breaks in the traffic, hoping for good news, he ripped the wrapper in two and licked the inside clean.

After eating, he hobbled back to the tree in the center of his island, still holding up his hind leg. Beside the tree, he resumed his watch duty, sitting upright and ignoring the biting pain in his leg because sitting gave him a better view than lying.

His stomach rumbled constantly. He couldn't remember the last time he'd eaten a proper meal, yet there was nothing else on his tiny island, so he had no choice but to ignore his cravings.

The sun set and streetlights bathed the area in a yellowy glow, and though nothing happened out of the ordinary, he still sat. Waiting and watching.

In the middle of the night, he gazed up at the sky and the white pinpricks shining like sparkling flowers in a meadow of black grass.

He remembered Dad and the beam of light arcing through the woods. Maybe the pinpricks weren't lights to guide loved ones home, as he'd thought so long ago, but tiny flashlights peering into the endless blackness for things that had been lost. If Mia wasn't in the red building, could she be holding one of those lights while she looked for him? It would explain why she'd been gone for so long, because they were so very far away. Even when he'd climbed the mountainside with her and been so very high, the lights hadn't gotten any closer, so the little things had to be as high as the clouds.

It was another mystery he had to solve. Another on a long, long list.

Finally, he drifted off to sleep. He dreamed of sitting with Mia to watch the green-sky-light dance above the lake and everyone who had ever lost anything found it beneath its magical glow.

The next day, while he was on duty, a silver car circled his island twice. When it came around a third time, Kai's heart pounded and his stomach clenched into a knot. He growled. Backing toward his protective thorny bush, he tensed his muscles as he pictured the Gray Man and his unbeatable pole stalking him for revenge.

The car window rolled down and a man leaned out.

Kai growled louder, slinking even farther back.

"Hey, dog!" the man shouted. "Catch!" He hurled something straight at Kai.

Kai tried to leap out of the way, but his injured leg buckled and he smashed into the ground. He yelped.

But then the strangest thing happened: a new scent ripped his thoughts away from the pain. He sniffed, then sniffed again, because what his nose was telling him didn't make any sense.

Wincing, he eased himself up and hobbled over to a flattened round lump lying next to his tree. His nose was never wrong, so he knew what it was, but he couldn't understand why it had appeared.

Pawing at it, Kai ripped away the wrapper with his claws. A fresh hamburger lay in the sun. He was so ravenous, its intoxicating smell made him dizzy.

Kai glanced around. He still remembered the cookie trick, so half expected to see a kick thundering toward him. But there wasn't one.

He sniffed the burger again, saliva stringing from his jaw onto it. No one else was on his island and the silver car was nowhere in sight, so...

He gobbled down the burger in just seconds, then returned to sit beside his tree on watch duty, the aching hollow in his stomach having disappeared for the first time in days.

* * *

The next morning, the silver car drove past again, and again the man threw a food parcel from his window.

Later that day, a chubby dark-skinned woman limped along the sidewalk, resting heavily on a cane as if it was a third leg. Her frizzy gray hair reminded Kai of the yellow flower that turned into a ball of white fluff after a few days. She stopped on the sidewalk opposite his island, swung her arm back, and hurled cooked sausages through the air. Most of them splattered onto the road, but three made it onto his island. He wolfed those down too.

Kai couldn't understand why these people were being kind to him. Mia and Dad had been, but that was because they were special. No one else had ever been special. Not one. Kai had met hundreds and hundreds of people on the street, so he knew that for a fact — a few had been cruel to him, yet most hadn't even noticed him. He was sure most people believed they were special, but did apathy qualify as a superpower?

* * *

Over the next few weeks, Kai's leg grew stronger until he was able to put his paw down when he walked, although his muscles were stiff and he still hobbled. Luckily, most days someone threw him something to eat, particularly the three-legged lady who came a few times per week. It was never enough to stop his stomach from regularly rumbling, but it was enough for him to fulfill his duty and sit beside his tree, waiting and watching.

One day, a green car stopped near the tiny glass-walled building. A man with no hair and a tall skinny man got out and walked closer and closer, finally stopping near where the Gray Man had stood all that time ago.

212

They waited for a break in the traffic and then jogged toward his island.

Kai spun around and darted under his thorny bush.

As the men came closer, Kai smelled meat. *Cookie trick. Danger! Danger!*

Kai crawled deeper into the undergrowth.

"It's okay, boy," Skinny Man said. "We're not going to hurt you."

Skinny Man crouched and reached in toward Kai, holding a piece of pork.

"Look. We have food for you." His voice was calm and gentle. "Come on out, boy. Come on."

Kai growled. He wasn't a naïve young dog anymore, so he wasn't falling for any tricks.

The other man crouched too and did happy-teeth. "Come on, dog. It's not safe for you here. Wouldn't you like a proper home?"

Kai shuffled even farther under the bush, spikes stabbing into his back. He was used to the pain of the thorns now, but he knew people weren't, which meant he was safe.

The men took a couple of steps away from the bush and stood staring down at it.

"I think we're onto a loser here, bud," said Skinny Man.

"If I go around the other side, maybe I can prod him out with a stick."

"Great." Skinny Man threw his hands up. "And I'll catch him without getting bitten, huh? A dog that size? Yeah, right."

"So what do you want to do?"

"I don't think we have much choice." Skinny Man pointed toward their car.

They threw the meat next to Kai's tree and went back to the car. He never saw them again.

As Kai watched from beside his tree one morning, a white flake drifted down from the sky and settled on his nose. For an instant, it was cold, then it magically changed into water. A warm glow filled Kai's chest as he remembered scampering in the white stuff with Mia, and how he always got a new box to play with around this time of

213

year. Oh, those boxes. Such wonderful gifts. Although, there was a mystery he'd never solved too: why Mia hid his boxes in colored paper and always filled them with junk. If he was lucky, one day she'd give him another box and maybe then he'd solve that riddle.

More white stuff fell — much more. Inches of it. The warm glow vanished, and Kai spent long, long days doing nothing but trembling. Though he moved into the thorny bush to sleep at night, he still shivered, but snuggled in a ball in all the brown leaves and shielded by the branches, it was warmer than outside.

Fewer people brought him food now. Whether it was because they were tired of doing it, or because the worsening weather meant they didn't want to make the trek to see him, he didn't know. Occasionally, the three-legged lady shuffled by and tossed him something, yet she seemed very unsteady on her feet, so he was sure it was a huge effort for her to make it to him.

When he wasn't watching for Mia, he watched the cars circling his island. He drooled as they went around and around, and he imagined what food those people might be eating and what they could throw him if they would only roll their window down. But it wasn't their fault — they were just people living easy lives, and such people didn't know what it was like to live a hard life, especially to be a dog all alone, so he couldn't blame them for not throwing him anything.

One morning, he woke up and couldn't stop shivering. The sky was one giant lump of gray and more and more bits of white just would not stop dropping on him. Kai was so cold. He couldn't bear to leave the underneath of the bush and the leaves into which he'd nestled. He was shaking so much he couldn't move his legs properly.

However, he had to do his duty.

He dragged himself out from under the bush. The white stuff was so deep it brushed his stomach as he lumbered through it to his tree.

Walking around in a circle, over and over and over, he gradually flattened a large enough area for him to sit and resume his watching and waiting. Peering over the wall of white, he shivered from the tip of his nose to the end of his tail.

As well as watching for Mia, Kai found himself watching for the

214

three-legged-woman, too. He prayed he'd see her hobbling along, see her arm pull back, then swing forward, and see food hurtling through the air. But no matter how hard he watched, or how hard he wished, she never came.

His stomach was so empty, it hurt like it was ripped open. As if to poke fun at him, his teeth knocked together, making clicking sounds like they were eating, even though he had nothing to eat.

White stuff fell and fell, and gloom closed in around him. Kai was so frozen through every part of his body hurt. Trembling, he sat hunched over, watching, as the gray day grew colder and colder, gnawing away every bit of warmth from his body.

Unable to feel his paws, he hoped walking around his island might warm him, so he pushed to stand but wavered and staggered sideways. After stumbling only a few steps, his legs gave way. Kai crashed into his tree and crumpled to the ground.

And all the while, the white stuff kept falling out of the sky.

Bit by bit, it buried him.

Chapter 39

Illuminated by the glow of the moon, two people lurched across Kai's tiny island toward a white mound near the tree, the white stuff crunching underfoot. At the mound, one knelt and scooped the freezing white away to reveal matted brown fur.

A woman's voice said, "Oh Lord, please don't let us be too late."

After more scooping, fingers gently worked their way underneath the motionless dog, then with the greatest care, powerful arms lifted the body up.

"I don't know, Mom," a man's voice said. "He's not moving. I can't tell if he's still breathing or not."

Mom draped a blue blanket over the dog in the man's arms, the man working it around the body to cocoon it.

"We've got to get him home, Ty," she said, "We can't be too late. We just can't."

The man cradled the dog to his chest as they tramped back through the knee-deep white stuff. A solitary car crept around the island, every so often its tires skidding on the compacted white. The pair let it pass, then crossed the road.

At a car parked nearby, the man placed the dog on the rear seat, Mom getting in the back at the other side while the man then got into the front.

"Put the heater on quick, Ty. On full," said Mom.

The car growled into action and the whooshing of air filled the interior.

Mom shuffled along the seat, closer to the dog. She eased up his head and laid it in her lap. After removing her gloves, she placed her warm hands on his head and neck.

"Come on, boy. Don't give up. Please, don't give up."

Kai's left eye flickered open. The three-legged lady who'd brought him food so many times did happy-teeth. Her round face was smothered in creases and sagged so much it looked like melted cheese.

"Ty, he's alive! Oh, thank God, he's alive."

A young man without a hair on his head glanced around from the front of the car, happy-teeth gleaming in the darkness.

Even though Kai recognized Mom and knew she must be kind to have brought him food, he wanted to run. They were taking him away from his island, where he waited for Mia. However, he struggled to keep one eye open, let alone stand.

The car crept along umpteen streets, then an icy wind bit at Kai as the back door opened and Ty reached in. He cradled Kai once more and carried him into a small house. Mom dashed to a black box with a glass door, pressed a switch, and flames shot up inside it.

"Lay him here." She pointed to the brown rug in front of the fire-box.

Ty laid Kai on the rug, still bundled in the blanket, but Mom pointed to the beige sofa.

"No, push that closer instead," she said, "so he can lay beside me."

Ty shoved the sofa closer to the fire-box and lifted Kai onto it.

Mom sat beside him and again rested her hand on his head.

"You're going to be okay now, boy." She stroked him. "You get warmed through and everything's going to be just fine, you'll see."

"Anything else before I take off?" said Ty.

"There's an empty cola bottle in the recycling bin. Fill it with hot water and wrap it in a towel, please."

Ty left the room, but Mom called after him. "Not boiling; hand hot. And bring a small bowl of the broth I prepared."

He came back a short time later, a bottle wrapped in a towel in one hand and a blue bowl with steam drifting up from the contents in the other. A smell similar to Kai's brown gunk wafted across the room.

Mom gently wedged the makeshift hot water bottle inside Kai's blanket with him, then held the bowl close to his snout.

"Can you manage to eat something?" She wafted the steam toward him. "Come on, boy, give it a try. It'll get you good and warm."

"It stinks," said Ty, opening his coat. "What is it?"

"A soup of dog food mixed with hot water, so it's easy to get down."

"Ewww, delicious."

Even though the food smelled delicious, Kai didn't have the strength to raise his head and lap up a single mouthful.

"No?" said Mom. "Do you need me to help?"

She placed the bowl in her lap, then cupped Kai's head in one hand and brought over a small spoonful of the warm broth with the other. Tipping it between his jaws, she let only a few drops dribble in so he didn't choke on it.

Kai swallowed.

"That's a good boy. We'll get you back on your feet in no time, won't we, hey?" She tipped in the last few drops, then got another spoonful and repeated the process.

Three spoons went down fine, but Kai was so weak he couldn't manage the fourth, and it dribbled out onto the sofa.

Mom dabbed it with a lacy white handkerchief. "Don't worry, boy, this will wash, and there's plenty more broth for later." She looked to Ty. "You be off now, we'll be fine."

She dragged a tartan throw from the back of the sofa and draped it over her knees.

Ty folded his arms. "Don't tell me you're thinking of sitting there all night."

"Of course not."

"Mom, you're not, are you?"

"I said not."

"So, you're going to go to bed and leave the dog here, right? You're not sitting up all night with him?"

She leaned closer to Kai and shielded her mouth from Ty with

218

her hand. "He thinks we're going to listen, but we're not, are we? We know what's best, don't we, boy, huh?"

"Mom."

"Tyrone, thanks for your help, but I've got it from here. Nothing you say is going to change that."

Ty rolled his eyes and heaved a breath. Zipping his coat back up, he strolled over to Mom, bent down, and kissed her on the cheek.

"Call me if you need anything." Ty headed for the door.

"Don't you worry about us now. We'll be fine, won't we, boy?" She leaned down to Kai and did happy-teeth.

Ty left.

Mom stayed with Kai in front of the fire-box. She stroked his head and talked to him in the gentlest of voices so he knew he wasn't alone.

"I don't know what kind of a life you've had, boy, but you're safe now. No more cold nights outside for you. I promise." She laid a hand on his side, his ribs visible. "And we'll soon have some meat back on those bones." She chuckled and patted her bulbous belly. "Though maybe not quite as much as on mine."

As the fire-box warmed his frozen body, her words warmed his frozen heart.

* * *

The next day, Kai woke up to find Mom asleep, her head drooping forward and mouth hanging open, but her hand still resting on his shoulder. He couldn't yet move enough to stand but could at least raise his head to see where he was.

Aside from the sofa and a matching chair, a rectangular black board faced into the room from one corner, while a long wooden box with small doors along the front hugged the wall underneath the window. An assortment of framed pictures was spread across the top of the unit, each showing people. The biggest one showed Mom and a white-haired man doing happy-teeth.

Kai twisted around to check what else he could see.

"Look who's awake." Mom stroked him. "How are we feeling today, boy? Well enough for a little breakfast?" She looked at a circular device hanging on the wall but did a double take. "Oh my! Maybe a little lunch, then."

She eased off the sofa, being careful not to disturb him, then left the room. Moments later, the smell of the soupy brown gunk drifted in, and she ambled back with a steaming bowl of it.

Lifting his head, she placed a stripy cloth under it and offered him the gunk soup. He tried to twist around onto his stomach to be in a better position to eat, so the food wouldn't fall out of his mouth, yet he didn't have the strength.

"It's okay." She smoothed the fur down his neck. "Don't struggle. You eat there. That's what the cloth's for."

Kai leaned forward and lapped a drop of the soup. It didn't just smell gorgeous but, it being hot, he could feel it gliding down inside him and radiating heat all the way through to warm him from the inside. He lapped again.

"That's it. Good boy. You eat it all up and you'll be running around again in no time."

Holding his head up well enough to finish his soup was so tiring that afterward, Kai dozed for the rest of the day.

Whenever he woke, the three-legged lady was there with him, never once abandoning him. Even though he didn't really know her, it made him feel safe.

* * *

Kai awoke the next morning to the sun glowing through the drapes. For the first time in days, he didn't feel cold. He stretched, pushing his forelegs out in front of him and thrusting his hind legs backward.

"Well, someone's feeling better, aren't they?" Mom did happy-teeth, gazing down from beside him. "Are we ready for breakfast?"

She left the room, and Kai again smelled brown gunk soup.

He twisted over onto his stomach and pushed his paws into the cushions of the sofa. Wavering, he managed to stand. He jumped down onto the floor, but still weak, collapsed in a heap on the carpet. Taking a deep breath, he pushed and stood again.

He sniffed. The gunk soup was somewhere through the door at

the back of the room on the left. He took a couple of teetering steps toward it, but Mom appeared in the doorway carrying a steaming bowl.

"Oh, someone certainly *is* feeling better. A lot better. Fantastic."

She placed the soup next to Kai and he wolfed it down.

"Now, let's see if we can avoid any little accidents, huh?"

Mom leaned down to support him and guided him to the front door, which she pushed open. Directly outside was a park even tinier than his island, with bushes down either side and a white fence at the front. Beyond that, cars tootled along.

With the ground still covered in white stuff, Kai took only three steps outside, then cocked his leg and peed on a plant pot that looked to have nothing but a lifeless brown twig poking up out of it.

After relieving himself, Kai sniffed the air. There wasn't a single scent he recognized.

With a tiny shiver, Kai hobbled back inside. When he was strong enough, he'd look for Mia once more, but to get to that point, he needed food and warmth. Lots of it.

Back in the living room, he plodded over to the sofa and managed to raise his front paws onto the sofa. However, when he tried to jump up, he just jerked forward an inch or two, lacking the strength to get off the floor. Mom stooped with a groan, then groaned again as she helped him up.

She let him settle, then sat beside him.

"Oh, I hadn't noticed you had a name tag." She took her reading glasses from a small table beside the sofa. "Now, let's see who you are."

Mom eased the disk on dangling from his blue-neck-band around and scrutinized it. "My name is Kai. If you find me, please call Mia Dubanowski: 555-4202."

Kai pricked his ears. Mia? Had she said Mia? Had he been brought here because Mom knew Mia?

Chapter 40

Mom lifted Kai's paw and shook it. "Hello, Kai, I'm Ellen. Pleased, to meet you. Now, let's see if we can't get you home."

His muscles weak, Kai struggled to sit up, but he managed, then he stared at Mom. She'd said the magic word: Mia. If he waited — and waiting was his specialty — he was sure she'd say it again and help him find her.

Mom took a fat sausage-shaped lump of black plastic from the small table, held it so its flat side faced up, and then tapped it with the index finger of her other hand. A small panel lit up. She checked the disk hanging from his neck again, then tapped the sausage numerous times before holding it to her ear.

An intermittent buzzing sound came from it. After a few seconds, a female voice spoke.

But the voice wasn't Mia's.

"Sorry, the number you have dialed is not in service. Sorry, the number you have dialed is not in service. Sorry..."

Mom rubbed his head. "Sorry, boy, but it looks like you're stuck with me."

Kai whined.

She did happy-teeth and patted him. "Oh, don't worry, I'll talk it through with Billy next time I visit him. He always helps me sort through problems."

Kai whined again.

Mia.

She'd said Mia, so where was she? Was she coming?

Mom lowered her face to his and kissed him on the nose.

"Now you're feeling better, Kai, maybe we'll have a short walk later. Would that cheer you up?"

Kai lay down, chin on his front paws, and stared at the door at the back of the room, praying it would open and Mia would saunter in. At least it was warm and safe at Mom's, making it an ideal place to wait while he healed.

Leaving him on the sofa, Mom busied herself by wiping a small yellow cloth over all the flat surfaces in the room, methodically working her way around as if it was an important ritual. After she'd wiped the top of the wooden box near the window, and Kai craned to look, yet he could see no difference. Mom was nice but had a bad case of people-crazy. Just his luck!

The wiping ritual complete, Mom bustled from the room and returned with a tatty brown walking-cord, which she fastened to Kai's blue-neck-band. She coaxed him from the sofa with a cookie, then they ventured outside together. Kai hobbled because the leg the car hit didn't like the cold and as if to keep him company, Mom hobbled too, using her cane as her third leg, which seemed a clever idea. He wondered if it was the same car that had hit her and hurt her leg.

There were no houses like Mia's around Mom's place. No woods either. But neither were there monstrous buildings rearing over him like around the hot dog truck. The buildings were small and low, each having only two floors and their own private minuscule park at the front. They were all pretty much the same, with a door between two windows on the bottom floor, then more windows above that. However, the minuscule parks were quite different, even under the blanket of white stuff. Some had large white mounds with twigs and greenery poking out, while others had nothing except a flat expanse of white.

Kai limped along the sidewalk, part of which was scraped clear of white stuff, arcing his head from side to side so he could sniff as many of the new scents bombarding him as possible: new people, new animals, new places. It was impossible to identify most of them, so he was just happy to relish all the new aromas, with the prospect of solving the mystery as to what object they belonged to being a treat for another day.

Together, Kai and Mom lurched down to the corner of the street where another road cut across it. By the time they stopped, Kai's tongue was lolling out and he panted.

Mom peered down at him. "Looks like that's enough for today, doesn't it, boy? Shall we go back?"

Kai slumped to the cold ground, his chest heaving as he gulped air.

"Well, I think that answers my question, doesn't it, Kai?"

Slowly, they ambled home, and within a few minutes, Kai was back in his place on the sofa.

* * *

Over the weeks, their walks took them farther and farther, especially once the white stuff disappeared and the days started getting warmer. With all the gunk soup, care, and gentle exercise, Kai got stronger and stronger, so hobbled less, yet he worried his back leg would never be as good as it had once been.

Mom puzzled him, though. She had her own warm soup, rested on the sofa most of the time too, and never walked faster than he did, and yet her bad leg never seemed to get any better. In fact, the farther they walked, the more she hobbled.

Kai felt a warmth blooming inside him. This was a mystery — a genuine mystery — and he loved solving mysteries.

One afternoon when the sun beamed from a glorious blue sky, they went for their longest walk yet and ended up in a huge park. The broken trees were starting to burst back into life, with tiny green blobs emerging from the ends of their lifeless limbs. In the patches of brown ground, small green shoots stuck up, some even having delicate white flowers that drooped downward.

"Let's see how good you're feeling, shall we?" said Mom.

She pulled a red ball from her big blue bag and threw it high into the air. Kai raced after it. The ball bounced and bounced, but the third time, Kai leapt up and snatched it in his jaws. He trotted back to Mom and dropped it at her feet.

"Oh, bravo, Kai. Your leg hardly seems to be bothering you at all now." She threw the ball again.

Kai raced after the ball time and again, while Mom stood in the one place, hurling it for him. After only a few minutes, they were both panting heavily, so Mom led them over to a wooden bench. Mom sat with a groan and Kai collapsed at her feet, his tongue dangling out of the side of his mouth. He was stronger, yet he still wasn't as strong as he had been back in those days with Mia in the woods. It seemed so long ago now. A lifetime ago.

For some time, the only close sound was Mom's labored breathing, but then that disappeared. Kai liked the silence. With the right companion, silence could say things that words would only spoil.

She leaned forward and tousled his fur. "I think it's time you met my Billy. I visit him once a month and tell him all my news but had to skip it last time because you were still so weak. Do you want to come with me next time?"

Chapter 41

Lounging on the sofa beside Mom, Kai studied her as she dozed. Could she be his new alpha? At least until he found Mia. She did everything a good alpha should do and more: she'd found a safe, warm home; she provided food; and she'd healed him when he was sick.

Yes, she was an alpha. A good alpha. It was strange she didn't have her own pack already. Maybe she'd lost everyone. Or maybe the Gray Man had stolen them. Whatever the reason, she didn't deserve to be alone. Maybe when Kai found Mia and Dad, Mom could live with them in one big pack.

Mia.

Now he was stronger, he needed to devise a new plan to find her — one that included Mom joining them. Formulating such a plan would take a lot of work, but luckily, he had plenty of time.

Her mouth agape, Mom made a strange rumbling grunting noise.

Kai winced. The noise wasn't as irritating as those Mia had made when she'd first gotten her hollow-wood-machine, but considering how sensitive his hearing was, this one really grated.

He shuffled around to face away from her.

The rumble came again, seeming to drill right through him to jar every bone in his body.

He winced again.

Most times, Kai was far too polite to disturb Mom when she

made this ungodly racket, but this time, the sound was so loud the sofa seemed to shake.

Kai barked, then pretended to be asleep.

Mom snorted and woke up with a jerk.

"Oh, look at me — asleep and it isn't even lunchtime."

Wanting to show how much he appreciated his temporary alpha, and feeling a little guilty at the trick he'd played, Kai licked Mom's hand.

She did happy-teeth and scratched him under the chin.

"Well, it's a big day today. Shall we have lunch and then be off?"

With a groan, she heaved up off the sofa and dawdled into the kitchen.

After Mom had her usual cup of hot brown water and two slices of bread spread with fruity purple goo, she went upstairs for quite some time. When she returned, she was dressed in matching blue clothes, her hair had been moved into a nice shape, so it curled more than usual, and she'd painted colors onto her face that made it look brighter and healthier.

"Are you ready, Kai? I just know Billy's going to love you."

On leaving the house, they headed out as if they were going to the park, but they didn't have the ball, so it looked like it was going to be an ordinary walk. Luckily, on the way, Mom tied his walking-cord to a streetlight and wandered into a stuff-building. Mom seemed to find every kind of stuff imaginable in stuff-buildings. It was like her magic power — no matter what stuff she wanted, she knew exactly in which building she'd find it and would amble out with her big blue bag looking heavier and bulkier. Kai never tired of watching this fascinating trick.

He stared at the door, hoping Mom had gone in for a new ball as theirs was at home.

Unfortunately, when Mom came out, she had nothing but a piece of plant in her hand, which seemed odd. It was a twig from some kind of thorny bush, but not the kind with the archway through it, nor the kind on his island. No, this one was a thin, thorny stick, about as long as Mom's arm, with a single red flower at one end.

What good was a thing like that?

He hoped she wasn't going to throw that for him to fetch. Apart from the spikes stabbing him, it would snap way too easily. When they all lived with Mia and Dad, Mr. Paget would have to give Mom lessons on finding the perfect stick. That was his magic power.

They strolled down the sidewalk and at the lights that stopped the cars, instead of turning right to go to the park, they turned left. Far from disappointed, Kai wagged his tail all the more — the scent of grass and flowers was blowing toward them, so there was obviously another park he didn't know about.

Eventually, they came to a fence made of black metal bars that stood in front of bushes so tall it was impossible to see anything beyond them. Luckily, Kai didn't have to see; he could smell. Grass, flowers, trees... It was a new park. Fantastic. A whole new world to explore.

Mom led them through an opening, only for Kai to frown. It was a very odd park. The oddest he'd ever seen.

Narrow paths crisscrossed a vast flat area with trees dotted here and there. Down each of these paths, on either side, were rows of big flat stones standing upright, each with strange scratched markings on them. Some of the stones had fresh flowers in front of them, while others had only brittle brown ones. Others leaned badly, as if they could fall over at any moment, or were dirty and broken, obviously long forgotten about by those who had put the scratches upon them.

Mom pointed into the center of the park. "Billy's on K4."

They strolled along one of the main tree-lined avenues, passing row after row after row of flat upright stones. Sadly, the scent of so many fresh flowers overpowered many of the other smells Kai longed to savor.

A few other people were scattered across the park, but they were too far away to smell or to see clearly. Most seemed to have brought even more blooms, as if the place didn't stink flowery enough.

All in all, this new park was a huge disappointment.

At a small marker on the ground, Mom led them along one of the narrower paths between the stones. Finally, she stopped and gazed down at a brown stone with scratches highlighted in white.

"Hello, Billy, my love."

Little pools of water formed in the bottoms of her eyes.

She stared at the stone for some time. Not moving, not talking, not doing anything except looking, as though she wasn't seeing what was there but something conjured by her mind. Turning away, Mom heaved a huge breath.

A small bench only big enough for one person to sit on sat a few feet away. Mom looped Kai's walking-cord over it.

"Stay," she said, an index finger raised to him.

Kai sat down.

"Good boy."

He didn't know why they were there, yet it had to be important, so he could wait until it was time to play.

Tottering over to the stone, Mom took a lacy white handkerchief from her pocket and dabbed at her eyes. She ran her hand over the stone's smooth surface the same way she did over Kai's back, then laid the thorny flower on top.

Her voice wavered. "Oh, Billy, you don't know how much I miss you."

After a moment of silence, she said, "I've brought a new friend I want you to meet. This is Kai, Billy. He was abandoned and all but died, so he lives with me now. You won't believe how good he is. No trouble at all. I couldn't ask for a better friend. Well..." Pools formed in her eyes again. "You know what I mean."

Kai glanced around, sniffing the air. So many new scents again. With the breeze blowing into his face, he could only sense the scents from in front of him, but that was more than enough to keep him occupied, especially as it was difficult to separate them all out because of the overpowering flowers.

However, Kai snapped back to the moment when Mom took a large candy bar from her pocket. He wagged his tail, smelling its sweetness.

Mom looked at him. "Don't you be getting excited, chocolate's bad for dogs. But don't worry, I haven't forgotten about you."

She took a plastic bag from her pocket and opened it. Kai wagged his tail even more, smelling its contents.

Mom threw him a yellow chewy stick that tasted meaty. She often found them in one of the stuff-buildings, and while they weren't strips of heaven, they tasted wonderful.

She opened the candy bar, broke off two squares, then put one on the stone next to the flower and ate the other herself.

She talked to the stone and shared the chocolate — one piece for her, one piece for it. Every so often, she dabbed her eyes with a handkerchief.

Growing restless with so many new sights and scents, Kai toddled around, investigating what he could reach with his nose before the walking-cord pulled taut, at which point he toddled another way. While smelling some particularly interesting footprints, he realized he'd wandered a surprising distance from Mom. Glancing around, he saw the walking-cord trailing on the ground.

Mom was far too busy to disturb, chatting away to the brown stone as she was, so he meandered away to entertain himself.

He'd only gone a few steps when the wind ruffled the fur on his shoulders, blowing from a different direction.

Kai gasped and froze. What was that?

He turned his face into the wind and sniffed, long and hard.

The faintest of scents wafted toward him. He arced his snout from side to side, gathering as much air as he could in his nostrils, partly to confirm the direction from which the scent was coming, but mainly to confirm it was what he thought it was.

The smell came from a long way off, so most of it was lost in the wind, but...

He sucked in more air.

That did smell remarkably like...

No, it couldn't be. Not after all this time. Surely not.

He ambled forward into the wind, toward the smell. Drawing in a huge breath, he sifted through all the different scents it contained — discarding all the ones from trees, bushes, birds, flowers, people, animals, dirt, stone...

230

His nose was never wrong, and right now, it was telling him someone he knew might be nearby. Someone from a life he thought was long gone.

Kai's heart hammered and something fluttered in his chest like a bird fluttering against the bars of a cage.

It couldn't be. It really couldn't be.

Could it?

Behind him, Mom continued her conversation, so Kai took another step forward. Then another. And another. With each step, the scent got stronger, until—

Kai gasped.

His nose was never wrong, and it was confirming what he rarely dared to even dream.

Chapter 42

Gravel crunching under his paws, Kai trotted along the path and away from Mom, deeper into the park. His mind whirled with the confusion of thoughts and possibilities. He glanced back; Mom was still distracted and chatting.

He glanced ahead again. Somewhere out there, amid all the stones, was Dad.

Mom was a good alpha, and she'd been so kind to him, but Dad... Dad meant only one thing: Mia.

The thought of seeing her again was more than Kai could take and his superpower for waiting deserted him.

He ran.

Ran as fast as his pumping legs would carry him, following his nose and the scent that would take him back to his beloved pack – the scent from a life he was beginning to fear he might never live again.

He shot past stone after stone after stone, ignoring the paths, ignoring the scratchings, ignoring everything except the primal instinct to be with those he truly belonged.

The scent grew stronger and stronger.

And he flew faster and faster

Way ahead, a figure lumbered into the distance along one of the other tree-lined avenues. Kai sniffed. His nose was never wrong, so he bolted along the path in pursuit.

Pictures swirled through Kai's head: Mia sitting by his fluffy-bowl,

Mia sneaking strips of heaven to him under the table, Mia scratching her metal wires in the wood...

Kai leapt over one of the stones, then another, and tore along another path. He had found Dad, and now he was going to find Mia.

"Help!" A shout came from behind him.

Kai ignored it. He wanted his old pack. He needed his old pack.

"Help! Please, someone!"

The shouting, the birds singing, the gravel crunching... it was all meaningless noise.

Kai pumped his legs harder and harder as the distant figure drew closer and closer.

"Help!"

Digging his claws into the gravel, Kai skidded to a halt, raking brown ruts across the ground. He turned and looked back. It wasn't meaningless noise — it was Mom. Something was wrong.

Kai peered at the figure slowly disappearing once more into the blurry distance. If he ran like the wind, Kai might catch Dad.

But Mom was in trouble. Big trouble, if the panic in her voice was any indication. He looked back.

What should he do? What should he do? What should he do?

Chapter 43

Kai glanced from the area in which he'd left Mom and back to Dad in the distance, then to Mom again.

It was an impossible choice, but he had to decide. Had to. Somehow.

He peered each way again. Dad was even smaller now, and soon, he'd be gone forever. Mom? Kai couldn't see her from where he stood. He sniffed. Nothing. Sniffed harder. Still nothing. The wind that had blown Dad's scent to him was blowing Mom's in the opposite direction away from him, and with it, whatever was causing the problem.

How could he decide? How?

In an instant, he knew. It was obvious, like waking from a dream and realizing what was real and what wasn't.

He had to do the only thing a good dog could do.

He shot along the path, head down, paws pounding the ground, back toward Mom.

Dad was his pack, yes, but Mom was his pack too, and she needed him because something was wrong. The pack was the important thing, more important than any individual member, and his pack was in trouble. Kai had no choice but to protect the pack. No matter what it cost him.

As he bolted back to her, he sniffed the air, desperately trying to solve the mystery of what was causing the trouble. However, he was still upwind of Mom, so all the scents were being blown in the wrong direction.

"Help!"

Kai leapt over a large black stone, then another. He shot along the path and swung a hard right onto another.

Mom whipped her cane through the air in front of her while cowering and staggering backward.

"Help!"

Before her, like a nightmare brought to life, growled Hound.

The fur on Hound's back stood on end and the beast's fangs gleamed in the sunlight. Hound snapped at Mom.

She shrieked and tottered back.

Trying to shield herself behind her arms, she said, "That's all I had. You've eaten it all." She flung the empty candy wrapper at Hound.

Daggerlike teeth snatched it out of the air, but then the dark beast spat the empty wrapper out.

Hound snarled and stalked closer.

Kai leapt, flying through the air and smashing into the big black dog. They tumbled across the ground, a mass of tails and flailing legs.

Breaking free, Kai scrambled to his feet. Hackles raised and teeth bared, he snarled.

Hound snarled back.

When they'd first met, Kai's nose had barely reached Hound's chest, but now, Kai was a fully grown dog — big, muscular, powerful. His nose still wasn't as high off the ground as Hound's, but it wasn't far off. Not that size mattered. What mattered was the strength gained from doing the right thing — protecting the pack.

Kai glowered at the monstrous dog, its right ear now ragged and a scar hugging its muzzle. A tough life gave it no right to terrorize the innocent.

Kai lunged, chomping at the black beast.

Hound dodged and swiped with its paw.

Claws raked Kai's ribs, but Kai twisted and sank his teeth into Hound's shoulder.

Hound yelped. He bucked and rammed his head into Kai. They rolled across the grass again, all gnashing teeth and slashing claws.

Mia's and Mom's love had worked miracles — Kai wasn't just bigger and stronger now, he was in far better condition than any street dog could ever hope to be.

Kai pummeled Hound and forced the animal onto its back. He snapped and snapped at the black dog as it squirmed in the dirt, struggling to evade the onslaught. However, it could only escape Kai's wrath for so long.

Kai clamped his jaws around one of Hound's forelegs. He crushed with all his might.

Hound shrieked.

But Kai hadn't finished. He had to be sure Hound knew to leave his pack alone and that, if it didn't, the punishment would be extreme. Kai shook his head from side to side, yanking on the leg as he bit it. Hound wailed all the more.

Finally, Kai let go.

Hound clambered to its feet. As if believing it could still win the battle, the big dog snarled again.

But Kai snarled back, then charged.

Turning tail, Hound shot away along the path. Kai raced after it. He had to ensure Hound never came back and never came near his pack again.

Hound swerved around three stones and onto another path. Kai tore after it. He needed one more bite — just one more stab of pain — so Hound was in no doubt about what would happen if they ever met again.

Kai closed in on the big dog as it bolted down one of the wider paths lined with trees.

Closer.

Closer.

So close Kai could almost bite the tuft at the end of Hound's tail.

Kai tensed his muscles to pounce and teach the black dog that if it ever showed its face again, Kai would rip it to pieces.

He leapt.

236

A pole swung out from behind one of the trees and a loop hooked over Kai's head, yanking him out of the air. He smashed into a big gray stone, then crashed to the ground. The noose tightened around his throat, so tight he couldn't breathe.

He kicked to stand up, but the Gray Man stepped out from behind the tree, raised his end of the pole, and shoved the other end against the ground to pin Kai down.

Hound skidded to a stop on the gravel path, then turned back. It pounced, locking its massive fangs around Kai's throat.

Kai kicked and bucked to break free. He writhed in the dirt, struggling to escape both the teeth and the noose, but he couldn't fight both of them at the same time.

"Let him go!" shouted Mom. "That's my dog! Let him go!"

Hobbling as quickly as she could, she lurched up behind the Gray Man and pounded him with her cane.

The man cowered as the cane hammered down on his head and back again and again, and he dropped his pole.

Released, Kai twisted back and forth, lashing out with his paws. He broke Hound's hold and sank his teeth into one of the dog's legs.

The Gray Man dashed in. He heaved a kick into Hound's side, sending the beast cartwheeling into the dirt. However, before the man could retrieve his pole, Hound turned to run.

Hound made it only a few steps, then the Gray Man's colleague arrived and snared it with his own pole.

Kai scrambled up.

His pack safe, he took a tottering step toward Mom but then collapsed.

Wincing with the pain, Mom crouched down to him.

"Oh, what have they done to you, boy? What have they done?"

Kai's neck felt wet and a thick liquid pooled in his mouth, so much that he gurgled as he struggled to breathe.

"Fetch the van. Quick," said the Gray Man to his colleague. "We need to get this dog to a vet as soon as possible."

He knelt beside Mom and squashed his hand over the wound in Kai's throat. "If we can stop the bleeding, he has a chance."

Salty-water streamed down Mom's face. "What the devil did you think you were doing? Look at him. Look what you've done."

"I'm so sorry. We were told there was a dangerous dog here menacing people for food."

"Does he *look* like a dangerous dog?" Mom stroked Kai's head. "Hold on, Kai. You hold on, you hear?"

Kai looked up at the old lady. She'd been so good to him, but she looked so upset, and he couldn't bear that. He hoped he hadn't done something bad to hurt her, because he never intended to be anything except the best dog he could be.

Worried Mom being in pain was his fault, he used what little energy he could muster and, trembling with the effort, turned his head and licked her hand. He didn't have a lot of his magic power left, but he had enough to help Mom. He'd brought a lot of worry and a lot of struggle into her life, but he hoped he'd brought a little joy too.

He licked her only once before the strain of holding his head up became too much and he slumped back down.

"Hold on, Kai. Please, hold on."

Salty-water dripped onto his snout. He couldn't feel it — strangely, he couldn't feel much of anything anymore — but he could smell it.

Then he sensed something else, though it didn't feel like it was his nose sensing it. Or his eyes or his ears. But what else could it be? He didn't understand why it was telling him what it was, but his nose was never wrong, so...

Though he didn't want to upset Mom even more, there was something he had to do. He didn't know why; it was just a feeling.

He struggled to push up but collapsed.

Mom eased a hand down on his shoulder. "Stay there, boy, till we can get help."

No. He had to get up. Had to.

He tried again.

Kai clambered to his feet, strings of thick red water running from his mouth. His legs trembling, he swayed, then collapsed again.

Panting, he reached out in front of him and heaved himself forward. He didn't know why, but something was drawing him, calling

238

him even though he couldn't hear any voice or smell any scent.

"Kai, stay still, boy. Help's coming." Mom caressed his side.

He pulled again and again. Scraping across the ground. Inch by inch.

"Can't you get him to stay still?" said the Gray Man.

"I don't know what to do." She looked up at the man, her face twisted with desperation. "Help me!"

The Gray Man laid his hand on Kai's back and eased down to pin Kai in that spot.

Kai snarled. The man whipped his hand away, jerking back beyond Kai's reach, and Kai crept forward again.

He said, "It's like he wants to go somewhere."

"Where? Where can he go like this?" Mom's voice broke as she spoke. "Please, Kai, don't move. Just wait."

Kai knew he could wait for Mom to heal him again, and though he was an expert at waiting — world-class — today was not a day for waiting. No, not today.

Kai kept hauling himself onward. He had to be somewhere. He didn't know why, he just did. As if an invisible thread reached deep down into him to lead him on, there was no way he could resist going where it was drawing him.

His legs didn't want to walk, and horrendous pain spread across his throat, but nothing was going to stop him from finding this special place that was calling to him.

He crawled. And crawled.

Mom and the Gray Man shuffled along behind him.

Finally, his trembling legs gave out and he crumpled in front of two matching big black stones. Though the searing pain from his throat drilled through his entire body like hot knives, he felt at peace — as if he'd come home after a long and arduous journey and finally sunk into his beloved fluffy-bowl. As if he was exactly where he always belonged.

The old lady gasped, looking at the gold-colored scratchings on one of the big black stones. She stared at it, eyes wide.

Her hand shaking, she clutched her mouth and read a single word, "Mia."

One word. A word Kai never thought he was going to hear again. One so soft, musical, and magical, he'd ached to hear it for such a long time. But the word now sounded distant. So, so far away. Like a whisper voiced at the far end of a long hallway.

He was tired. So tired. His eyelids drooped like someone was pulling them down, and no matter how hard he fought, they wouldn't stay up. He shook his head and managed to pry his eyes open again, yet the light started growing dim, as if the day was coming to an end. And he felt so unbelievably tired.

Maybe if he rested, for just a moment, he'd feel better.

At the foot of the big black stone, he laid his head on his front paws. He gazed at the fresh pink flowers in a vase and imagined the happy-teeth Mia would do if she could see them.

The old lady crouched beside him with salty-water streaming down her face.

"No. No. No." She stroked his back. "No, Kai. No. Stay with me, boy. Stay with me till help comes. Please, Kai."

Kai's eyelids drooped lower and lower.

What a day it had been. The best of days. He couldn't have asked for a better day than one in which he could prove what a good dog he was by fighting to defend his pack. Yes, a wonderful day. If he was lucky, maybe tomorrow would be even better.

Kai closed his eyes, and the world turned black. And all the scents faded...

... faded...

... faded...

Gone.

Chapter 44

Kai's eyes flickered open. Mom and the Gray Man had disappeared. All the big stones had disappeared. In fact, everything that had been there had disappeared. Including the crushing pain in his throat.

Kai pushed to his feet. His bad leg that had always felt so stiff since the car incident didn't feel stiff. That was good. But where was he?

He glanced around.

Before him, a meadow speckled with different-colored flowers stretched away toward mountains, their jagged peaks clawing at the sky. To his right, a rainbow swept down to brush the leaves of woodland trees.

The place felt like somewhere he should know, somewhere safe, yet he knew he'd never been here.

However, it wasn't the sights that tantalized his senses.

There was a noise. A noise he remembered from long, long ago. He listened as it drifted on the wind toward him. More a blur of sound than something coherent.

"... lived in a moldy...

... take you out for walks."

It couldn't be...

Could it?

Something else drifted toward him too. A scent.

A scent that made his heart pound with joy and warmth fill his body, as if he were lying in their special place on a glorious summer's morning.

He ran, following his nose, because his nose was never wrong.

He bounded through the long grass and the tall green stems with bright flowers on the ends. The noise grew louder, and the scent grew stronger.

"But now I'll be your true best friend,
And love you till time meets its end."

The mystery driving him on faster and faster, he raced toward what he hoped was the solution.

A breeze parted the grass ahead, and for just an instant, he saw the back of a girl with long, flowing black hair.

He flew toward her. Flew faster than he'd ever run before.

And suddenly...

... he was there.

"Then as the stars fall from the sky,
I'll sing to you this lullaby."

He stood, heart thumping, staring at the girl from behind.

Could it really be? Or was his nose really, really wrong?

She turned.

Did happy-teeth.

Happy-teeth just for him.

She knelt, holding her arms out wide. Kai bounded over to her, feeling like he just couldn't run quickly enough. As she flung her arms around him to hug him, he pushed his front paws up onto her shoulders, and entwined, they fell over into the grass and flowers.

She lay on her back, hacking and hacking and hacking, while Kai stood over her, licking and licking and licking.

He'd been a good dog. He'd waited and waited and waited, like he knew a good dog was supposed to, and now, all that waiting had paid off — his dream had come true.

It was Mia. It was Mia. IT WAS MIA!

The End.

As The Skies Cry

If you enjoyed *As The Stars Fall*, you must read *As The Skies Cry*!

To Win in Life, Sometimes Your Only Choice is to Lose.

When his master dies, Harley loses everything: his home, his best friend, his reason for living. Alone on the city streets, he whimpers, while struggling to evade the dangers that lurk in the shadows.

Across town, Rachel aches to hug her autistic son, yet he's so withdrawn he pulls away if she reaches out. She cries about it at night. The last thing she needs is another headache, such as a stray dog latching onto her.

However, when her son and Harley meet, magic happens — suddenly, the boy talks and plays and loves. He's the son she'd always dreamed of, but never thought she'd meet.

But just when her gloomy future bursts into dazzling color, an unexpected phone call tears her world apart...

Read *As The Skies Cry*. Use this link:
www.stevenleebooks.com/sx9s

FREE Book

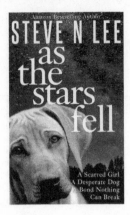

This is an exclusive ebook for *As The Stars Fall* readers only.

If you enjoyed *As The Stars Fall*, you need the accompanying ebook written by Steve especially for you. In this ebook, you will:

> discover how the story started out as something completely different

> unravel how the characters were created

> learn why the cover was a huge problem

> read never-before-seen example texts from the story's very first incarnation

> enjoy a revealing extended interview with Steve

> choose from a whole new selection of Book Club Questions

> find exclusive images from Steve's personal collection

> and uncover much, much more.

To get *As The Stars Fall*, please use this link:
www.stevenleebooks.com/7r6y

Interview with Steve N. Lee

You're known for your gritty crime thrillers, so what inspired you to write As The Stars Fall?

I think it was a number of things. Firstly, donkey's years ago, my partner, Ania, told me about an abandoned dog that had lived on a traffic island for some time. I'd always liked that as a story idea but could never see how it could translate into something of book length.

Secondly, last year, we lost our three-year-old cat in a road accident. We'd had him since he was a kitten, when we'd discovered that he wasn't just visiting our garden every day but actually living under one of the bushes, presumably because some monster had kicked him out. We're both huge animal lovers, so we took him in and named him Trouble. Losing him was devastating. Like losing family.

On top of losing Trouble, we also lost a number of other people around that time, so on some level, I think the story came about as some sort of subconscious catharsis. Once I got the idea, I set out to write the kind of story I'd enjoy reading — one that's funny, yet insightful; heartbreaking, yet heartwarming. One that can move even a hard-hearted Yorkshireman like me!

How did the story develop?

Well, amazingly, it came to me one morning in bed. I do a lot of my best brainstorming first thing in the morning, and this story came more or less fully formed after lying there for an hour or so. I haven't a clue why I suddenly thought of Ania's story of the dog on the traffic island for my mind to get working piecing it all together.

The weird thing is that it started as an idea for a kid's picture book, so that's how I developed it to begin with. I even researched picture book artists. It was only when I realized that it might be too dark and too complex for that medium that I thought about expanding it.

Was it touching as you were writing it?
Oh, you better believe it!

Even though I'd created every word, I still found it incredibly moving. Some parts, I just couldn't work on without welling up.

Had you read many dog stories beforehand?

Not a single one. I didn't even know such things existed outside children's fiction. I'd heard of *Marley & Me* because I like Jennifer Aniston (I was a big *Friends* fan!), but I didn't know it was adapted from a book. I was shocked when I discovered there were dog books that had sold millions of copies.

It was only after I'd mapped out my story that I discovered these other books. However, I didn't want anything to influence my work, so I completed my first novel-length draft before reading any of them. Then in January 2020, confident I had a good, solid draft, I bought around eight dog stories to see what other authors had done, starting with the "big three": *The Art of Racing in the Rain* by Garth Stein, *Marley & Me* by John Grogan, and *A Dog's Purpose* by W. Bruce Cameron.

Was it easy writing from an animal's perspective?

In some ways, it was very freeing. I especially liked being able to look at our world in a lopsided way. However, in other ways, it created a number of problems. For example, dogs can't see red, so if I created the world accurately, it would make the color palette very boring, with some things being blue or yellow but everything else being gray. Dogs make their world more interesting with scents, but of course, you don't have that option with a book, so because this is fiction, I forsook accuracy in favor of creating a colorful world for the reader to enjoy.

Ultimately, Kai was a character like any other, so I didn't think of him as a dog but a person with some dog-like tendencies, which any dog lover will tell us is pretty much what a dog is anyway.

Is there a religious element to the ending?

No. I have a spiritual side, but I'm not religious (as will be obvious to readers of my thrillers which are crammed with dark, gritty realism). I'd like to think that if there is some sort of heaven, we'll meet not only the people we've loved again but the animals that shared our lives and made them so special. If my four-legged loved ones aren't there waiting for me, I tell you, the "big guy" better expect protest marches!

So what do you say to people who think the ending is mushy fantasy that ruins a good story?

Simple. I say, prove that isn't what really happens when you die and I'll delete it.

What breed of dog is Kai?

The cover shows a Rhodesian ridgeback, which I chose simply because that one has such a wonderfully expressive face.

That aside, I picture Kai as a mutt, not a pedigree. Quite a big dog, with thick but not long or curly fur. Mainly brown. So more some sort of Lab or German shepherd cross than anything like a Chihuahua, poodle, or boxer. Truth be told, once I got into his head and his wonderful way of seeing the world, looks didn't come into it — he became any dog and every dog.

Do you have a dog?

Not currently. At the moment, we have two black cats. One was a stray that arrived in our garden one day and never left, just like Trouble, while the other was an abused kitten we adopted from a rescue center.

What's next? A sequel/prequel to As the Stars Fall?

For a long time, the answer was always a hard No. Unless a book or movie can be improved upon by continuing the story, I believe it's best to leave well enough alone. For me, *As The Stars Fall* is the perfect dog story, so because I felt I could never better it, I was determined to get back to my thrillers. And then came October 13th, 2020.

You had an idea for another dog story?

Wouldn't you just know it! An idea came to me when I didn't want it to.

Anyway, this idea had serious potential, so I spent a few days playing with it and... As The Skies Cry was born.

So is it like a 'Kai and Mia II', but with different characters?
The story is just as simultaneously heartwarming and heartbreaking as As The Stars Fall, but it's a very different tale. There was no way I was going to rehash a story I loved so much because it would be doing it a disservice. Like I said, I wanted something original, something that explored different ideas.

Obviously, it's in the same vein as As The Stars Fall, but it's wholly original, because I made some crucial changes, the biggest one being that only part of it is told from the dog's point of view.

This story focuses on a mother, her autistic son, and a dog, but is much more of an ensemble piece – the dog is still vital to the story and much of it centers around him, but the mother and child get their chance to shine too. I'm really excited about it. Especially about writing as Mom because she's such a fascinating character.

Does that mean your thrillers are on the back burner again?
Well, I'm hoping to write As The Skies Cry and the next book in my Angel of Darkness thriller series at the same time. I love my anti-hero, Tess, not least because she has a slanted view of the world. I think that's what draws me to those books – not the high-octane action, which is an absolute blast to write, but being able to see the world through her eyes. I think it's that combination of action and character development that keeps readers coming back to the series, too.

I've also got other ideas in various stages of development, from rough notes to completed drafts – a psychological thriller, a comedy, a zombie apocalypse, a ghost story... I'm aching get to those.

So you want to branch out into even more genres? Like James Patterson
Oh, yeah. Just one problem: so many ideas, so little time!

To enjoy an extended interview with Steve, please use this link
www.stevenleebooks.com/7r6y

Will You Help?

I'm just an ordinary person like you, so don't have some big New York publishing house to spread the word about my work, but instead, rely on kind readers taking just a moment to post a short review online.

If you enjoyed *As The Stars Fall*, will you help me spread the word about it, please? It will only take a few seconds to post a short review and yet it will make a tremendous difference.

But please remember to keep the story's secrets, so others can discover the magic for themselves.

Thank you!

www.stevenleebooks.com/s9p4
(Either search for the title yourself or use this link which will take you straight to it.)

Book Club Questions

SPOILERS!

Some plot elements have been revealed in order to provide interesting questions, including the ending. If you have not yet finished the book, please read no further.

Below is a varied selection of questions from which you can pick and choose the most suitable ones for your particular club. Want more questions? Click here!

1. Kai is badly injured by fighting a dog against which he obviously had no chance. Why was he so determined to prove himself in such an unequal matchup?

2. When they meet, Kai and Mia are both suffering horrendous loss, but later, each finds comfort in the companionship of the other. Do you believe animals can play a role in the healing process, and if so, how?

3. Kai and Mia comfort each other after both experiencing nightmares, which strengthens their bond, making these two events a significant turning point in the story. What are the other major turning points?

4. Kai searches tirelessly for Mia, not understanding what has happened to her, finally keeping vigil outside her old school. How common do you feel such loyalty is in a dog? (If you think never, here are just three to start you off: Greyfriars Bobby in Edinburgh; Scotland; Shep in Fort Benton, Montana, USA; Hachiko in Tokyo, Japan.)

5. The story is told entirely from Kai's point of view. How different would it be if it was told from Mia's, Daddy's, and Mom's instead?

6. When Kai and Mia are reunited at the end, do you believe that is a wishful dream as Kai is dying, a pain-induced delusion, or real?

7. Throughout the book, many elements foreshadow the ending – how many can you name?

8. Has reading *As The Stars Fall* changed how you look at animals and at dogs in particular?

9. If there is a heaven, would you want to go if it is only for people and doesn't have animals?

10. What lasting impression has the book left you with? In particular, is it positive or negative, hopeful or despairing, uplifted or saddened?

11 Do you have a favorite quote, passage, or theme?

12. If this book becomes a movie, who would play Mia, Daddy, Mom, and the voice of Kai?

13. How do you think the title ties in with what happens in the story?

If you'd like a much larger selection of questions, please use this link:
www.stevenleebooks.com/7r6y

Crime Thrillers

⭐⭐⭐⭐⭐ Karen Bryan   ⭐⭐⭐⭐⭐ J. Alexander   ⭐⭐⭐⭐⭐ Stephen Crowe
"Absolutely loved it!"   "Fast-paced and action-packed"   "Bloody fantastic"

As The Stars Fall is a clean, relatively gentle story. If you also enjoy dark, fast-paced thrillers laced with gritty realism, you'll love my action-packed *Angel of Darkness Series* (book #1, *Kill Switch*, has over 1,000 5-star ratings).

★★★★★ *"Fast-paced and action-packed, it takes you on a ride you don't want to stop!"* J. Alexander

★★★★★ *"Reacher fans should enjoy this ... a thrill-packed adrenaline rush."* AJ Norton

★★★★★ *"A good fast-paced read with a fabulous female lead."* Julie Elizabeth Powell

★★★★★ *"Fast paced thriller with suspense packed onto every page. Loved it."* Michael Miller

★★★★★ *"Gripping stuff — I couldn't put this one down, read it in one go."* Jan Simmons

Dive into this pulse-pounding action series today with this link:
www.stevenleebooks.com/qf3z

Steve N. Lee

Apart from animals and writing, Steve's passion is travel. He's visited 58 countries and enjoyed some amazing experiences, including cage-diving with great white sharks, sparring with a monk at a Shaolin temple, and watching a turtle lay eggs on a moonlit beach. He's explored Machu Picchu, Pompeii, and the Great Wall of China, yet for all that, he's a man of simple tastes — give him a sandwich and the TV remote control, and he'll be happy for hours!

He lives in the North of England with his partner, Ania, and their two cats.

To learn more about Steve and his books, please use this link:
www.stevenleebooks.com

53453536R00152